D0827315

FROM HELL TO BREAKFAST

ALSO BY MEGHAN TIFFT

The Long Fire

meghan tifft

FROM HELL

TO

BREAKFAST

a novel

The Unnamed Press
Los Angeles, CA

AN UNNAMED PRESS BOOK

Copyright © 2019 Meghan Tifft

Published in North America by the Unnamed Press.

Unnamed Press and the colophon are registered trademarks of
Unnamed Media LLC.

Library of Congress Cataloging-in-Publication Data:
Tifft, Meghan, author.
From hell to breakfast : a novel / Meghan Tifft.
First Edition. | Los Angeles, CA : Unnamed Press, [2019]
LCCN 2019030205 | ISBN 9781944700621 (paperback) |
ISBN 9781944700638 (ebook)
LCC PS3620.I46 F76 2019 | DDC 813/.6--dc23
LC record available at https://lccn.loc.gov/2019030205

Distributed by Publishers Group West

Printed in the United States of America

www.unnamedpress.com

First Edition
Designed and typeset by Jaya Nicely

1 2 3 4 5 6 7 8 9 10

To my husband and daughter

Now that the dawn has come and there is no danger that I might meet myself...
—Walter Simonson

FROM HELL TO BREAKFAST

The Pigeons

*B*efore the coffin lid parts, before he has a chance even to congeal from the bright liquid motion of his dreams—slick and vivid dreams of sunlit beaches and chiseled blue skies into which he drifts, weightless, with the blithe surrender of a child—Dracula can already hear the sounds of fretting, the stifled currents of atmospheric disturbance in the close and mouthy air beyond his sleeping chamber. He knows that his girlfriend is out there. She is waiting for him, probably standing in the open door of the closet in which he is carefully propped, upright—and as he imagines this he also recognizes the broken gasp of air vaguely chafing his trapped interior. His girlfriend is crying.

But Dracula must wait, first for the lid to open, then his eyes. The ritual proceeds with the utmost languor and rigidity.

"What's the matter?" he finally asks her, stepping out into the dim lamplit room.

"My mother caught me," she says, her voice glubbed in tears. "My mother is a grubby hag from hell."

Every minute his girlfriend lives Dracula wants to bite her, with a softening of all his bones. Always it begins with the same stunned weakness the moment his eyelids curl back and there she is, as she was moments ago, planted in the doorway, the burled roots of her feet stippled into the scuffed wooden floor, the white sprigs of her fingers laced frozen across her face.

"Oh darling," says Dracula, opening his arms to her. "Oh my delicious dove—"

"I wish you would kill her," she says. He can smell the flush of red coming into her face, her beautiful bullion eyes all simmering hot. "With a knife or something. Not the way you normally kill people. I want her to die."

He wants to show her that he can be there for her but he can't help himself. His tongue in the cold mist of his mouth slithers out and licks a tear, and the smooth bisque of her skin warms him like a meal.

"Oh get off me," she says, pushing him away. "I know what you're thinking. Can't you listen to what I'm saying for just a second?"

Dracula's girlfriend has raw rustling currents of golden hair, some of it dark and some of it light. It smells like fallen leaves burning in the autumn sun, floating into crisp warm piles against gravestones.

"Okay." His jaw flutters. "I'm sorry." Dracula shakes off like a sodden dog. He always wakes like this, to his own dark carnival of embarrassment, as if he's been swilling all night in someone else's smarmy dramatics, and woken up in their costume. He lets the lingering scent of her hair float up his nose. He breathes while Lucinda speaks. Why does she always have to incite him like this? Why is his love for her so tender and obscene, such a bruised tumor that he has to carry around so delicately, cradling it away from the lacerating whip of her anger? It makes him feel so good. And so bad. It's a good-bad feeling, he thinks, an exquisite soreness that he wants to touch over and over.

"I didn't even hear her come in. Did you know she made a copy of our key when she was bringing in our mail last month? I should have never let her do that." Dracula's girlfriend plugs her fingers into her temples and holds them there affixed to some electric current. "I'm so stupid! Why would she want to bring our mail in? Do you know what she did?"

He wants to kiss her leeched lips, stop her fevered fretting once and for all. Except his girlfriend is leaving. She's going to the bedroom. Now she's back with some letters. Now she has the letter opener.

"Can I at least kiss you?" he says, accidentally tilting his head toward her tensed neck.

"Oh my God." She's flapping the letters in his face. "I must be crazy. Why do I do this to myself?" She dodges past and splats the envelopes on the pressboard table that holds their mail by the door. The pits and gouges look so bad there. "She brought it back. It's nothing but junk mail. Why would she take it in the first place?"

"Hmm," says Dracula, smoothing the static that's carrying off wisps of her hair.

Lucinda has only dropped the letters, not the opener. "You're not helping with this. Do you want me to be like this all the time?"

She pops a piece of gum in her mouth. A pink fat cube. The letter opener she flicks open and begins to jab mercilessly into the rest of the pack on the table.

"No, no, of course not," he says, patting pillows into the air. They don't really use the letter opener to open letters. Dracula doesn't know why she has such a thing with this.

"Are you sure?" Lucinda is cupping her words away from him, her eyes looming with new tears. A sweet warm smell syrups the air. "Because I know that's why you like me. I know that's the only reason you don't kill me every night when you wake up all jiggy for blood," she says, chewing. "Sometimes I feel like one of your scummy pigeons."

"Don't say that," Dracula says, somehow enamored at this, and feeling sorry for her. "Let me just go get a sip of water."

"She took your pigeons. That's what I was trying to tell you. She's probably calling animal control right now," she says loudly from the other room.

Dracula fills his glass from the tap, thinking tenderly of her spazzy, sadsack brutality. It's true, he thinks. It was the reason he had fallen in love with her, the reason he had followed her into this life they now live. She has no choice but to be here now.

He had found her at the public library, late into the night, her bramble of hair bent low into a cubicle desk in front of a second-floor window, the air around her spiked with toxic concentration. He floated among the bookshelves, feeling delicious shudders of anticipation. He could wait. And while he did, he wondered what she was reading. What fantasy, what menagerie of dreams, would still be lingering in her mind with its wisps of wonder and romance and horror, soon to waft her off to eternity? Was she a student? No. She was much too shrewishly bent to be broadening her mind right now. That book was being devoured, violated with a dark, spastic acumen. Her fingers kept dicing the space in front of her face and she would jolt suddenly forward as if the book had sent a hard spark of current through her. He was very close to her now and could see her watered reflection in the window, where of course his reflection was absent. And then she lifted her face and her private peering eyes were like those of a deeply satisfied predator looking out of itself in the middle of a delicious meal. There was something in her mouth, too. It looked like a moth wing. Maybe it was a scrap of gum.

Dracula felt warm as a fresh splat of blood. If he had a reflection, they would have been staring at each other. But instead, she was blank-faced, looking past her own reflection and through the glass into the funnel of black beyond, poised in such a bare attentive stillness that she seemed more and more elaborately savage every second he looked at her. Slowly, as if the sensation hung suspended in him, he felt a dull puncture of surprise. Then her pointed tongue came out and she folded the gum behind her teeth.

When she got up to leave, all his original intent drained away like a seepage of dirty rainwater. By the time she clawed her way out among the desks he was a little soggy about the knees. He noticed that she had left a pile of shredded paper over a book, enough for a tatty nest. It was a scummed-up paperback called *The Dead Stars*, and the bottom corner of the soft cover had been ripped almost off and it was tacky under his thumb. He sniffed at it. He realized, then, that she had stuck her wet wad of gum here and torn it when prising it off. Had she put it back in her mouth? That was when Dracula flipped through the pages and found all the source material for her shredding.

It was a freakshow inside of feisty feathered frills, and then—more queerly—mushy places, like she had licked the pages to better hack at the pulp inside, possibly trying to hew out a secret storage compartment for hiding something. There was sort of a square shape in there. But she had also written screwy commentary all along the margins. Or else that was already in the margins before her. Maybe it was what had inspired the ecstatic hacking. Either way it brained him to look at such a rabid fracas, all scrambled with the tidy typesetting. There were comments about egg breakfasts and stage assembly on adjacent pages, and then some spinoff thoughts on one of the biographies sharing the second page. It looked like a book of celebrity profiles and presumably by this commentator's rantings they were worth attention.

Dracula blew a breath. He was obviously drinking in the pure and lofty industry of a lunatic. He was just about to let it go—not, after all, hanker after this girl's harebrained blood and instead let the open maw of night have her—when a librarian happened to run up on him. Dracula's spine quilled. The lady gave him a look of quaint surveillance, and he felt implicated, yanked into collusion, swinging with that girl on her rafter of madness.

It wasn't until later that Lucinda told him. She wasn't crazy. Nor was she a vandal. Just severely furious, about something her mother had done. Her mother, Dracula wagered, and wagered correctly, was always maddening her to spasms. But before he knew any of this he had stood in the library, the small, thorn-haired librarian going on her way over the buttered linoleum. He imagined her thoughts still wondering after him, later maybe returning to find the book and falling through a trapdoor of revulsion. What was this? What deviations and recollections would it cleave free from her interior? Who knew what byzantine imaginings she might have, pondering after him? Dracula was indulging himself here. He put his tongue to the cover and tasted. He had to give this back to her. He had to see what she would do. Sweet.

Walking through the library he felt more and more urgent, down the wide shoe-buffed steps and through the bandaged echo of the place to get to her, out in the open aching night, that black tremor of terror, where she might already be fiending down alleys of her own, just like he was apt to do.

At the corner he caught up to her. She had paused to riffle through her purse, her leg switched out in front of her like a foldout blade.

"Hello, miss?"

She looked at him.

"Are you—"

"What?" She was definitely chewing gum. She seemed to crystal over under his gaze. "Oh, I'm not a hooker," she said, folding her leg back under her.

"No. I'm not—" It sounded malicious, whatever it was. "I'm not either," he said, hoping this would splinter the tension.

Her mouth smeared oddly. "That's a good one." Her voice had a candlelit waver, a blue orange hue that flickered warm and cold, like the key he loved best on his harpsichord. That was the key that he played before and after a satisfying evening, still licking his lips for traces of that deep, delirious birdsong of blood. She started walking. Well, now, what could he do? He fell into step beside her.

"I want to see you again?" he said, trying to emulate something he may have seen on TV.

"Don't you need to see me first?" She took a chomp of her gum and grimaced. "Look I—this isn't—"

"But I *have* seen you," he fumbled to interrupt her. "In the library."

Her face climbed into panic. "In the library?" She looked at him and reached down and shook her keys out of her purse, smacking her gum industriously. Her steps seemed to quicken.

"You were. You were reading—" He felt the book in his hand and held it up, not exactly realizing he had carried it with him. His finger grazed the dangling flap on the cover, and he thought of her mouth, her flesh, the delicate fog of his breath unfurling on the spare supple planes of her body.

"Oh my God." She looked at the book. "You were watching me—" She shook her head and turned the corner, and Dracula hurried up beside her. They were hastening under shivering spores of lamplight, drifting through downtown in a damp and deserted city at the edge of a polluted wood, two shadows thrusting raggedly up the sides of pink buildings.

"Wait," he said. "I didn't mean to—"

"No," she turned on him, her dark eyes boiling. "I'm not a freak."

He thought, maybe, that he caught a wary glance from her as she turned right along a side street, where a row of shabby Victorians slumped into weedy sidewalks.

"Okay. May I introduce myself?"

She flicked him a thin, tisky look. "I don't really—"

"Dracula," he said, holding out his hand to shake.

She looked at it. "Oh," she said dryly. "Shucks. This is not—okay." She gave up a breath. "Are you planning to slay me or something?"

He wanted to say no, of course not, but instead a noise bulged out of his throat, something like a startled laugh. He hoped that was what she thought it was.

She idled, warily, in front of a porch with sooty stone columns and gave him a sting of a smile—tiny and totally unreadable. "Maybe you should do it right now and get it over with—" she flitted her eyes back and forth between him and the peeling door behind her. "My mother's about to do it anyway, soon as I go in there."

"Your mother." Dracula was surprised.

She was licking her apparently anesthetized lips. "You should meet my mother, ha ha."

Why did she seem so mumbled and drunk all of a sudden?

"She's a bloodsucker too. You'd probably like her." Then she dashed at the stairs.

"Wait. I didn't—" He was on her when he noticed the knife. She seemed to slump back in a browbeaten way. But she was the one holding it.

"I can't believe I just showed you where I live," she said, to herself. The knife was held. Just held. She never held the knife on him again. Though she could have a million times.

"Not like this will do any good," she said.

Then Dracula understood that he had bungled this completely.

"So, I've read the books," she said. "Does that mean I can call you Vlad?"

He almost went and opened her fresh lily neck right there, just because he felt sorry for her, and since she so expected it, but something held him back. Something in the song and dance of her misfit defense, some rare vial spilled by her hasty choreography and spritzing the night air. He was standing in it, facing likely the blackened symphony of her home life, wondering why she wasn't even wearing a coat. It was complex and confounding, this moment. It definitely wanted to thwart him. Dracula could barely flap his tongue to beg himself off. "Where's your coat?" he heard himself blather. Now who was the drunk and mumbling one? She was wearing a dress that looked like a costume.

Lucinda laughed at this, but not happily.

Dracula always tried to keep her in the limbo of that laugh—or better, if on some days he can manage it.

Now, returning from the kitchen, having occluded himself with the rusty water from the tap, he finds his girlfriend draped over the couch in the living room. She is smiling that same unhealthy smile. It drops like a stale body off her face when she sees him. "So," she says. "Have you decided to bite me tonight? To get this whole thing over with? Or should I keep stabbing things until I turn you on, huh?"

"Okay, okay."

"All your snacks are gone. You're going to have to go out and bite some pretty girls instead."

He lifts her legs and sits under them on the couch. "You're my pretty girl."

"Thank you for saying that." Her voice is cagey and tight and it makes Dracula nervous. "She's such a fat angry mammoth. I couldn't stop her. I didn't even hear her come in. I was practicing my lines. Do you know what she did?" She looks suddenly drugged and horrified at once.

Dracula isn't really aching to ask.

Lucinda's eyes come to rest on him with a beautiful, battlefield stillness. "I'll show you."

She takes his wrist and stretches across the room with him, pulling him like reluctant rubber, until he's with her at the chair that came with their dining nook. "Sit there," she says, and then she gets some twine out of the bottom drawer in the kitchen. Standing over him, she unwinds it.

"She tied you up?" Dracula is incredulous. His girlfriend is arranging his hand against the arm of the chair and wrapping the twine around it. "Is this another of your theater homework assignments?" he asks, preferring that. "Are you just practicing or did your mother really come over?" He hates the theater but her mother is way worse.

Dracula's girlfriend is too busy grinding the twine into the flesh of his wrist. "Ow," Dracula says. "That hurts." She is leaning over him now to tie the other hand, white cords of tension pushing up through the skin at her throat, her hair singed like kindling. He feels almost a tantalizing amorousness in the throes of her despotic calm. What really happened?

Dracula's girlfriend stands back and screws her face. "You filthy bitch," she says, raising her hand.

"Wait a second," Dracula says.

She flicks her hand down and slaps him, stingingly.

"You sick, sick, creature."

"Is that what your mother said to you? It seems like you're more talking to me."

She slaps him again, this time more bluntly. Her clammy hand leaves a trace of dew on his cheek.

"I'm confused," Dracula says, but she is concentrating on the performance now.

"Don't you know what you are?" she hisses at him. "Don't you know? It's about time." She holds up a finger—as if to politely signal he wait—and retreats to pull an eyebrow pencil from her purse at the particleboard table. "Sit still now." She grows a monstrous grin. He can't tell if this is reenactment—what her mother said to her—or instruction—what she's saying and doing to him for the demonstration to be accurate. Lucinda's not using her voice or her mother's. Then she begins to dig greasy lines into his face with a frenzied look of animal greed.

"Ow. This is scratching. Did she really use a makeup pencil? Or are you doing this to—" He can't think of why she would be doing it. "I can't see anything on your face," he says into her milky complexion.

Her gum blots pink in her mouth, and then all at once, as if the words just hit her, she stops, the stalled operation of her mouth seeming to throw a hitch in her whole industry. She pours a sorry look over him, either false or forthcoming he can't tell, and hovers with the point of the pencil still denting his cheek. She turns and sits down sideways in his lap.

"I'm sorry." She breaks out into breath. Without looking at him she reaches out and holds his head against the flutter of her heart.

"I don't like being toyed with." Did he really just say that? "I mean tricked or lied—" he still can't figure out what exactly she did.

Lucinda sighs, like she agrees. "I just kept thinking about how you were going to go out and suck on all those girls to-night." Now her voice seems to be blowing cool air at his sparks of indictment. "I get so tired of it."

He's silent, letting her pat his ire away for several moments, breathing deeply against her fragile chest, sniffing at the blue white skin. "So, my pigeons are really gone?"

"Those are the ones I couldn't get to fly away."

She points outside the window, where two pigeons flap on the railing, looking like frazzled witnesses, flustered and disheveled and too enfeebled to flee. "I feel sorry for those pigeons," she says. "More so than the girls."

Dracula tries to sift through her bare-branch words, to make sense of the admission that seems to be budding there. "Was it really your mother that let them out?"

His girlfriend's eyes have glazed over. Her breathing is quiet. "I can't stand hearing them in there," she says. "All those wing sounds."

"I understand." Dracula sighs. He leans back and his hairline goes up with his brows. It's one of those fifties hairlines, so he's been told, severe and handsome.

"I just wish you weren't Dracula."

It occurs to him, wiping her hair off his face, that she could any night have killed him with a wooden stake, that she is not the hanged one here so much as he is, that even that eyebrow pencil could do the deed. He isn't even sure if she loves him. What a silly predicament for someone of his infernal status to walk himself into. How did he take such tasteless and lackadaisical terms here, heading right into apartment living with the first girl he spares, and leaving the night a mere curio outside his window—a place he visits only when he wants to shop for the strange and arcane. He even dreams now of daytime, things he sees on TV. Lucinda isn't having it either. She isn't having him. Not really. He can tell.

"Are you mad at me?" she says.

He is hanging here on her mercy. "I love you," he says, unconsoled and unrelenting like always.

"I sort of wish you were," she says, daubing his wound with her hand. They watch the pigeons. "I love you too," she remembers to say. "I have to tell you—" she breaks off to toss her hair out of her face. The pigeons continue to snoop, like secret agents in everyday plumage. Lucinda still can't seem to say something. "I can't believe her."

"Your mother?"

Time wafts. Lucinda is looking down at a strand of ragged hair. What had her mother done? "My mother is a monster."

He pats her thigh, waiting.

In a quiet voice, through crisp tendrils, she says, "She is the mother of all monsters."

Dracula hesitates, turning this over in the slow, immortal folds of his mind. Is this what she was going to say? Just before? "You mean..." Dracula trails off. He thinks she's being metaphorical. He thinks.

His girlfriend looks at him, eyes dark as a sitting cauldron, and also far away, lost in the prim postulations of stars. Or is he just once again grafting his own eternal fixations on her?

"She says she wants to have you for dinner."

The Coffee Table

*L*ucinda's mother has a new coffee table. It's a wire cage
with a dog in it. She puts her magazines on top of it—
stolen copies of *Bait and Lure* and *Game and Trophy*—and a
scalloped wooden tray from the pawn shop she sometimes
manages, a spot for her husband to put his can of beer on
when he watches TV. The TV is also from the pawn shop, and
it tends to display a jolting picture embellished with digital
hieroglyphs that pop up sporadically in the upper right
corner of the screen in laser-green bars—B, ^, PL, :P, B | |.
Lucinda's father likes to write these symbols down on a
notepad for later examination.

His job is to interpret the seemingly inexplicable and
random phenomena in the universe—all the cryptic and in-
cidental outpourings of material happenstance that suggest
a hideous tendency toward entropy—and find a logic that
knits them together, a pattern that uncovers the grand plan, a
fabric profound enough to underpin the extrapolations of all
apparent chaos. Lucinda's father used to be a mathematical
genius, but then he hit his head in a fishing accident some
years ago and has been on disability ever since. His current
studies include electronics, the ancient wisdom of various
Masonic groups—a few to which he still maintains an emeri-
tus membership—obsolete computer information systems—
preferably the archaic ones that display DOS commands and
a blinking cursor, and which are in abundance at the pawn
shop—and the entrails of dead animals washed up on the
beach. Dead animals are a rare gift and necessitate a beach
scouring at least twice a week.

The dog is of little interest to him because it's alive. It came with the cage and though the door is always open this is where it settles to while away its days. The dog is old. Lucinda named it Vlad and she takes it on walks every afternoon. During his fifteen minutes of release Vlad is in spasms of uneasy animation, though one decipherable only to the empathetic eye. He waddles around on sleep-stiffened legs taking huge gulping yawns. His bobbed tail vibrates. When he arrives again at the recognizable charred stone columns of their porch he poops out with a wheeze and sits looking into the tarry dusk with Lucinda.

When she catches a glimpse of his eyes, the darkening luster there, it tells her he's astonished to be free. And it's that look that reminds her of his namesake, which is not exactly the right term, she knows, because she named the dog before she even met him, but somehow it feels like it was through some prophetic foresight that she named the dog ahead of time after the guy who she would end up dating with all the timorous uncertainty of a lamb to the slaughter.

It has come to her attention that the man she is dating really is Dracula—and if he isn't, well then he's even worse than Dracula—a deranged moron who sleeps in a coffin by day and hunts pigeons all night in a show of unsolicited loyalty to her. He doesn't want to make her jealous. Biting all those dewy-eyed young professionals drifting home from a long day of work. There are a lot of young professionals in this city. It's up and coming again.

Lucinda sighs, and Vlad looks up, his mouth stretched wide in a whining yawn. He seems to understand her melancholy. When she's ready to go inside he escorts her back down the hallway and trundles back into his cage, lifting his nose to the delicate complexity of Lucinda's father's feet, which are bare and propped overhead. One of the big, cheesy loaves twitches, and Lucinda's father laughs.

"That tickles," he says.

This, thinks the dog, is where it all ends, and it closes its eyes, living mostly in dreams—places of dappled shadow and light, vast continuous breezes swept down from the gory firmaments, the howling urgency of deepening night and the musky bouquet of morning shadow. The company of other dogs, the surrender and ecstasy—tumbling, romping, breathing in the deep assembly of scents—all those richly hued and moist exchanges of energy and spirit that cling to a different life.

The dog's paws and eyelids twitch.

"Dad," says Lucinda. "I'm dating a monster."

Her father scuds his glasses up on his forehead, where they ogle her. He is busy with his notepad. He is not even Lucinda's dad. "Huh," he says. He scratches his armpit with the capped end of his pen and puts it in his mouth, thinking hard. "PBJ, volume bar, absolute value, cardinality set x. That coincides with yesterday's luncheon at the lodge. Arlo made sandwiches without the crust."

"Dad—" Lucinda likes the word Dad.

But it's her mother that answers, loudly, from the kitchen. "What? Come in here."

Her mother hocks noisily over the sudden rush of sink-water.

"Hey," says Lucinda, getting up to talk to her. "Is Warren my real brother?"

Lucinda is still gazing back through the doorway at her mother's husband who is quietly puffing out a series of belches.

"I don't know."

"Why don't you know? It's not normal not to know."

Her mother can look at her with an ember in her eye that actually glows. It makes Lucinda twitch like a bug with plucked wings. It makes her suspect that some kind of huge force is at work around her, and she can't always say how she feels it, or why it slides off like a warm bathwater every time she leaves the house.

"I'm dating a guy who says he's Dracula."

"Oh, I know." Her mother scratches in her hair.

"You don't care?"

"The guy in the hall?" She tilts her head and pricks up a smile, still scratching. "No, he's cute. Why should I care?"

Lucinda remembers the day in the hall. How he followed her all the way up the walk to the porch as if he had no idea how unnerving, how utterly horrendous, this was. She opened the outer door and stood in front of it, afraid and furious that going inside might offend him. Why did she always attract crazy people? She hated it. She hated crazy people. They were hazardous and unpredictable. And who was this guy? What would he try to do to her? Maybe if she invited him further in he would get jumpy and go away.

"So you want to meet my mom? She's psycho," she said, stepping into the entryway. To her surprise he came spryly up the steps.

"Oh—this isn't a house," he said in a slightly flat, smoked voice, like a corpse.

"It's an apartment conversion." Her tongue fumbled nervously in her mouth. He was actually following her into the hall. She found herself two steps ahead of him, scuttling down the gummy blue carpet to her apartment.

"You haven't told me your name," he said.

"Oh, I haven't?" She stopped with the keys in the lock, her heart traipsing up into her throat. "I'm Lucinda," she swallowed. "So are you sure you want to come in? Because you don't know me or anything. You could find something atrocious behind this door."

He seemed shyly amused. She was trying not to mention her qualms about what he had said. He was not the type.

His teeth were big and squarish. They looked like bones, not teeth—not even regular teeth, let alone the chiseled little points required to pierce flesh. And he wasn't very tall. Wasn't Dracula supposed to be tall and sallow, floating lugubriously over the land like a gloomy vulture? And shouldn't he have been varnished in everything black, a veritable pothole of oily, sinister stealth? This guy was in a plaid flannel coat. His skin wasn't a traditional chalky white. It had a stale brown tint like the pages in an old book. Maybe that was how eastern Europeans looked.

"If you want me to," he said, spreading his palms out. "I could just take your phone number."

"You know, maybe you should just do that." She glanced uneasily at her apartment door. Her key was having problems in the slot.

"Are you afraid to take me into your house? Your mother—is something bad going to happen?"

"Oh, no," she said. "I was just joking about all that. My mom's cool." She let him look at her. Now the slow petroleum of his eyes did seem to spill from him and into the hallway, gathering some shadows. Was she imagining that?

"You're afraid of something," he said.

"Well, actually—" she looked down at her key. "I just—"

As she spoke the door opened a crack and her mother peeped out. "Be quiet you. Your father is sleeping and if you wake him up so help me."

The blunt heavy slab of her mother's voice was like a hand steadying her.

"Oh, Mom. Hi." She whooshed out a breath. "I was just coming inside." But her mother wouldn't let her through the door. The raised cloth bolt of her arm held it resolutely cracked, letting the pungent odor of catfish boil past her into the hallway. "I have an idea to leave you here," she said, looking past her at Dracula. "Who's this?"

"I don't know," Lucinda said.

Her mother snorted. "What the hell's he doing in the hallway then?"

"I just met him here," she said, trying not to meet his eyes, trying to flatten herself and her voice into something discreet and inoffensive so she could get past the doorway.

"Is he a delivery man? We didn't order any food. You're delivering something?"

"No," he said, and pointed a girlish finger at Lucinda. "I was invited to meet you by your daughter."

Lucinda felt her knees quake with dismay. Why was he such an idiot? He acted like a foreigner.

"Oh isn't that nice," said her mother, and she reached out and flicked her daughter hard on the forehead. "Well I can't meet you tonight because I'm busy cooking fish for my dimwit husband. He went on a trip with his friends and came home with a shitload of the little stinkers. I've been gutting all day," she said to Lucinda. "Little missy ran away right when he came home because she likes to hide from us. Don't you?" her mother asked her.

"No," she said in a threadbare voice.

Behind her, Dracula stood in his swirl of darkness. She could feel its cold oil spreading across her back, slicking her down. Oh please, she thought.

"Well if she doesn't like to be my daughter she doesn't have to be."

"No Mom," she said.

"*No Mom,*" her mother repeated. "She's a pain isn't she? A pretty little pain."

Lucinda patted her sides with dread. When was her mother going to let her in?

"Give it," she said, crabbing her hand at the air.

Lucinda sucked in her breath. She fumbled the knife out of her pocket. Now could she go inside?

Her mother snatched it away. "It's not yours. That reminds me," she said, "I've got a surprise for you." Her face left the crack and reappeared smiling as her free hand stuck something out into the hallway. It was the barrel of a shotgun. It was pointed at Lucinda's acquaintance. "Your father came home with this. I don't know where he got it but it's mine now."

This was like a bad movie, Lucinda thought—she out here, her mother in there with a castaway armory, aiming the shotgun while the monster pressed all the shadows together behind her. Just like when she was a little kid and she woke up from a nightmare and stood at the sloppy darkness of her mother's bed, afraid her mother would claw her back if she tried to climb in and afraid to stay away in the crushing darkness of her room, strung on an invisible cord of terror in the middle of the night, alone and incubating in her own unending dread.

"Mom, please," she heard herself say, but she knew desperation would only egg her mother on. "Can you please let me in?"

Now this man was seeing everything. She hated him for making her need her mother.

"You can just stay out here tonight," her mother said, "and sleep on the doorstep for all I care." And she closed the door. Lucinda knew it wouldn't be opened again for hours.

"I hate you," she said, to her or to him, and pushed him backwards into the hallway. Now a baby was crying somewhere. "You did this." She was stumbling away from him. She and the baby were both crying.

"You're going to kill me."

"No I won't. I promise."

"I don't understand," she said after batting back the outer door, and from the avid look on his face she wasn't even sure that he did.

He didn't kill her that night—he sat on a bench with her and played cards. She took him to the bus depot, where it was warm. Match after match of War and Go Fish in the dead, waystation light. Why wouldn't he leave her be? Why couldn't he say goodnight and go? How much worse was this going to get?

Now that she was dating him, it was the same sense of peril but she had started to notice a fading indifference to it, like a cup of tea gone tepid on her desk. It was there, she could drink it, and it was no longer blowing its curtain of steam. She couldn't decide if he was Dracula or he wasn't. She didn't know if it even mattered. If he wanted to murder her he would murder her.

"You don't mind?" she said to her mother in the kitchen.

"Why should I mind? It's your life."

"What if he murders me?"

Her mother stopped the sink and looked at her. She seemed to be whittling out a private thought. "Oh, you're not scared of him." Her mother graveled in her throat and batted her hand. "You have no reason to be. You're his problem and he don't even know it yet!"

"No I'm not." Lucinda went to the plant alcove and picked up the shotgun. She aimed it at her bedroom wall.

"Who put that there?" said her mother.

"What?"

"Who put that there?"

Lucinda looked at the gun and then at the alcove, with its dripping greens in front of a whitewashed window. "I don't know." Lucinda turned back. "Would this go through if I shot it?"

Her mother smiled. "Oh I love you," she said.

"What is that supposed to mean?" Lucinda asked.

Her mother seemed to be waiting for something, an answer to another question in the air. "Why is that window always so scummy?"

Lucinda found herself unable to go here or there in her mother's line of questioning. "I washed it."

And then Lucinda had a feeling. Her mother's smile opened a great gory chasm in her.

"Did you," said her mother.

"Did I what?"

"You know," her mother repeated.

"No I don't," said Lucinda.

"Oh, no." The ember fairly baked her to ash.

"What are you talking about?" said Lucinda. "I *did* wash the window yesterday. I was doing it. The gun wasn't even here."

"You weren't either. For a while."

"What? Wait a second," Lucinda was slowly realizing that what her mother had done was make a liar of her. She hated when her mother did this—her favorite crafty line of questioning that turned her upside down by the toe only to dangle her over the pot of her own hooliganism. Except most of the time it was only Warren's hooliganism and Lucinda was getting blamed for it.

"You took it out of the house."

"No I didn't." Who knew who took it out of the house? Probably Warren.

"*No I didn't,*" her mother mocked her. "You're following him. I know you want to see what he does."

That part was true. And there was nothing wrong with that. "I just *told* you," Lucinda said. "I have to stay safe."

"Oh but you're not safe."

Before Lucinda could argue with this direct contradiction of her mother's former pronouncement, her mother salted out a shaker of laughter as if she thought this was actually a joke. "Did you like that?" she asked, as if she had just accomplished some clever wordplay that had gone over Lucinda's head. Lucinda was so over this conversation, but her mother was still going. "You are your mother's daughter, missy! Don't you know it! Washing windows!" She wiped a tear and then without preparation her hand grabbed out and pushed the gun backward with Lucinda attached. It was a love push. Lucinda dropped the gun. The sludgy feet propped across the room then spasmed with a rake of surprise. The dog sprang into its delirious expanse of air and broke its dream against the wire of its cage.

"That isn't even loaded." Her mother beamed with vicious pride. "And here you are toting it around in the dark, ready to get yourself arrested. Oh, you're ready," she said.

"I did not—"

"You're all grown up and ready!"

"What?" said Lucinda, recoiling further like a beast from a poker. "What are you talking about?" She hated how her mother made her feel like she was crazy. There was just no arguing with her.

Her mother dived at her with a rabid smile. "Pack your bags," she said. "You're moving out!"

The Apples

"*I*'m going to call Warren," Dracula says, coming out of the shower. He smells something.

"I have to tell you something," his girlfriend says.

"Again?" The blitzing floodlight outside the window turns the air to mechanical torchlight. The birds have flown away. He can't stop thinking about her mother wanting him for dinner.

"I've been following you."

This, thinks Dracula, is bluntly discomfiting. Maybe this is what she was trying to tell him before.

"Okay," he says. He waits for more. It seems like there's going to be more. His girlfriend still has not turned on a light. She's sitting in the dark and he can see the book of matches on the table with the bills.

"You were following me?"

"You're not—" Now his girlfriend is biting at the nubs of her fingers, like a busy raccoon. "You're not really doing anything."

Why does she seem embarrassed?

"Why do you go to the bus depot?"

It doesn't seem like something he should be ashamed of. "They have a TV there I like," he says.

"You like a TV?" Lucinda has dropped her hand to prowl at him with her eyes. She seems almost to think there's a revelation in this.

"No. It's just—a show. I like a show." Is he clamming up now under her fidgety attention? "It's not—I just go and sit—" he doesn't feel like this is at all important. "It's almost dark in this one—where the lighting is—"

"Squalid," she says.

She seems edgy, and not very nice about any of this. Dracula remembers that *she* was the one following *him*.

"We should just get a TV," she says.

Dracula blows a brisk breath. "We don't have money for a TV."

Lucinda nods. "I quit my job," she says, as if to corroborate.

"What? You quit your job?" Now his girlfriend is back to her biting—a glum, spacey look on her face. "You did?" he says. He finds himself realizing that they will not have enough money to pay rent this month.

Lucinda doesn't even answer him. "I've been meaning to tell you this for a long time."

"A long time? You mean this didn't happen today?" Dracula scuffs the beads of water from his brow, finally exasperated.

"No—" Lucinda flutters this off with her fingers. Apparently that's not what she meant. Apparently she meant the other thing. The one she wanted to tell him. "I mean, I saw you," she says.

"You saw me?"

"In the window," says his girlfriend.

Dracula looks out the window. He tries to think of a window. "I don't understand."

"That day," she says.

Dracula knows she means night. "What *day*?"

He gives all his knuckles a crack. He can't stand around waiting to see how her salt-and-peppering of fact and innuendo will eventually taste—it's time for her to tell him something. "Can you please just tell me?"

She opens her mouth. He knows she doesn't like his tone. Her eyes appear to dirty on something behind him and Dracula can't help it. He looks over his shoulder. The bedroom door with its many little holes is hanging partway open as usual. The dart is there in the wood. He turns back.

"You said you're going to call Warren?" His girlfriend is reaching for the matches.

"Yeah," says Dracula. "Does that have to do with something?"

"I just realized." She pokes her tongue out and pinches something off with her fingers. A flake of fingernail. She puts it back in her mouth. "That's exactly what he wants you to do."

Dracula is at his end. "Well, what else am I supposed to do? What does this have to do with anything?" He can't stand her pigeonholing him right here in this place and then giving him exactly the runaround that keeps him in the dark.

Lucinda looks at him. She seems to want to make a suggestion. A real one. He skids a snippy breath, waiting, telling her he's waiting. Then she clams up and doesn't say anything. Her mouth goes to clabber and for an answer she lights another match and plucks a single hair out in front of her face. She watches it fizzle away. Lucinda seems to find this exquisitely satisfying. She's pretending he's not here.

"Please. Come on," says Dracula, and she doesn't seem to like this either. It's his tone. It's his terrible tone.

"Fine," she says, "call Warren." Her voice is brittle as burnt plastic. She puts the match out on the table.

Dracula shakes his head.

"You're really in a sour mood," he says. He knows it's not the right thing to say. Not after what she told him. She seems to want him to know already what she means. It's whenever she tries to be direct, when there seems to be something important to say, that she climbs to the edge of this pit and lurches all the way over before she even gets the words out. She's somehow irretrievable after that, like an animal in a well. Dracula blames her mother for this. Her mother has put her down that irretrievable well and, Dracula reminds himself, her mother has been here today. Doing something. He tries to find temperance in this.

"You know I'm doing this for you," he says.

"Gee thanks." She razors this out without expression. "I love it when you hunt birds and not girls."

"I wouldn't have to if you hadn't let them out." Had she let them out? Dracula's breath is scuffing out in abject annoyance. He doesn't understand why they are having an argument right now. "I thought this is what you wanted me to do," he says and picks up the phone. Lucinda can't give him any corroboration. She shrugs, but her eyes seem to be brimming with ripe, bruisy panic. He is not sure why she would look like this. "Warren," he says, when her brother's loping hello comes through the line at him. A brief fraternal feeling trots up on him. "I need your help tonight."

"I'm driving the truck," Warren says. Lucinda's brother works for UPS, just like Dracula. Dracula was the one who got him the job. "I'm meeting someone after so we have to do it while I'm on shift."

They make plans to meet at eight. Dracula offers to get Lucinda takeout. He just wants to see what she'll say.

She's putting the book of matches in the drawer. "I'll just call one of my friends. Maybe go down to that noodle place." She has arranged her face. She seems to be trying to give him a nice enough goodbye. "Good luck," she says. "Knock 'em dead."

"Ha ha," he says. "Theater humor." He gives her a kiss, only a peck on the temple, and he can't help thinking they have both just slighted each other.

Outside, the moon is hung low and tarnished over the buildings, like a doorknob stuck up there to taunt him. Dracula goes down the cantilevered steps and feels them tremble slightly under his weight. He feels too unsteady, floating away from that inside abyss into this tilted void. He feels just like that moon, dangling on a door that's open all akimbo.

A white owl sits atop one of the vacated dorms, watching. The unfallen apples dangle in poison clusters from the trees. Rotten ones freeze at his feet. Dracula has been juggling three of them.

"Skank, where's your cage?" Warren is walking up.

"Missing," says Dracula, suspicious. He's gotten somewhat used to Warren's way of talking. "You didn't see it earlier at your mother's house?"

"No. Wait a second." Warren appears to think, his blond hair slung like sheet metal over his eyes, his mouth fading to a contemplative slit. "No."

The cage started out as Lucinda's mother's, and the dog used to sleep in it. But the dog is dead now.

"I didn't see it," says Warren, as if Dracula still needs convincing.

Dracula is not convinced, especially now that Warren has tried on purpose. He never knows what to think about this family. They don't seem to like each other and yet they seem to be telling protective lies around each other all the time. They're actors in some cheap intrigue he can't decode. Warren often seems the most delinquent and also the least calculating of the bunch, which ought to make him the easiest to deal with, and maybe he is. Dracula hates to be thinking of Lucinda now, because she isn't that bad, not in the way Warren is.

They are all actors, but Lucinda is the only one with actual acting aspirations, and it shows. The classes she takes at the local community college, the campus upon which Dracula and Warren are currently loitering, seem to fill her entire life these days. Dracula supposes that's normal, for a theater group that's putting on a play. Dracula stanches his distaste and flaps open a black garbage bag as Warren makes a hammock of his brown uniform shirt. He plops the fruit into the hammock with gloved hands.

"Come on," he says. "Hurry up. I thought you'd have done this by now."

Dracula should have. He has been lost in preoccupation. He still can't think of a time Lucinda could have seen him, not one where he was doing something unseemly. This bothers him in a way he didn't expect.

Without a cage, Dracula will only get tonight's meal. He appreciates Warren's help but he knows there's a rank opportunism in it. Tomorrow he'll have to do this all over again, and the next day and the next until he finds a cage. As they walk toward the library with their ammunition, Dracula can already feel the fidgety stillness sifting the air, the frail open current of little wingbeats, soft rearrangements in the dark. It makes him twitchy and dismal with appetite.

He isn't a big fan of the next part. The bleat of distress, the feathered commotion, the body plummeting like a podgy pouch of coins, the dull plop in the dirt. It's worse without a cage because after each one he has to run up and sink into it right there, like some gory ghoul, squatting on his haunches to hide himself from all the windows. As they creep up under the eaves, Warren cocks his arm and sends an apple soaring, catching a dull stony light. Dracula doesn't even see the target until a body flounders and pro-pellers to the ground. His aim is uncanny.

"Got one." He looks at Dracula. "Go do," he says, his eyes lit up with frisky interest.

Wishing he had a little more privacy, Dracula approaches the stunned lump, its wings twitching faintly, its breast heaving, and imagines it brained into some beautiful dream, swinging through clean, cold skies, a ruby sun off in the distance, and he probes past the soft ashy purse of feathers and the tender sleeve of flesh until the breath of heat touches him, and his teeth roll past the sinews of nerve and vessel and break into the bag of blood. A tingling fury pixilates the seconds as he siphons it off.

Fifty minutes later there's a pile to his knee and he and Warren stop throwing fruit and stand over it. In the dark it looks sculpted of some metal alloy, the glimmering flint of bellies and heads and the black cast iron of beaks and backs. The beady augur of many eyes looks out and beyond.

Dracula flaps open the mouth of his garbage bag.

"What are you doing?"

"Taking them to the dumpsters."

"Oh no. No. We had a deal."

Dracula stands back, already lit to combustion. He was afraid this was coming. He wants right now to sear some indictment into this before Warren gets out of hand. He is pretty sure they never had a deal. Only that the first time they did this Warren had an idea.

"This is fucking phat!" he said that time. This time his slang is much less corpulent, more relaxed and calculated. "We'll just do it neat this time," he says. "Easy on the eyes, so they want to see it and sling it."

Okay. Dracula scorches breath. He wants to shout his veto but he seems mismatched to the mood already and unable to intervene. Warren takes off his backpack and kneels down. Just like he did the first day.

That day, he said, "I just had a fucking gorgeous idea. This is perfect." Warren unzipped his bag and pulled out two spray cans. He shook them both at the same time, like a beer commercial.

"You're going to spray paint them?"

He walked around and around the pile of birds, as if deciding on an angle of incursion, eyes hooded and looking in with quiet introspection.

"I'm confused," Dracula said.

Warren shook his head, not looking at him, his gaze grossly slickened with lust. "It's art, man! It's fucked up!" He hissed out a jet of glowing pink and began to paint the birds.

Dracula stood there, transfixed, as Warren circled the pile on bouncing haunches, absorbed in his project, kneeling down and tilting his head and thrusting back up to his feet to study its progress and stooping back down until the fumes of his labor were dizzying both of them.

"Wow," Dracula said when he was done, not sure what to think or how to feel. The pile frothed with candy-acid hues. "That's..." He did not want to be caught anywhere near it.

Warren was drizzling his name on the cement beside it in green paint. "Let's go."

Ever since then he'd been begging Dracula to do it again. "I need to do it regularly, like installments, for people to catch on."

"Catch on?" said Dracula. He'd had a cage to put the stunned birds into by then.

"Like Banksy."

While he didn't like the laboratory disaster of doing the thing in the bathroom it was better than the congested dog runs of the inner city. "Banksy? What are you talking about?" said Dracula. He wasn't really listening. The polluted wood was the only place he could do this with any dignity but it was too far to go every night. Every now and then he did a camping trip.

"Come on. This is art. This is massive!"

"It's not," said Dracula.

"Yes it is. It's half yours too. I'll credit you."

Dracula spat his vexation. His anger lapped at him like a heavy tongue. One day if he wasn't careful he would do something to Warren. "You want to out me as Dracula?"

"No no no." Warren practically rolled his eyes. "Okay. Let me think. I'll come up with a good angle. We can shank it in all sorts of Disneyland places"—with this he actually did a little piratey thrust and twist—"shopping malls, strip outlets, post offices, churches. And what about the kids? Gotta do the parks." Warren was giggling as if he was making new play equipment. "It's commentary. On the whole fucking fallacy of life! Ha ha! It's so bolted down I can't even explain it!"

Dracula didn't know how to call Warren off, to make him see the recoil it gave him, the shame and drainage of seeing his own existence groping back at him, the pitiful pitilessness of all things. "It's just—no," he said.

"You can make money off it." Dracula assumed that Warren meant he himself could. "I'll cut you in. It'll be so fucking famous! The illuminati will hunt me. I'll dress like a hipster carny and be anonymous, like in those videos."

"I don't—" Dracula was not liking the blather now sudsing the air. "No."

"You have to do it."

"I do?" said Dracula. "I have to?"

A crisp silence schismed the air, during which Dracula tried to figure out if Warren had threatened him or he had threatened Warren. It was confusing. They left it hovering there between them, heavy as lead.

Now here he is watching it happen all over again and all he can do is stagnate like a bog while Warren makes haste with his art and locks down their supposed deal. He finds himself in a trance when he watches Warren. It's like a bloodletting that part of him thinks he deserves.

"There," says Warren. "Now I'm going to call somebody."

"What in the fire and brimstone?"

They both turn. The campus cops are pulling up on their bicycles, asses high and heads low, gears slick and ticking, helmets of swift molded plastic riding up on them like cresting waves.

Dracula is briefly arrested by the sight, and by the colorful phrasing. Warren has already put toe to ground and bounded off. Now it is Dracula's turn to run. He sees it's too late, even as he feels the surge. He is Dracula. It would be no effort to wipe the night behind him. He can feel his limbs already going to gloss. But he just doesn't feel like it. He's not himself these days. He crosses his arms. One of the bicycles has whizzed off after Warren. The other one catches its kickstand as the official dismounts and strides up on him.

"What's this?" It isn't the voice that spoke before.

Dracula shrugs. "I just saw this guy doing it. I came over to look."

The cop looks down at the sidewalk without seeming at all to look away from Dracula. "Warren. Is that his name?"

Dracula licks his fingers and wipes at his mouth. "I don't know his name."

"Why did you do that?"

"Do what?"

The man is now considering his protocol. Dracula can sense the hassled millisecond of thought. "Sir, can you please show some identification?"

"I don't have my wallet on me."

The man has a divot in his chin. He doesn't seem to want to pursue this part of the reconnaissance. He seems to be distracted by the chase he's not making. There's a shafted restlessness blowing off him. "What are you doing on the grounds, sir?" he says uncuriously. His head is tilted to some secret inaudible pitch.

"Just walking through. I told him it was illegal if that's any help."

"Not really," says the cop. He's young, and probably has a dog at home that he jogs with. "What's in that bag?"

Dracula looks down. "Oh. I'm going to pick apples."

"You're going to pick apples?"

"At the colonnade." Dracula points with his chin. "There's a bunch of them still on the trees."

The cop actually sighs. "Please don't pick apples, sir." Dracula can feel his smile spreading even though he doesn't want to make the cop feel mocked.

"Okay," he says. "Why not?"

"They're not edible." Now the cop seems to know something out of his jurisdiction.

"Is that so?"

"That's what you're doing here?"

"That's what I'm doing here. Good thing you caught me."

The man is tired of him and he doesn't think he's funny. "Please leave the campus grounds. Don't pick the apples."

"Fine. Hope you catch him." The man pretends he said nothing and makes a note. What else can he do? He's not a real cop so he has to let guys like this go with their fibs and calculations. This apple picker was probably here with the other vandal who ran off. Probably his indolent accomplice. But there's no way to know. That's the crux of it. Dracula can see all this in the set of his face. It makes him brim with a sticky sort of kinship, for the man and the whole lineage he came from, all its staunch mistakes, its doomed Excalibur dignity. Every little thing is so much bigger than it seems. He feels that way too.

Warren catches up to him at the edge of the grounds. "That was sick," he says in a pant. Dracula can't tell by his tone if he's satisfied or incensed. "We have to do it all over again. They're going to trash my piece before anybody sees it."

Dracula gives a noncommittal grunt.

"Don't you need my help tomorrow?"

They have reached the truck.

"You don't have a cage, right?"

Dracula looks over. Warren shrugs with the complacency of someone who has always gotten away with everything he has ever done. All his petty and minor delinquencies, piling up behind his closet door. Who is he, anyway? What has he done? He bends and rolls up the back door. This is what it has come to, Dracula thinks, glancing into the empty cargo hold.

"Got your deliveries done early," he says.

"Yep." Warren checks his watch. "Got to get the truck back." Dracula has to get in the back of the truck now. He knows that if he doesn't Warren could lose his job.

Dracula swaddles down into a disgusted silence.

"Your turn," says Warren, prodding him in.

"I can go buy another cage," he says.

"Do you have the money?" Warren showcases a glib smile.

No. Not since he started paying for Lucinda's acting classes.

"Hey—you need me to make you some money so you can buy another cage," says Warren, pointing at him like a gaudy salesman, working his dumb wiles at a blowout bonanza— everything must go. He rolls the door down over him and Dracula balls up the empty garbage bag in his fist. One apple is left lolling in the bag.

It's one of the rotten ones. He can tell.

The Bill

D racula has a rubber mouth guard for when they have sex. It's clumsy and bludgeoning, but an absolute necessity. He once tried a mere foam sheath to slip only his teeth into and that almost got her killed. It came off and he has a very, very strong jaw that could have hinged a whole hunk out of her neck. The mouth guard is bulky enough to obstruct his hinging action and jammed in deep enough to resist his tongue's ejection. It's not sexy. It is not at all what she thought it would be. It's like a mallard prodding and snipping at her with brute affection, doing something diffident with her other body parts. She can hear his breath snuffling inside the rubber, and they can't kiss at all. Of course, if they kissed during that climax of passion he would mangle the tongue right out of her mouth. Supposedly. If he really is Dracula. This is what she tells her girlfriend Vanessa. Vanessa dangles her jaw in stupefied disapproval.

"You're not serious."

"I am serious."

"You actually for a second believe him?"

Lucinda flutters her crisp, false eyelashes. They're bothering her. "There's something in him. He has an aura."

"An aura. You should test him."

"Test him? Like, what, ask him lore or something?"

"Ask him what would happen if he drank AIDS blood. Tell him you have AIDS."

"Tell him I have AIDS," she says in a plummeting voice. She squeezes the cellophane sleeve from the celery she just unwrapped and feels it compress under pressure. This is how her mind works. Now she thinks she has AIDS. She feels herself gripped by panic. If somebody suggests she tell a lie about herself she will instantly interpret it as possibly true. Why shouldn't it be possibly true? She knows there is something wrong with her.

"Stop messing with your eye. It's fine."

"I think it's coming off."

Vanessa leans in and gives Lucinda a squint that snags up her whole upper lip. Lucinda can see the glint of her tongue stud in her open mouth, like a stone in a dirty pond. "Oh, yeah, it is coming off. You want me to—?" Vanessa lunges at her with pincer fingers and Lucinda dodges back.

She peels the eyelash off herself. It's the silver one. The other one is gold. She just came from rehearsal, where she saw the stack of playbills for the first time, ready for dispersal around town. There was her name listed in the cast, *Lucinda Linde*, wafting out at her in light italics. It gave her a rash of virulent chills. Now she keeps thinking, it's too late to back out. It's always there in her mind, like a cyst that never stops growing.

"You should totally leave the other one for our next appointment," says Vanessa.

Lucinda tries to laugh. Her breath feels like a crust of ice.

She and Vanessa are apartment hunting. This is what she reminds herself, trying to throw a sandbag at the other thing. Lucinda's mother has kicked her out of the house and she hasn't even retrieved all of her things. That's how fast this fumigation happened. Why does she feel like such a crisped abomination right now? She's all dressed up for a play she never really aspired to be in. She has no money and soon maybe no job. And she's shacking up with an actual Dracula until she can figure out what to do with herself. The dog at least had come with her.

"This is stupid." The other eyelash cleaves briefly to its adhesive before tugging away.

"What, this?" Vanessa showcases Lucinda's current fashion statement with a wave of her hand. "Your wacky play? Or your dangerous liaisons with Ducky? Because either way I agree."

Lucinda sighs. She told Vanessa about the play. Rehearsal ran late and she didn't have time to change.

"I just mean." She takes a whiff of air. She tries to swipe a lid on the absolute breadth of her feeling. "I can't afford any of the good ones," she says with a swallow.

Vanessa snorts. "You can't afford any of them at all. You probably won't even have a job next week."

The pitiless way that Vanessa says this annoys Lucinda. It's partly Vanessa's fault that Lucinda might lose her job. They work together at the smoothie shop. Lucinda got the job on no experience and no recommendation, because she was young and lived within walking distance, and this is how the owner likes to hire his minions. He wants gophers with nothing on their mind but spending money and no way of not getting to work. Lucinda has been there for three months and is well into the groove of it. Grind. Scoop. Flick. Pour. These are her professional gestures. They are brisk, and in no other aspect of her life is she able to be so vigorous and proficient. It gives her a pure and seamless feeling. It's not like the play, where she strays into her role like a shaft of lost light. Here, she stands sturdy, with her legs planted apart. When the blender gets an air bubble and stiffens and clogs, she pounds it with the heel of her hand to make it move. There's nothing more satisfying than that whirring column of emptiness, that perfect ovoid space down the center of a blender cup telling her that the mixture's in motion, the solids are going to liquid, the switchblade axis is spinning.

Last week, she was working with Vanessa and Richard, the owner. Vanessa's hair is always the same at work—like hardshell chocolate on a round white scoop of vanilla—because she spends an hour every morning straightening it with an iron. She says that she wakes up with a Jewfro, and then she points at Lucinda's hair. "Like that only shorter. I can't stand working with hair in my face. Are you sure you aren't Jewish?" Then she says that by-the-way she has massive cramps today because she just had her eggs harvested, so she apologizes if she's in a bitchy mood.

"What is that?" says Lucinda.

"Egg harvesting?" Vanessa tamps down a talon of hair. "They pay you a shitload of money so somebody can use your genetic material to make a baby." She puts finger quotes around the words *genetic material*. "It's not like I don't have enough eggs to spare, I mean, God. Somebody up there doesn't get supply and demand." Sometimes her voice reverberates in the small space of the smoothie shop with a painfully metallic clatter, like a pot dropping in the stainless sink. Sometimes she even notices it herself. Sometimes she breaks into bright song. The lofted ceilings and polished wood floors are a perfect echo chamber. She says she wants to be a singer.

"Did it hurt?" Lucinda says, patting her voice down with her hand, trying to exert a sly influence on Vanessa.

Vanessa opens her mouth like, *what do you think?* "You know how every month you drop one egg? Well, I just dropped thirty. My ovaries are like heaps of rubble after some demolition project. It's absolutely immobilizing."

It doesn't look very immobilizing to Lucinda as she watches Vanessa tromp to the sink and drop in a blender cup. The lights overhead shear out bits of her vision. They're roosting in shallow silver bowls all over the ceiling. A wet lacquer slides endlessly over sheets of glass and polished steel. It's like being stuck inside a revolving bottle.

Richard chuckles. "Yeah right," he says. "Miss slam-bam-thank-you-ma'am." His hands are crossed over the top of his stomach and he's leaning back on the counter to watch.

Vanessa rolls her eyes. She proceeds to peel skins out of the veggie grinder and plop them into a rag. "Shut up, Richard," she says.

Lucinda can see Richard's laughter parting the curtain of his festive Hawaiian shirt, at the bottom where his belly bulges, hard and white as a peeled potato. Her own Hawaiian shirt is humongous, hanging in a steep flat plane that stops mid-thigh. She wonders if she should ask a question. She knows Richard thinks she is strange. He's not sure about her. She should ask a question.

"What's he blabbing about?" she says to Vanessa, hooking her thumb, thinking she got it about right with the gabby tones. It's all good practice for her.

Vanessa pats at her wool helmet. "It's a long story," she says, then turns to Richard. "I *had* to." Her voice goes rich with extravagant regret.

"Don't tell Harvard," he says. "He'd kill you if he knew." He seems to be quoting Vanessa back to herself.

"Who's Harvard?" Lucinda asks.

"My boyfriend." Vanessa says this with a stitch in her mouth. Her voice goes slightly surly, as if she is saying yuck at something. She flicks her rag over the trashcan. Lucinda can tell that something is off about the boyfriend. Or else she just doesn't like the job she's doing. "He goes to Harvard."

"Why don't you tell her how you cheated on him? She slept with someone," Richard blurts gaily. "Twice."

"Well"—Vanessa flings up her hands in protest—"they kept giving me huge injections of estrogen to get the eggs to grow, and I was horny. My friend set it up." She kicks the trash back under the counter and rolls a private look at Lucinda. *His daughter,* she mouths, finger pointing under her chin, then turns back. "It didn't mean anything," she says loudly. "Obviously we used protection."

"I heard you called the fire station to come put your fire out." Richard rattles out a few more coins of laughter.

"Right," says Vanessa. "Because I told you that."

He pushes off the counter. Someone is coming in. A thin figure with a foam of white hair.

Lucinda feels the air perforate. Why should it matter? Vanessa tilts her head to Lucinda. "The guy worked for the fire department," she says as they all watch the figure squint at the menu board. She taps Lucinda with a confidential elbow. "What a creep."

Lucinda nods. She doesn't know which one she is talking about—Richard or the customer or the guy. Richard pokes the order into the register.

"Even his daughter thinks he's a creep."

Lucinda has tipped her head lightly to take this in. "You know his daughter?" she murmurs. She thinks she's putting on the right inflection.

Vanessa flutters her eyes and taps her fingers on the machine for the order slips, waiting to receive their commands. "It's how I got this wonderful job. She's in my math class now. Or was." Her hand is aloft, poised in the air to snatch the incoming ticket. "I haven't seen her since our 'double date,' probably because she couldn't look me in the face anymore." She shrugs. Now Lucinda senses that she feels a little skeezy over the date. "Then again, it's math class. Nobody comes." Now it's slithering out. "Banana-Rama," she says.

Richard turns and says the same thing.

"We have a machine right here that tells us."

Richard gives her one vapid look and slumps to the swinging door.

After he goes Vanessa blows out a sigh. "God I need money. If I didn't need it I would quit. I'm selling my human parts, for Christ's sake." As Vanessa digs in the vanilla tub, Lucinda shovels in the banana. It's a lot of banana.

Lucinda can see the empty shop behind her in the two-way mirror. Upon inspection, the customer's silhouette is outside, bent intimately over her cell phone. She can tell it's a her now. "You can go," she says. Vanessa's shift ends in only six minutes, and Lucinda wants to be nice. "I got this."

With a groan of gratitude Vanessa plunks down the scoop and goes to the tip jar. "Why did my family have to go broke right when I came to college?" Change clatters across the counter and Vanessa flattens it with her palm. Lucinda fits the blender cup onto the power spinner and flips the plexiglass hood to mute the sound and watches Vanessa put a dollar back in—just in case the lady had left something. That was nice. She concurs that family is a nuisance.

Vanessa death-levers her head back at the ceiling. "All I do is pay for their wine and doctor's bills. Anyway, whatever. At least I'm not selling actual *sex* yet. I wish Igor over there would stop talking about my embarrassing self-compromises." She flicks a glance at the mirror. "It's beyond gross. And he totally wants to sleep with me."

Lucinda opens the blender hood. She makes a disgraced face for Vanessa's benefit and pounds a bubble out of the roaring cup and returns Vanessa's wave goodbye. Then she spends the rest of the day wondering if Richard really wants to sleep with Vanessa. That's something that had not occurred to her until Vanessa said it. Now it seems obvious. Is that why he always stands around like such a hobgoblin whenever they are all working together? He never loiters out front talking to Lucinda when she's alone. He always sits behind the mirrored glass in his office, poking at his calculator and making phone calls, swiveling his chair around to face the wall. At least that's what she usually saw him doing whenever she had to dash back to get the bins out of the freezer when supplies got low up front.

Richard was not all that bad. If there was a rush he always came out to help her, so she knew he did look out the glass.

Sometimes she couldn't help herself. She stared into the mirror when she didn't know if he was back there or not, mesmerized by the dirty smoke of her reflection. It was like the glass was a secret panel in some magic trick, giving her a view of herself from far away. It told her something. Sometimes, imagining that Richard might be looking up and seeing her, she lifted her hand in a vague, viscid wave. She never knew if he was waving back. It always looked like a hand lifted on a dead woman by a slow current of water. Strangely, seeing herself whisking that watery hello was like saying something other than hello to herself. She couldn't stop doing it. That was probably why he thought she was strange.

She could see him through the mirror sometimes too, whenever he went to his lamp in the corner to scribble the signatures on paychecks.

"Got your paycheck," he would wave it in the air, coming out afterwards.

This time she took it and he nosed out a chuckle. "Yeah," he said, as if she was already in the middle of a conversation with him.

Lucinda split him a quick glance. She was allowed to take one food item home for free at the end of her shift, and she was preparing herself a baked potato—one of several new additions to the menu meant to lure the college dinner crowd.

"That Vanessa," Richard said.

"What?" she said, wondering what from earlier he wanted to revisit. Before he could say anything a soft sashay of steps came up on them.

Lucinda turned as the customer pawed at her own chest. "Hey—fancy that!"

Lucinda was startled and a little wobbled. "Oh. Hi," she said.

"It's you!" said Lauren, from the play.

Lucinda's cheeks split into an ungainly smile. She liked Lauren, but the gash of smile she gave scared her.

"My heart just did a drum roll! I didn't know you worked here!"

Richard expelled a gas of unctuous laughter. "Reunion," he said, swiping his hands together.

"Marty gave me a stack of these," Lauren said, brandishing a sheaf of paper. "Is it okay if I put one up here?" She aimed this question at Richard.

"Uh," Richard poked his nose up politely. "What is it?"

"A bill for a play? Down the street? It's going to be *other-worldly*." Her voice bounced into a trippy tenor. "At the Im*a*go." She gave the word frills.

Richard aimed a ferret's grin at her. "Sure. No problem." He seemed muted by her enthusiasm, almost normal.

Lucinda tried to look placid. She did not want that up on the board but Lauren was not to be deterred. There were a lot of people like this in her theater class, who seemed to flit about with some perky omnipresence, turning up in various unrelated precincts of her life. The other day she had seen another one, Rory, in the parking lot at the apartment building, smacking his gum through the driver's window of a pickup. What was he doing there? Lucinda liked the people in her acting class, but there was a weird, showy ardor about them that could strike her like a bad chime.

Lauren, who seemed to like Lucinda oddly a lot, actually came up to Lucinda halfway through class on the first day and said, "I'll be your friend," with emphasis on the *your*, as if she were picking her out of a lineup. Since then Lucinda has felt a little singled out, a little trespassed upon.

Today Lauren looked like Peter Pan, in a soft suede tunic with little moccasins. It occurred to Lucinda that she'd only ever seen Lauren in costume.

Lauren was already stepping back now and seemed to be taking a big enjoyable swig of the whole exhibit: Lucinda, skullcapped and wallpapered in tropical vegetation, her boss tufting coconut into his mouth and swiping his hands down his voluminous shirt. Can she see Lucinda's mute lapse into nervy discomfort? Her apparent embarrassment? "Well," her eyes swing over them with voluptuous ease. She has gone, without so much as a see you soon.

For some reason, Lucinda turns to Richard. "That was my friend."

"Yeah?" He's leaning back again, busily working coconut out of his teeth with his tongue. He pulls down on his nose.

"Going home?" His eyes settle on her like a fly.

Lucinda nods. Her hands fumble at her potato. She doesn't know why she's still nervous.

"That for your boyfriend?"

She glances over at him. Did she tell him she had a boyfriend? "No." Lucinda smiles at the idea of her boyfriend eating a potato. It's for the dog.

"Yeah," says Richard, as if disagreeing with her, as if he wants her to be making a potato for her boyfriend. He sniffs. "What a catch," he says, insinuating something she can't quite follow. Does he mean him or her?

"Vanessa told me you're living with him," he says. His smile is plucked up like a snarl.

"Oh." Lucinda sprinkles bacon and cheese onto her potato. She's not sure how she feels knowing this about Vanessa.

Richard wags his head. "She's a pistol all right."

Lucinda makes a sound in her throat, just enough to show she's listening.

"You wouldn't ever do that, would you?"

"What?" She seems to have lost the thread of the conversation.

"Cheat on your boyfriend."

It takes Lucinda a second to trawl all the way back to where he is.

When she gets there, she's swarmed by his germy intrigue. Richard is sifting out a low chuckle. "I don't know what that girl is thinking." Now Lucinda is morbidly curious. She wants to know what Richard is thinking. Is he going to talk with her about Vanessa? Is he going to ask her opinion of Vanessa's sexual accessibility? What will Richard find fit to say? She feels like his smile is crumbling out a secret he wants to confess.

"No," she says. "I don't even really think she has a boyfriend."

"Eh. You think he's made up?" Richard seems to take this without any surprise. "I don't know—she told me a lot about him."

She nods. "But she doesn't seem to like him."

Hairs come out of his nose like the legs of crushed spiders. He pinches it with his fingers. "Yeah. I did that once and my wife went berserk."

Lucinda looks up. "What?"

Richard pushes at his glasses and she sees he has a folded bill in his hand. "Cheated."

Lucinda's brow just went briskly up her forehead. She looks at Richard and the bill. She can't tell if he's gloating or looking guilty right now. "I didn't know you were married."

"Not anymore." He sniffs out a laugh. "She was not a nice woman. But still, cheating." He shakes his head. "Never a good idea." He puts his fist with the bill in it on the counter. "Just get out of it. Don't sit around and make it worse." Lucinda is feeling somewhat crowded. Why is he telling her this? "But—" Richard charbroils a breath. "I guess I'm a free agent now." Now he isn't saying anything and he has his head tilted at an inquisitive angle. His smile hooks her with a wincing stillness.

Lucinda wraps the foil around her potato.

"A bad relationship—it's not the bed you want to make in the morning, right?" She thinks she nods. "I heard you need cash for a security deposit on another apartment." He has a knowing smile on his face. "Can't live with him can't live without him, huh?"

Lucinda is a little perturbed. Apparently Vanessa told him everything. "It's not like that." And then she realizes it's exactly like that. But not in the way that he thinks.

"Uh-huh." Richard clears his throat. "You should work more hours if you need cash. Minimum wage," he says, wagging his head. "That's not the fast track."

Lucinda gives him a brief smile.

She clocks out and Richard watches her. He seems to be probing at her with his eyes, waiting for something. A breeze flaps the playbill on the bulletin board. It's like Lauren is laughing at her. Daintily, she picks up her smoothie and potato.

"You know," Richard says, pointing. "Somebody's been taking things without paying for them."

She stops walking. "What?"

"Like what you're doing right there." A barb in his voice snags an invisible curtain off the conversation, as if it's really been hiding something else under there this whole time. What is going on? "You're not trying to set the table for someone at home are you?"

"What?" She looks down at her potato and smoothie, utterly discombobulated.

"Saving money?" says Richard. His tone has so barely shifted that she can't yet tell if he's joking.

"I thought I was allowed to take one food item for free," she plays along.

"That's two food items."

"Oh—" Lucinda grimaces in surprise. As she does she realizes something. "I didn't think the smoothie counted. I thought the free smoothie was separate." She realizes she's lying.

Richard shakes his head. "It was one free smoothie when that was all we sold. Now it's one free food item—smoothie or potato or pretzel or soup bowl. Not both." He really does seem dead serious.

"Oh, I'm sorry." It's barely all she can say. She has been taking right in front of him like this for weeks. All along she had been perfectly aware that she was getting away with something. Lucinda had thought that somehow her actions were exerting some kind of compliance over him, since it was too blatant to even look like stealing. Vanessa did it too. Now it seemed like Richard had been paying attention all this time, building up some kind of collateral.

Richard pushed off the counter. "I'm warning everybody," he said. He went to the register to put the bill underneath the tray in the drawer. It was a hundred-dollar bill. "I'm putting this—" Lucinda watched him flick the fold out before he put it in. "If you need." He put it in. "Here," he said, his voice at a queer tilt. She waited, shaken, for the rest of his explanation about the bill, but he seemed to sniff up the rest of her angst like a bitter, iffy odor that he couldn't get rid of any other way. "All right," he said, to himself, swinging his head away from her, and then he aped his way back to the swinging door.

On her way out, Lucinda snatched down the playbill with shaking hands.

"Wait a second," Vanessa says at the bench, where Lucinda has just told her about it. "Are you saying he was offering it to you? Like here's a hundred dollars?"

Lucinda is making a crinkle face. It's all she can do after having this admission dug out of her. Vanessa had done most of the work, clawing and excavating the exchange as if she had some prior knowledge of it. All Lucinda had said was that Richard seemed sketchy.

"He didn't do anything to you, did he?"

Lucinda still has to work on the way her voice goes pale and dank in times of distress—coming out of her like steam from a manhole. It seems to creep people.

"Maybe he was just putting it there for some other reason," she says now, smoothing her thin satin dress for the play.

"No. He was totally coming on to you." Vanessa's hand comes up and flutters at her bangs. "He was feeling you out. And then he was totally threatening you when you didn't take the bait. Like you shouldn't tell anybody about his come-on or else he'll fire you for being a food thief." She seems slightly miffed at some part of this, and not exactly shocked. "And what's with the hundred?" she says. "He didn't give me one."

"Give you one for what?"

"For—I don't know. For always coming on to me? Why do you think he gave it to you?"

"He didn't give it to me. He just said he was putting it there," winces Lucinda.

"Well, why would he say that?" Vanessa wrinkles her lip. "I think he's bribing you to have sex. Like if you change your mind the offer still stands. He should bribe me to have sex. Kidding," she says, slicing air with two flat hands, before Lucinda can even open a gory look on her. It occurs to Lucinda that she doesn't think Vanessa is kidding.

"He is *way* more pervy than I thought," Vanessa says, avoiding her eye and looking out at the patio with a squint.

"Maybe he was just trying to make me feel exposed. For stealing."

"You're taking *snack* food. *Everybody* does it." Vanessa was the one who told her she could. "And he's not warning everybody. Christ, sometimes he helps me bag mine up." Vanessa is wagging her head with a slow, showy consternation. "No. If I were you I would tell this Dracula guy to take off his duck bill and come meet you after work. It's not safe there. Jesus—he wants to rape us."

"You know, he doesn't wear it all the time."

Vanessa keels forward, her mouth a silent leer. "That would be funny if he did."

Lucinda can't help it. After a bout of infectious laughter, she begs Vanessa's confidence. "Don't tell," she says.

"What, about the killer duck you live with? Or the boss who wants to ram-bam you? Let me have one of those if you're not going to eat them."

Lucinda tries not to recoil as Vanessa dives at her celery. She can be so brusque. With a queasy feeling, Lucinda looks down at her watch. Her eyelids feel tacky. She thinks about the play. "It's time for the next appointment." She doesn't know why she told Vanessa all that. Vanessa is not exactly her friend, though she does like her. Lucinda has never exactly had friends and it is because she does things like this. She seems to attract people who don't know the type of person she really is. She feels a vanishing guilt all the time, like a faint breath on her neck. It's as if she hovers off to her own periphery, watching and waiting to become what they see. She knows she's something else.

She knows Vanessa will check for the bill the next time she is at work. Vanessa will tell Lucinda, not Richard, that it is gone. She'll say that she looked and she'll swear she didn't take it. Did somebody else? Who would steal a hundred-dollar bill they knew nothing about? They will confer over this. Lucinda will say nothing about having taken it herself. Together they will speculate over whether Richard took it back or not. If he calls Lucinda to the back to explain herself, she will say that the only person she told about the bill was Vanessa. He will look out through the two-way mirror, his dismal squint turned on her. He probably won't fire Lucinda. Maybe he'll proposition Vanessa. Lucinda wants to know what he will do. She wants him to wonder what he is doing, who he is paying and why. She doesn't know why she wants this but she will wait now to see what he will do. Maybe he'll put another bill under there. She has a feeling he might. And if he does, then it'll also be hers for the snatching.

Vanessa tilts forward with a groan. "God, I feel like a hag."

Lucinda stares at her, momentarily abashed.

"*You* know," says Vanessa with a roll of her eyes. "My ovaries have just been eaten out with a spoon? Jesus," she says. "I hope there really is more in there. Someday I want to have kids." She grimaces. "If I'm not made into meat first."

The Window

*D*racula can hear the neighbors fighting through the walls. He is surprised that Lucinda sleeps through it. It's three A.M., and afterwards he finds the neighbor outside smoking a cigarette. The door to his apartment is ajar and he keeps dribbling a stream of sulky comments in through the opening. The neighbor is standing over the ashtray between their doors in gray sweatshorts and a baseball cap. His calves are huge and his cheeks are huger. Dracula takes all this in and hunches further into his coat. His neighbor is Russian, and most of what he says is incomprehensible.

"I'm sorry. That's terrible of me." The Russian pats his hand over his mouth when he sees Dracula, like a little girl. His voice is a flat high tenor that reminds Dracula of a Muppet rendition he once saw of a frog. He has seen the Muppet rendition of himself. It's a little bit accurate. "Such a mess," says the Russian, tsking his tongue. That makes him seem more foreign. Dracula shrugs, politely. He doesn't want a conversation. The Russian is speaking much louder than he needs to and Dracula suspects it's because of the woman in the apartment. Dracula doesn't see her come to the door and he doesn't hear her say anything back to him.

This is how it is. The Russian is always speaking much louder than he needs to, either yelling across the courtyard at the live-in manager about the broken stove or shouting up to the third-floor windows about the scratch mysteriously marring his car. The thing about the woman inside is that Dracula has never seen her or heard her. He is not sure she exists.

Somebody next door is always singing songs by Whitney Houston, and he is pretty sure it is the Russian himself.

"Is that Russian?" Dracula asks.

The Russian nods. "Yes it is."

It's obvious that the Russian yells because he thinks that no one understands him. He enjoys a privacy that allows him full latitude in front of everybody. He is an exhibitionist.

"Yeah. I thought so."

"Why? You know it?" The Russian's head moves to a grim tilt.

Dracula shakes his head, somewhat vaguely. "I used to know somebody who did. That's how he sounded."

The Russian blows out a vaudeville sigh. "Yes. All of the consonants, none of the vowels." He flaps his cigarette hand. "Learn the bad words for when you get angry. They're good to say." He turns to close the door and belts three words into the crack, which translate plainly to *I love you*. Dracula knows that the Russian would not have said those words in that way, in that tone, if he wanted the woman inside to think that he meant them. The woman probably knows that too.

"Those are a few for you."

Dracula pretends along with a smile. He wonders how he so effortlessly translated that phrase. Then he wonders why he remembers nothing else of his Russian.

The Russian puffs his lips benignly. Now he looks like that pig, Dracula thinks, the one who's in love with the frog. He's a little surprised that he even knows this.

In general, Dracula is surprised by how much he has absorbed of pop culture since he has been dating Lucinda. He has not been inside of this weave for a long time. He is not sure that it's good for him, for the plane of existence he occupies. It does make him feel less foreign. It seems strange that a Russian can seem more foreign than him.

Lucinda has other thoughts about the Russian. She thinks he is not merely foreign, but genuinely certifiable. "He talks to himself in there. There's *no* woman," she says. Dracula is not sure how she can be so certain, but she is. It makes him wonder if she's been in the apartment.

As much as Dracula considers the Russian a nuisance, Lucinda seems to despise him and avoid him at all costs. If he ever comes up the stairs and says hello she pretends he's not there. Dracula can't get her to say why she hates him so much.

"Don't make me talk about him."

"But your whole family is worse than him."

"I know." She says it like she doesn't understand it herself. "He just won't stop singing," she tries, in a belated explanation.

"Maybe he'll stop when the news dies down."

"What?" she says.

"The singer—Whitney Houston." The dead one. "Isn't that who it is?" He already knows who it is. The only reason he knows is because they won't stop talking about it on the radio. This is what's diverting him these days. He has to listen to the radio if he wants any diversion on his work route. He is starting to wonder why he is becoming so dependent on diversion. Another tic in the dial of his assimilation.

Dracula is having a hard time with this. He's having a hard time with all of it. His new domestic entrenchment. The moods and misgivings that have crept their way in. This confession the other night. How she said she saw him somewhere. *In the window,* she said. *That day.* How she also inexplicably quit her job, for entirely unrelated reasons. She now won't talk to him about any of this.

"Okay, fine," she says, when he returns to the subject again. For the third time he has refused to let her go to sleep. "I *saw* you," she says, flopping her arms out on the pillows. They are bare and long, glossy as entrails freshly dragged from a corpse. "Your reflection. In the library."

The Russian pounds his fist on the wall. "I hear you!"

They look at each other. "Is he talking to us?" They can't tell if he pounded on their wall or the neighboring wall.

Every bedroom in this complex has a Four Corners and this is theirs. Dracula and his girlfriend are not even talking that loud.

The fist thuds again, this time more obliquely, like a scuff more than a thud.

"Maybe he's talking to her?" Dracula means the woman inside the apartment. His head is full right now of a distracted static. Had she really just said what he thought she said? There is no way.

Lucinda groans, softly. "There is no *her*, Vlad. What if you're not really Dracula? What if you're just a maniac?" she whispers fiercely. "All you do is kill pigeons. I don't know if you're Dracula if all you do is kill pigeons."

"I'm Dracula," he says, fixedly.

"I don't know which I'd rather you be." Lucinda doesn't seem to have heard him yet. "If you're not him, then we're both crazy. If you are, then I'm just as much a monster as you because I *saw* you."

The fist clops the wall again, almost socially, and Lucinda stuffs the pillow over her face.

"He can't possibly hear us," says Dracula. He is too disoriented to focus. He looks at her, trying to find a strand in this web of revelation and follow it. "Okay," he says. He realizes that he is so used to not exactly believing her that he has to concentrate. "So you're saying you saw me." The fist is now thumping a gentle tempo on the wall, as if keeping time to a song. "In the window." It is beginning to dawn on him. "At the library." Dracula's voice dribbles out like gruel. He can't believe what he's hearing.

"It's pretty simple." Lucinda snatches the pillow off her face impatiently. "Either I am a monster or you are not Dracula. That's what I've been trying to tell you. Either way we're screwed."

Dracula lets this work its way in.

"I de-ci-ded long ago, not to fall on anyone's sha-dow."

"Oh my God," says Lucinda.

"Wait," Dracula tries not to be thrown. "But I am Dracula," he says fixedly.

"I *wanted* you to go out and do your Dracula thing the other night. With the girls. When my mother took the cage, I was going to follow you. But then you called Warren instead."

"At least I live as I will be."

Lucinda wags her head. Her face is soggy as an old bandage. Is it the song?

"You were going to follow me?" Dracula says.

"If you can drain one whole girl then I believe you. You're Dracula," she says limply.

"They can-not ac-cept my dig-ni-ty."

"Wait a second." Dracula pats the air, chafing at this. Something's not right here. "How is that... ?" He tries to sink down into his uninterrupted thoughts, staring at the slump of Lucinda's face. Did she want to watch him? Why does that seem unnerving? "You... want me to?"

"No, I don't. It makes me sick."

"But—" Why then? "You—" He blinks himself back into focus. "You're saying you really saw me?"

"It hap-pened so to me."

"Is that the *same* song again?" Lucinda huffs. "Is that even how it goes? I don't think that's how it goes."

He can't help it, the instantaneous tripping on tangled contradictions. That is definitely not how it goes. "Just wait a second," he says again. He can barely catch his breath. "Do you always see my reflection or was it just that once?"

Lucinda gives him a glassy look. The Russian's voice mercifully subsides, his murmurs a sultry serenade to their grim consultations. They listen for a deaf second.

"I don't know," Lucinda says. "The first time it was definitely a reflection. I was not expecting it and you were there, behind me. I just thought you were some gross guy checking himself out."

"I didn't even notice you. I mean I didn't notice you noticing," Dracula says, disgruntled. He feels almost as if he's lost the memory altogether. "You didn't even blink."

"But then you told me you were Dracula, and after that every time I looked for it I could see it, and every time I didn't look for it I noticed I didn't see it. It's like I can't tell if what I'm seeing is real or if I'm doing it all myself."

Dracula lets out a grizzled breath.

"Quiet!" the Russian shouts.

They peer at each other, utterly beside themselves. They wonder how in the world they got on this diametric, this perfect seesaw of monstrosity. They decide to make a plan. They have to make a plan. Eventually. They will stage a test. It's the only way.

"Okay," says Dracula.

"I don't want to do it," says Lucinda, in the voice that says they must.

The song is there again, the smallest of campfire wisps.

"The big-gest love for all, is hap-pen-ing in me."

Lucinda snorts forlornly. "What, he couldn't secure the rights or something?"

Dracula tries to smile. Now he can't help it. He's thinking about the corpse in the bathtub, the silent white porcelain, all the tragic manglings of lyrics and life.

He puts his arm around Lucinda. "What's all this in the bed?"

"Oh."

It looks like gum, all these confetti bits.

"I was doing that last night, when I couldn't sleep."

Dracula gathers them up. The song trails out again. The way it fades, they can tell the Russian has walked out of the room. Dracula feeds the bits of gum to Lucinda. He feels bad for keeping her up.

"Sorry," she says to him. He knows she won't sleep now. "I couldn't figure out how to say it."

The silence seems to be holding on to their bated breath. Then Lucinda gives Dracula a kiss. She tastes like Hubba Bubba.

For some reason Dracula finds he needs this—he needs her to need it. Do they really feel like it? That's what his look asks her. He doesn't put on his mouth guard. The gum is a floating gonad that soon loses all flavor between them, and somebody eventually swallows it, and it isn't until afterward that they notice the Russian has kept them in a loud dismal silence the whole time.

Dracula is suspicious of the Russian, and more and more as the days and weeks go by. He just went downstairs to try to catch the apartment manager in the office and discuss the new rent predicament they now face, and the Russian was in his window staring out his curtain the whole time. He was looking down into the inside courtyard, apparently at Dracula and the manager, but he never waved back. Dracula had just missed the apartment manager at the office because he arrived barely beyond the end of business hours, and he had to go to his apartment door. He can only observe this archaic ritual of nine-to-five business around the time of the winter solstice, when it gets dark early enough for him to pry himself awake in haste, and even then he's cutting in a few minutes before the office closes and still syrupy with sleep. It's not early winter right now, the solstice was some time ago, and that leaky zodiacal light is lingering at the horizon, keeping him cranked in tight till well after five P.M. The manager lives in the complex, but he only wants to be disturbed outside his apartment door if there's an emergency. He has made that clear. Business hours are for business. But it's either that or an unnegotiated nonpayment. There is indeed a crisis unfolding here, Dracula has decided, even if most of it does not concern the manager.

"Lucinda lost her job," he says. "So—"

"Who's Lucinda?"

"My girlfriend?" Dracula is momentarily disoriented. He cocks his head back, like a hammer on a revolver. "The one who's living with me?" He turns to point, as if she'll be there. The apartment manager follows his motion and his eyes seem to gutter on something and he lofts his hand reluctantly. Dracula scrambles for the missed visual input. It's the Russian, next door, not waving back.

"What is with that guy," says the apartment manager.

"I don't know," says Dracula. He takes this moment to mention that the Russian kept him up last night pounding his fist on the wall. It's a conversational tactic he finds useful, to get the manager's annoyance preemptively directed elsewhere. "He kept yelling at somebody to be quiet."

The manager turns with a squint. "He was pounding?"

Dracula bares his teeth affirmatively.

"Was he yelling at you?"

"Uh—"

"Well, I don't want him breaking a wall. Let me know if he does it again. I'll talk to him if it's going to damage property."

Dracula hesitates, trying to formulate his next sentence, and the apartment manager adopts a wooden expression. "I don't want to get in people's business. You have your girlfriend in there, apparently"—he jams his arm out. *Apparently?* "I don't say anything as long as you both pay your rent and don't disrupt anybody or do damage—"

At the mention of paying rent, Dracula fumbles out a few words and the manager pats them out of the air, not even waiting, "you have somebody living with you—she's not on the lease. That's fine, I say nothing. If things get out of hand with him, then maybe I'll call somebody. The guy's a little loud at times. I don't want the police coming over and complicating things."

"Oh, yeah," says Dracula, "I'm not even—I don't—" He swipes his hand over his face. The rent. How can he get back to the rent?

When finally he stumbles over it the manager scoffs. "Now here you are asking for an extension on your rent. You're knocking on my personal door and you're not talking to me during business hours. Who's a disturbance now? Now you're a disturbance to me because you don't have your money and I need to pay my bills and you're knocking on my door when I should be eating my dinner."

"I—" says Dracula. He's clenching his jaw. The manager has some vinegar in him. The manager seems to have gone a bit caustic.

"I mean, here I thought you were paying the rent all by yourself. That's what you were doing however long ago before she came—whatever you said her name was." He flails his hand up in her direction again—"Look, I don't want to know about her. I'm just saying, this is how it is. Your circumstances change but mine don't. I need rent on time."

"Okay," says Dracula, restraining himself. He has paid rent on time every month that he has lived here, "except, I'm just asking, this month—"

"On time," repeats the manager, and Dracula can't believe he's actually going to stiff-arm him. He is so close to drilling two holes in this guy's neck. Except that he is thinking this entirely in his mind, and his body stands there severed from thought while the door closes in his face.

As he is walking back up the steps, still feeling the effects of this faulty connection, the Russian is gone and instead it's Lucinda standing in their window looking at him. She shakes her head as if she already knows. She probably saw the apartment manager gesture at her. He might have even been explicitly pointing her out for all Dracula knows. All this time, he has been a model tenant, he thinks. He's trying to remember how long he has lived here. How many lease renewals has he signed? He's never made so much as a peep and now he can't get any leniency? The apartment manager has even insinuated that he might be as much a disturbance as the Russian. Passing the Russian's window he sees a slit in the curtains, and in it sits a cat on the back of a chair. He tries discreetly to peer past it and sees only the brown broth of a shaded lamp. He thinks of the cooking odors he and Lucinda sometimes smell from his apartment, foreign food dishes that smell bad because they can't recognize them. He and Lucinda have already speculated that it might be the cat he's talking to in there. It really doesn't seem that way.

At the window he kisses his thumb and plants it over Lucinda's mouth. It gives him a strange sensation because nothing in the gesture matches at all how he feels.

Nothing right now seems to match up. Nothing seems like what it is. Ever since she told him she saw his reflection in the library that day. All this time he thought he knew exactly what they were. It was the oldest story. Now he doesn't know what the story is.

The scary part is that he can't remember the time before they were dating. The slippery nights he spent out alone. When was the last time he even had a human victim? He can no longer revisit or conjure the memories.

"How long have we been dating?" he asks Lucinda. She shrugs. Neither of them is very good with time. "How long have we been living together?" Their gazes slide off each other, inscrutably. The Russian has been here as long as Dracula has. He remembers the day they both moved in—the Russian hauling boxes along the breezeway while Dracula stood on the doorsill, airing out a freshly painted apartment. He could always ask him. But it has somehow become a matter of self-respect not to talk to the Russian. As the days go by, it seems as though they are out to get each other. The

Russian flicks a dozen crushed cigarettes onto his doormat and Dracula scoops ashtray sand into the Russian's mailbox. Dracula wonders who started this—him, the Russian, or the apartment manager. Or was it Lucinda? Her cold-shouldering? He still wonders at her insistence that the Russian has no live-in companion. He is sure that he has heard a female murmur at least once or twice. Sometimes people are there that you don't see. She should know this.

Now he stands over the pressboard table with the curtains drawn over his contested reflection and thinks about the manager's comments about damage. Lucinda has done some damage. There are burn and stab marks in the table, dart holes in the door, blots of old blood in the bedroom curtains. He once thought those curtains were just abundant and convenient absorbency for the various self-inflictions she performed, usually to put herself to sleep when he was driving a shipment overnight, which he didn't think she did as often as this except that he's been going out on a lot more overnights now to try to make rent, and now he's grossly disturbed to find that they almost look like a pattern, one that he can possibly imagine the manager overlooking upon inspection, if she ever fills in a few strategic areas and then has the restraint to desist. Then, grimacing further, he ascertains that maybe she is actually making a design, something torturously decorative, a perfect collection of Rorschachs to study by moonlight. He pulls the curtain out flat. He sees that, no, what she's been doing is stenciling the slow calligraphy of words, words he can't make out. A lot of it looks like it's done in felt-tip pen. Well that's a relief.

When he asks, his girlfriend heaves a deserted sigh. "He's always drilling that foreign chitchat at me through the wall. I'm sure he's talking to me. He's talking to *me*. I'm the one," she says, as if it's an answer to an earlier question. "I thought you knew I was doing that."

"Why would I know?"

"It's kind of obvious. There's a Russian-English dictionary beside the bed."

"There is?" How did he not notice that?

She shakes her head as if to dismiss his obliviousness. "I write it down so I can translate later. I can't help thinking it's a message, or a code, or something"—she ratchets her finger back and forth between them—"like maybe he's a messenger and he doesn't even know it. Stranger things have happened."

Dracula stares at her. One of the Russian's meals comes wafting through the walls. A deep fungal smell.

"Sometimes I get the words wrong. Usually," she says.

Dracula seems to be lost for words. He tries to close off his nose to the odors. He is aware that his freezer is currently crammed beak to toe with frozen bird carcasses that he thaws and sips inside brown paper bags on his delivery route. He knows he shouldn't judge.

"You know I get insomnia," Lucinda says. "Basically I'm just learning Russian. The hard way."

Dracula doesn't know what he wants to say. When he thinks about how his girlfriend is learning to speak the language of his old-world neighbors, of his own abandoned liaisons—through the conduit of his boorish neighbor—Dracula feels a hot poker jab him in the gut. Why does this scandalize him so? How long has she been doing this? What words has she learned? She recites a few pleas and admonishments. *Stop. Don't hurt me like this.* She now knows more than he does of the language he is pretty sure is still lapping somewhere at the deserted grottoes of his mind.

Lucinda plugs her nose. "God. What awful thing is he cooking in there?"

The Russian has been lately admonishing somebody to eat. "Eat why don't you!" he says. "Why are you starving yourself like this? You're killing me!"

"By the way," Lucinda says, "my mom's still bugging me about dinner. When will you have a night off?"

"When I make enough money for rent," Dracula says, grimly. He won't make enough money for rent.

He's been picking up extra shifts whenever he can. He drives the overnights between the drop-off stations, a perfect job for him. It's flu season, and somebody is always looking for a sub. Lucinda is still looking for a job to replace the one she left. She won't say much about why she quit. She also bought a TV, a cheap one, with money Dracula didn't know they had. That does not make him feel good. They get just enough reception off the rabbit ears to pick up the syndicated shows he likes. Lucinda hates the TV. But then again, she says, maybe she should watch. She can't decide if she should begin living like they're nitwit degenerates and just drift into the slow doldrums of insanity, or if she should be doing something more avidly aggressive about her impending monstrosity. *What could they do?* she asks over and over again, looking for ideas.

Dracula keeps working overtime.

One night, coming home late, he clipped in just before daybreak and it made him feel alive and invigorated in a way that gave him a glimpse of something liberating, his own slim aperture, opening up. Was this what Lucinda was talking about? He found Lucinda on the couch, doing something different too, awake and looking at the TV with wide serious owl eyes. The TV was uncharacteristically on. "I heard the song again," she said.

The song? "What song?"

Lucinda pointed at the wall.

"Oh, his? The Russian's?" Dracula picked up the remote. "I'm going to turn this off."

When Dracula does, he feels bathed in a new and soupy silence. The sound wasn't on, and all that thin static cling from the back of the box is gone.

"It's such a morbid song."

"Morbid?" says Dracula. That is not how he'd describe that song.

"Well, for a funeral," she says. She looks away. "For how she died."

Dracula gives her a puzzled look. "Wait—" Is she talking about the singer who died or somebody whose funeral she went to? "You went to a funeral?"

"It was in the bathtub," Lucinda finishes her thought.

That did not clarify anything.

"Who died?" Dracula asks, trying to draw straight the kink in the conversation.

Lucinda nibbles at her nails. "The girl I worked with. Vanessa. You never met her."

He is still standing next to the open front door.

"She said her boyfriend was going to kill her. Harvard. But that was just a figure of speech."

Dracula feels a swoop of dread. He perches on the table. He stares at the dead TV. "You mean, she was murdered?"

"No," Lucinda says, watching him closely. "I don't think so. I don't know."

Dracula thinks about the bathtub. "She was in the bath?"

Lucinda nods. "She was a singer, and now every time he sings it I'll hear her voice. *Her* voice." After a pinched and desolate silence, she says, "I think it was my fault."

Dracula props his chin on the tips of his fingers. He realizes that he is not surprised to hear her say this.

"I should not have quit my job," Lucinda says.

"What does that have to do with it?"

Lucinda pauses. She seems a little affronted by his tone. "I just stopped talking to her," she mutters, as if she knows this is no answer.

Dracula sits and breathes. He thinks about the dead co-worker and what this means. He thinks about how she won't discuss her reasons for quitting.

Lucinda clamps her hands in prayer between her knees. He looks at her, wishing he wasn't so stuck all the time on himself. There is still so much he doesn't know about her.

The Door

*D*oors always open. That's what Lucinda's father used to say. Her other father, not the one she lives with now. Lived with. She keeps forgetting she moved out. It's all new to her, this situation. Being Dracula's girlfriend. Living with Dracula. Doing his laundry. Doors always open. She hasn't thought of that in a long time.

She doesn't like doing the laundry. It's in the basement of the building and there's only two machines and the foundation walls are literally dissolving into pink sand heaps on the floor. There must be some animal down here digging away. The only hiding place is underneath the bicycles, a huge rabble of all broken parts.

It reminds her of her childhood at home. Her first home. The one before the apartment. The one from those years with her father—her first father. She barely remembers her first father but she does remember that he wasn't the same as her second father.

Sometimes, when she thinks about it, it seems to Lucinda like she's had three fathers, the second one being both of the last two. Because of the accident. Now she wonders if it wasn't he who had the rule about the doors—the second one. The one before the accident. She knows she hasn't heard it said in a long time.

Lucinda pulls Dracula's jeans from the wash, a damp heavy handful. She has to hang them, from a hanger she hooks to a bare iron pipe, because he can't abide any sort of machine- in- stilled shrinkage.

Then she gets out of there fast, holding her breath. Now she's at the bottom of the stairwell, looking at the door directly across from the laundry room door. That one is always closed and the other one is always open. It's why she always thinks of her father—whichever one it was—every time she comes down here.

"I'm afraid something bad is going to happen," she sometimes says to Dracula.

He looks up from his mending. He squeezes her knee. "Something bad is always going to happen," he says. "You just have to live with it."

Lucinda has come to like living in Dracula's apartment. She prefers being outside to being inside. What she likes best, what gives it the uncanny feel of sanctuary, is the inside feeling of the outdoor space. The inner courtyard—that's what she loves. It makes her think she does want to stay here. Maybe she won't bother with another apartment. It's like being in a diorama without its lid—sitting inside an airy museum exhibit and enjoying a companionable coexistence with others who won't bother her. The hedge sculptures, she means. There are figures all over this little open-air cubicle. They help her. She focuses on the play out here. It's like some oblique preparation for the moment she steps into statuary onstage, and then ceases to be herself. Every day she comes out and sits, feeling enclosed and ventilated at the same time, the sky dropping away above her and the walls closing in around her and the hedges cozying up like eternal little friends. Right now a centaur and a mermaid are keeping her company. They are at the center of a small meditation path looking out with their backs to each other. Though mermaids are deceitful and lascivious creatures Lucinda feels certain that this one is still young and unspoiled, leaning out for open armfuls of love. She is fresh and green. Lucinda has seen the manager meticulously trimming her forked tail.

Lucinda often comes out here to the courtyard to wake up. It takes her a long time. Sometimes, she wakes to a version of herself she doesn't exactly recognize. She has to sit until she's familiar again.

Right now, she is taking her time to get her bearings. Lately she's been arriving at work before she's even aware of herself and then it takes a cold glass of water to really plant her in the ground. She often looks into the register drawer minutes after just having done it and then finds the bill on her person somewhere and recalls that she already took it. She doesn't understand why she is taking money from her boss. Why does the register continue to harbor hundred-dollar bills at random and why does she continue to retrieve them? As long as they keep this up they seem to be knitting together the fabric of some inaccessible deal. She doesn't know what the deal is. Maybe this is the deal. Maybe the deal is what they are doing already.

Whatever is happening, Lucinda hasn't told Dracula yet about the hundred-dollar bills. She has been quietly hoarding them away, because she can't add them to their funds without causing cataclysmic ripples. Five bills in all now, and she continues to wonder whether her boss is ever going to try to redeem them. "You're too skinny," he told her one day, out of the blue. It's like he wants to fatten her like a pig. She can't tell when or if the cash-in will come or what she will do in response. She can't tell if she will keep the money or give it back. At first she was saving it for another apartment but now she doesn't want to leave this one. She wants to stay in the rejuvenating stillness of this open box. She wants the centaur and the mermaid to go on guarding each other in eternal commemoration of their mutual solitude. It doesn't matter that they don't go together at all. They are both here.

Sometimes, looking down from their window, Lucinda says to Dracula, "Do you ever feel like we're leaning on a door that's about to open? That's how I feel. Like we're about to fall into some hidden pit." She feels stupid saying it but Dracula looks at her with intense scrutiny, the kind that makes her spine stiffen pleasantly.

"Yes," he says, "yes." It seems they momentarily get each other, in a way they don't have to discuss.

Her father used to say it too.

"You're going to disappear," he said.

Dracula is coming to meet her now at the end of her shifts, whenever they end after dark, but he doesn't ever come inside. She can't tell if Richard senses him out there, deepening and harrowing the night air. She almost wonders sometimes if he does and is afraid. Lately he paces behind the counter like a rat in a laboratory simulation—pushing back and forth through the swinging door and darting looks at the glass windows and bumping between the sink and the mirror. When she sees him under the lamp at his desk, his hand is methodically rubbing his head, as if to soothe away the pain. He hardly talks to her and when he does it's in uneasy expulsions out of the side of his mouth. He is finalizing the divorce with his wife, after six years of separation. It is not pretty, he says to Lucinda. She is reaming me. This makes Lucinda grim with suspicion—the fact that he is wasting petty cash on her in the midst of some intimate gouging. Maybe it's what Vanessa says and he feels compelled to pay her to keep quiet about his earlier come-on, if that's even what it was. Maybe he is tossing reckless sandbags at a flood he knows will bring him to total disaster.

When he comes out of the back room, he's always rubbing at his eyes, almost as if he has been sleeping back there.

"Oh my God," he says, smearing his face. He never looks at her anymore.

"The divorce?" says Lucinda, politely. She doesn't really want to know.

Richard's breath rattles in his throat. "I don't know. I didn't know this was going to happen."

Lucinda is not sure what to make of this. Does he mean the divorce itself? The bitter enmity, the loss of spirit, the bleeding out of all feeling and fund? Or does he mean something else that happened because of the divorce? She gets the sense he wants to tell somebody.

"Didn't know what?" she says, patting lightly at the register keys, hoping he might not answer.

The boss stands in silence. "Oh," he says, behind his hands. Hollowly, he draws a ragged breath. "Oh, my daughter," he says.

For a second, it sounds just like he is saying it directly to her, calling her his daughter, his voice a wobbling plea or appeal.

Lucinda is speechless. She feels her throat slab up like meat. For a second, she imagines that he actually is her father.

The hands slide off his face and he stares out the open door. He likes to prop it wide on winter nights to snag passersby who might not otherwise be tempted by a smoothie, and he places a space heater right beside it, blowing out waves of heat. "I didn't even find out from my wife. I found out from my wife's legal aide. Acting in her capacity."

Lucinda is trying to put two and two together. Does this mean he is finding out something about his daughter? Does this mean his wife is a lawyer?

"I didn't know you had a daughter," she says, even as she remembers. Vanessa said she knew her. Lucinda has her arms crossed over her Hawaiian shirt. It gets cold in here at night with the door open. The heater is a tremendous waste of energy. It sends Dracula into paroxysms of dank despair.

Her boss sniffs and shakes his head. "She used to run away. This time she's really missing."

"Oh—" Lucinda swallows her next word. "That's—" She tries to sound sorry. She is sorry.

Lucinda's boss looks at her. He seems keenly aware of her in some deep way she isn't even aware of herself, and almost as if he pities her for it. She can feel a sprinkling of ice on her spine. "I can't—I have to stop," he says.

"Stop what?" she says quickly back, feeling an earnest need to have him tell her.

But his look seems to weasel further into her and makes her feel suddenly like they've been doing more than she realizes.

"I'm quitting," she says. Her mind is bucking in her head. "Right now, I'll quit."

It's impossible, she thinks. They've not been doing anything. "Okay?" she says, scurrying to get her apron off and clock out.

Her boss blinks at the air. He doesn't say anything.

"I'll just go right now."

Lucinda now has to write her new address down if she wants to get her last paycheck. She's been meaning to do this and she does so with a trembling hand, on a scrap of receipt paper that she puts under the register tray. "It's here," she says, wobbling out the words. In the drawer. "My new address," she tries to clarify. Now her boss has it. He can send the money to the apartment where she lives with Dracula. "You can mail me my last paycheck."

On her way out after hanging her apron she sees her boss reading it, scrutinizing it mutely as if it might mean something.

"What is this?"

"It's—where I live." She thinks he might not have heard her.

Richard pinches the bridge of his nose, as if this is the last thing he wants to hear. "Do you know something about this?"

Lucinda clutches her throat. "About what?"

"You've been here all this time," Richard says, flapping the paper.

"I—well, since I—" moved in, she wants to say. But she can't say exactly when that was.

"Is this who you call Dracula? This guy you're living with?"

Lucinda darts a disturbed hand to her mouth. Vanessa has been talking about her then. Again.

Richard has a look like he's blaming somebody for something. Whether it's her or Vanessa she can't tell.

Barely able to scrape up a murmur in the looming silence, she still feels she has to say something, some last words to finalize this goodbye, so he knows she isn't coming back. He hasn't moved from his place behind the counter. He is a shabby dilapidated sculpture, a wrecked and desperate version of himself, and she quickly, with a sliver of uninvited feeling, memorizes the angle of repose. It almost dignifies him. "I'm—" Should she say she's sorry? She doesn't know what she's being blamed for.

Richard looks at her. He opens his mouth to speak, as if some thought or fragment of lost speech is thorning through the thistle of his mind. "You don't know about this," he says. It's like he's verifying something he's already sure of.

"I don't—" She's halfway out the door. "I'm—" she says, not finishing. "About your daughter." She has no idea what she means.

Out on the street, she thinks about what he said. After she's been walking she begins to feel drastically on edge about giving him the address. There was something about that address. She has never claimed it in any official capacity before tonight, and his reaction upsided her. It's still twenty-eight minutes prior to the end of her shift and she walks briskly, wondering if she'll meet Dracula on the way, coming to meet her from home. She doesn't, and she finds herself in front of the portcullis, using her key, the one she duplicated from Dracula. The apartment manager is inside looking at her as if he doesn't know who she is. Often he has looked at her sitting in the courtyard, poised out there while he is at his work or is escorting last night's date over his doormat, and he doesn't seem to see her at all. She's a twig lost in a verdant copse of green. The women he accompanies to and from his apartment all bear a certain kind of fruit, and the unseeing look he gives Lucinda is familiar. Men like him don't see people like her. When he is out here trimming his hedges, he is already off in a world of his own, whatever place he goes to when he wants to make his boxwood monuments. She doesn't hold it against him. Years and years she has been ignored like this. Women are just the opposite. They tell her she should model.

"Where'd you get that key?" he says to her now, not ignoring her at all.

"It's mine." She holds it up shyly. "I live here."

He pauses, puzzled. "I've never seen you before."

"2B," she says, as unassumingly as possible.

He looks up there. His hair is like a ragged dandelion spore chewed over by the wind. "You live in 2B?"

She nods. She realizes Dracula might yet be up there—not having left to get her. He doesn't need much lead time. When he's alone he moves fast.

The manager shrugs. "Okay, I guess." He speaks to his own skepticism. He goes inside.

Lucinda sits for a while in the courtyard.

She thinks of her boss. She doesn't remember anything. Does that mean that there is nothing to remember? She looks at the apartment door. She thinks of her father, far away and somewhere else. She thinks of Doors Always Open, of being seen and unseen at all times. She used to play a game in the old house when her father was away, alternately closing and opening doors to make different configurations of space for sitting in. Often she did this just for the feeling of being prismed somewhere else, right inside her own home. The house was a warren of rooms and hallways and doors back then, a claustrophobic maze. She wouldn't have even noticed if her father hadn't called her attention to it with his rule.

"I can't see you," he used to say. "You're too skinny." It was either her first father or her second father who said this, crossing his arms in her open doorway, as if to blot out her whole budding being. It seemed to work, in a way. She is still thin and dilute, strained to the slithery liquid she always and ever was. What does Dracula see when he looks at her? What does he think? She wonders if he'll even notice her sitting here when he comes back from going to meet her at work. Lucinda stares down at the key she just used. She probably should have waited for him at the smoothie shop.

She hears a click-click-clicking. A man is walking his bike to the basement stairs. He looks like some kind of hale authority, a bicycle cop, riding home on his municipal issue at the end of his long day. The day is just beginning for Dracula. He is out there, or about to be out there, looking for her. She wonders if Richard will look for his daughter. The man uses his key to open the door and shoulders the bike down the steps. She wonders why she has never tried her key on the door at the bottom of the stairs.

Lucinda can't tell what she wants that basement door to do. She wants it to creak monumentally open and she wants it to stay monumentally closed. She wants to know and she wants to never have known.

Except now she's already on her way, into the mildew gloom of the stairwell, her legs stiff and spidery under her as she picks her way down through the pickled light. She can hear the metal wheeze of a tire spinning. She doesn't want to be doing this. And also she does. Lucinda is realizing, beyond a doubt, what she really wants. More than anything she wants that door to be open already. She wants it to just be resting ajar without the disturbance of opening on her. She has never felt more humbly destined than she does right now. In front of her, she can see the soft form moving through the darkness. Behind her, she can feel the swift hiss of spinning metal.

"Hi." The voice is three in one. It's his and hers and his.

The Shirt

"*H*ow do I look?" It's hard to not see yourself in the mirror. It's hard to perform routine hygiene and dress for stylistic conformity. It's hard in this way to know yourself. He can see almost every part of himself below the neck, but only in pieces and planes. He can't see his face. His self-esteem waxes and wanes on a barometer of partial blindness. There have been centuries that he's felt invisible to women and centuries that he's felt like the lady-killer he is. At least that's how he remembers it, vaguely. This is one of those in-between times, when women may look at him, but they have to be the right type.

"You have a kind of reserved hipster vibe," Lucinda assures him. "Like an IT guy who goes partway in for the fashion. It pretty much works."

They're talking about his sense of style because of Warren. Warren has made some underground traction with his street art. Two parties have photographed and disseminated it— the police and The Grannies. The Grannies are a group Dracula still wants some clarity on from Warren. There was also an unambiguous capsule in the arts weekly, asking *Art or Atrocity?* Warren has a name now in certain circles. Curiosity is fanning it out. He's planning a gallery show.

In the meantime, he needs more fresh outdoor installations, and he's having a party. It's for his housewarming. They wouldn't be going except that they are now about to ask Warren if he can loan them rent for next month. They are one paycheck away from having enough. It was either that or ask Lucinda's parents.

Friday is the party. Tonight and all the nights this week Dracula is working and then Sunday he is going with Lucinda to her parents' for dinner. He is trying on the shirt that she bought for him, or took or borrowed. It is unclear how she came by the shirt. It is unclear whether it is for the party or the family dinner on Sunday, or both. The shirt is "programmer plaid"—white with crosshatchings of blue and maroon—and soft as fog. Someone has washed it a lot. When he changes over into his brown uniform she hands him his overnight sack lunch. What she doesn't know and what he doesn't tell her is that tonight he is going to try something. He is going to take a victim—the old way, privately, and without consultation.

It is much better that Lucinda doesn't know because just having her know on the nights he has gone out has been giving him diuretic bouts of performance anxiety. Every time he has returned hungry and humiliated because he can feel her neurotic silhouette scintillating the air somewhere nearby, whether she is really there following him or not. She used to follow him. She says she doesn't anymore. Now that she knows that he knows, the whole thing is real and she doesn't want a part of it. She almost wishes that they were insane, in the nonviolent way. Dracula understands. He feels like he's going mad, for the first time in his immortal life. What if he isn't Dracula anymore? What if he was once and he has domesticated himself right out of his eternal curse and never noticed it?

"I have this feeling," he says on bad nights, "that my successor is coming to retire me."

"What does that even mean?" says Lucinda. "Is that how it even works?"

"I have no idea."

"What would your successor look like?" she says with a squint in her eye that can only be described as cagey and provocative. "Like you?" It makes Dracula insanely suspicious.

"I don't know—why?" he says, trying to be cool.

"I don't know," she says, equally as cool.

It occurs to him, dismally, that if he saw somebody who looked like him he wouldn't even know it.

But there's a woman—barely that—who works at the all-night diner on his route. She looks something like Lucinda, and that is why his mind seems to cleave her out of the many anonymous others. It's as if Lucinda's is the only face that ever sticks with him, and all her many approximates out in the world are linked to her in an oblique and peripheral intimacy, like the diminishing replicas he sees of her in the facing planes of their bathroom mirror. It's one of those mirrors that wraps behind the sink and around the two adjacent walls and produces an unending corridor of reflected selves. That's what Lucinda sees anyway. Dracula sees Lucinda. Is it face blindness? This is what she asks, leaning in to look at herself. Lucinda still doesn't think he's Dracula. She still suffers paranoid and increasingly debilitating attacks that they are both dysfunctional and deranged, like the Russian next door and her boss at work and her whole family and the actors at theater class and probably everybody else they have ever come into contact with, all of them grubbing around in their domesticated degeneracy. She hopes they don't kill anyone. She really does. She does not feel anything close to the purifying inferno of monstrosity that he says has possessed him in former lives. Neither has Dracula felt it in a long time. Look at us, she says. *What if?* she says, until Dracula feels all his own elemental clarity sliding away from him. Maybe we need to volunteer ourselves. Volunteer ourselves? To the nuthouse. It's a term he's never heard before. Another term he's never heard before that she keeps using is face blindness. A peculiar form. That's what she keeps saying.

"Can you see me?" he says, holding up his toothbrush hand.

"Yes and no," she says, "but that's me."

Dracula waits, willing her once again to explain her paradox.

"I already said, I'm too impressionable. What if we get someone else to look?"

"Then they'd know I was Dracula."

Lucinda's gaze goes imperceptibly opaque, like a sheet of water streaking down glass.

"What?" he says.

"I could—never mind," she says.

"You could what?" Dracula cinches his brows. "Nobody knows I'm Dracula but you and your delinquent family, right?"

The nod she gives to her reflection, and not him, is a fuzzy one.

"Who did you tell?" Clearly, this is something she wants to confess.

"It's not like anybody believes me. They all think I'm doing some kinky role-playing thing."

"Okay," says Dracula, prodding her with his tone.

"My theater class."

"You told your whole theater class?" Dracula stares at her. He can't believe she might actually mean what she says. "They know I'm Dracula?" This is when it hits him. She really doesn't think he's Dracula. If she ever did, she doesn't now.

"I also told Vanessa. And she's dead now. And I'm freaked out," she says, the wicks of her fingers splayed out in the air. In the mirror, her waxen pallor is drastic. She looks more and more like a dead bride in a horror movie. "I don't know what's going on," she says. "Let's just get this over with. Can we please get this over with?"

Dracula knows what she means. But it's complicated. "Soon," he says. He doesn't tell her his other plans for tonight.

His logic is all up in knots right now. There's no way out of it but into it.

Dracula brings along another shirt to change into so that nobody can trace him to his UPS job. It's the one she left out on the bed when she went drooping from the room. Dracula finds it fitting that he now has a shirt to wear incognito that he has never worn before in his life.

The other Lucinda, dependably, is here tonight. Dracula likes that the diner is simply called The Diner. Its name is timeless and plodding, and he can sense this is what makes it hip. His shirt fits right in here. Two guys on adjacent dates wear those plastic glasses that are supposed to look nerdy. The obligatory pierced and dog-collared teens cluster at the far booth, where the light is black and effluvious beside an open waste bin. The diner is always slowly gloaming and moist with common cuisine. It seems to percolate its own rich and pungent humidity, the booths and linoleum smearing down glops of dark brown, the windows blurred with grease and condensation that salves off the dry, wintry cold that sups slowly on them from space. The waitress twines up from the shadows, droll and slow, sinewing along on faulty ankles that knob out over platform wedges, a glossy helix of straps winding partway up her legs. The caresses of one dead animal upon another. She stops at a booth. Her hair is like silt dragged across her back. Her nose is devastatingly razored. She is like Lucinda and so not like her at all. She reminds him of a dead mermaid.

"Hi there," she says, coming with the menu. It's the kind of place where you seat yourself.

Dracula scabs the air with his hello. It startles him to realize how dry his mouth is.

The waitress makes reluctant eye contact. "Anything to drink?"

Her voice is bland and weary, for it is a great effort to be friendly this late at night. That's what she is telling him by also not wanting to meet his eyes at all. Dracula tries to smile and instead feels his mouth stretching into a wide rubbery grimace. He stops it by clearing his throat.

"Agh." He breaks into a short series of rude coughs. "Some water?" he croaks uneasily.

The waitress's eyebrow lifts and she looks at him as if she's coming to certain conclusions. "Okay," she says in a bright, stark voice that sounds deliberately judgmental. "Just a minute."

He watches her slink off into the lagoon lighting, feeling vaguely chafed. She probably thinks he's a pervert. Like many other men who try to enter a restaurant alone and after someone else's bedtime. Dracula is tucking in his lip. It seems that all these graveyard waitresses want to dislike men in his situation. He and men like him are always getting prematurely condemned. Dracula has had this happen a lot. He sees it all the time. It's like an epidemic. He can't help hating women who want automatically to hate men like him. It isn't his fault if she has a good reason for it.

Dracula shakes his head, trying to clear it. This is no time for petty agitation. He doesn't want to render himself ineffectual. He is not a man in the usual sense. He is not at bottom impotent or indolent or inconsequential. He is Dracula. There are practical matters he has to work out. He has to find out when she gets off work. If her shift ends too late, he has to get her out on one of her cigarette breaks. If she doesn't smoke he has to dredge her out somehow by dawdling in that unlit cove by the bathroom, where the back door is. Maybe he can pretend to be using his phone.

He gnashes his teeth and squeezes his hands together on top of the table to relieve some of the pressure. After a minute it seems that the teenagers at the far booth are turning one at a time to peer at him. Is he emitting some feral vibe? That makes him feel better and worse. He has abandoned his train of thought and now all he can do is smolder blankly. What is wrong with everybody? Is he such a spectacle? He looks down at himself. The shirt is fine. His pasty skin is fine, fore-arms smooth with muscle as if fish are swimming beneath the surface. He imagines octopuses knotted in his biceps. This is about all he can do to scrutinize himself. He feels alright. But the teens are still taking little squalid looks of him that are making him gristle with rage. Then here comes the waitress, blatting through the swinging door and past them, making her way toward him like a rare and spindly insect, and he can't help it. Her face is so aloof. In his vague and meaningless contempt he wants to stamp her flat with his foot and rid the world of her despicable existence.

"Here you go," she says. "Are you ready?"

For a moment he only stares at her, grinding his teeth as if it will help him to fiercely chew up the huge rising lump of hatred within him so he can speak again. "Yes," he spits when he sees her expression, and snaps the menu closed. "Steak and eggs. Please," he adds, when he sees her head kick back at his tone. "Rare," he adds over that. A glib smile tells him she sees this as amusing. She thinks he's posturing. "Bleeding," he says, furious.

"Got it." She makes a note in her pad. He can't infer any-thing from the delicate way she pinches the menu off the table. "Anything else?"

He breathes out air like a blast from a steam cooker. What is wrong with him? "No," and then, "thank you," he says, sensing his own near implosion. He looks down to diffuse himself. The corner of his eye catches on the coil of her shoe straps. They are slick and incendiary.

"Okay then," she says, with disparaging brightness. "I'll go put that in for you."

She didn't need to say that, he thinks. She could have just walked away. Maybe he is just being thin-skinned. When she comes past him again with menus for another table, he stubs out his finger.

"Can I ask you something?"

Her look tells him that she would rather he not. She's on her way somewhere.

"What are those shoes made of?"

"Oh—actually, they're eel." She says this almost with some embarrassment, and he can't tell why. Is eel expensive? Is it unseemly? He's one instant away from asking this when he realizes it's probably not polite.

"My girlfriend would like those," he says, feeling his chest fill with hot jacuzzi water. He tells himself he can do this.

The girl nods, primly. Giving away that she's trying not to show that she thinks he's lying. Dracula sees it. She is definitely sure he has no girlfriend.

Dracula tries, so hard, not to let this get to him. "You get those anywhere nearby?"

"In Europe."

"Europe. That's where I'm from." That sounds stupid. She doesn't ask him to specify. Instead she smiles obligingly.

"Long night, huh?"

She raises her eyebrows, then appears to focus on doing a scan of the table, as if it's a tactic she has for getting out of these conversations.

"So when does a shift like this end?"

"Not soon enough," she says. "Are you going to want Tabasco?"

"What?"

"With your eggs—Tabasco?"

"Oh, sure," he says, giving her the excuse. He is already exhausted by working so hard to sound nice, and it feels like two sticks rubbing together, the heat singeing him all along his insides.

"Red or green?" she asks flatly.

Dracula shakes his head. He passes his hand over his face. He wonders if he's already giving this thing up. "Oh, let me see. Red, I guess."

She turns again and leaves. Dracula looks around, feeling like he's about to laugh this battered feeling right out of him, and catches the eye of a fat bearded kid in the back who's been staring at him. He can tell he's been staring at him by the stagnant slump of his parked jowl. Why? He raises his eyebrows and waits for the kid to look away, but now he seems to be talking and staring at the same time, with a look of smug indifference on his bear-cub face.

Dracula sighs at the ambiguous stare-down. To be young, he thinks. To be out this late. To look that way at a world you hardly know. He's probably no older than twenty. He's probably just looking past him, he tells himself. Dracula stares until he turns away. He can't help noticing that the girl across from him is wearing nothing but a pink kerchief around her chest in twenty-degree weather. Her coat is shrugged off on the booth behind her. At least she has one. Dracula watches her stick her finger out at her companion's face—oh, now she's picking his nose and squealing. How old are these kids? He has no concept of that anymore. Lucinda is twenty or something like it but she seems age-less, utterly outside of her generation. Dracula's too tired to contemplate the implications. All these kids out at night, drunk and dumbstruck by the brief and misleading promise of adulthood. He sees them over and over, everywhere he goes. They're like an epidemic.

The steak and eggs come out on a heavy white platter in a great big hemorrhaging heap and the waitress walks behind it like she can hardly keep up. For a moment Dracula feels a throb of alarm at her momentum, as if she's preparing to throw the dish at him. Her face is hardened into a little, calcified smile as she dumps it down on the table and follows with the bottle of Tabasco.

"Okay?" she says.

"Ah—" says Dracula, and she smiles and walks off again, interpreting his utterance to be an affirmation—or else making clear she doesn't care. Either way she did it on purpose. He is now struck by the saucy dismissal of her hips as she saunters away, as if she expects him to watch and wants him to feel rebuffed. He doesn't have a napkin. He's watching because she left him in the middle of a sentence—more like a word. Not because he wants to watch but because he wants a napkin. He looks around his table. All of this would amuse him if he wasn't actually trying to do what she presumed he was, at least by half.

He turns the bottle of Tabasco upside down and shakes it vigorously. Are those kids sniggering? He thinks he hears them. He knows so well what she's doing. She made him look after her by walking away before he was prepared and then tried to make him think he was a pervert for watching. This was supposed to mortify him out of talking to her. What a scam, Dracula thinks. What a self-fulfilling punishment it all is.

Dracula is taking large heavy forkfuls of the bleeding heap before him and thrusting them into his mouth. Now what? He continues to violate the meat on the front half of his plate while behind it the egg yolks jiggle. He's aware of the dull, heavy clamor his cutlery is making on the stoneware, and after a while he rotates the plate and continues eating. What would his girlfriend say if she were here? She would probably say the woman was beautiful. She was always appreciating the weird looks of strangers. She could do that because she herself was beautiful. Dracula pauses a moment to think of the soft hiss of her hair, floating behind her like spun sugar as she left the bedroom, and he has this sudden feeling she was leaving him forever in that moment, that she may or may not be home when he gets back but either way she will be gone, unreachable, and he can't swallow the bite of food in his mouth. He gapes quietly into his plate and sits very still, feeling the late hour, feeling as if any movement might cause him sudden inexplicable agony.

When he looks up from his plate he sees the waitress at the other booth delivering a hamburger to the girl and an enormous bowl of cereal to the fat kid across from her. He had seen that stupid item on the menu, and it seems appropriate that some podgy bear kid would indulge in something so showy and gargantuan. The dour waitress can barely support the bowl with her feeble wrist. She's surely one of those hollow, anemic girls who never eats. Her blood would be tangy and acerbic. He swallows a bite of food. Her teeth have that leached granular look that Lucinda's have, like eggs dipped in vinegar. That acid streaking—as if their throat is a leaky valve for constant reflux. Lucinda has to take pills. Sometimes he can hear her gagging in the bathroom. Dracula puts down his fork.

The grease he has just consumed is sliding warmly down his stomach, and he feels it ripple up in a wave of anxious anticipation when the waitress turns and comes toward him, tearing the ticket from her pad and pretending not to see him looking at her. Lucinda would say she was beautiful. She was so ugly she was beautiful, he thinks, feeling the same confusion and resentment he had felt when she made him watch her walk away from his table. He loves her. Lucinda. This is what love is, he thinks. It's a sickness that is starving him and stuffing him full.

The ticket comes fluttering down on his table and the words come blurting out. "I have a girlfriend," he says. "You're like her." He watches several taut cords spring up in her wrist as she lifts his plate off the table.

"Okay." Her voice corrodes into scrap.

Dracula is sparking like a ripped wire. "She's bulimic. Anorexic," he says.

She looks up at him in surprise, her dry lip snagged by the two points of her teeth. "What?" she says.

He clears his throat. He watches the bleak vacancy of her expression sour into confusion and disbelief. Then her look goes to brine. "What are you talking about?" she says sharply.

For an instant she gazes at him, and her acid expression holds such a power that he goes blank. "It's a disease you know." He fumbles to regain himself. "My girlfriend," he says. "You can get help."

"Oh my God." She shakes her head. A smile spreads up her face and hangs there, and he knows she is privately damning him to hell.

"You might think you look okay but to the rest of us you don't look healthy," he says, hardly knowing where he's going. He realizes this is something he has heard her father say. Lucinda's.

The waitress blanches. She is still shaking her head, even as the smile goes to slush and slips from her face. "I can't believe this." Her face sags and for a moment she stands very still, as if any movement will destroy her. With a sudden guilty panic Dracula realizes she is about to cry.

"I'm sorry," he says. "I didn't mean—"

She mutters something under her breath.

"Wait," he says, and she brushes her hand across her face and turns and walks away. When she's gone Dracula sits a moment in the pummeling silence. The murmuring patrons all seem to be mouthing soundless scoldings at each other. He fishes his wallet from the chest pocket of his new shirt and pinches out a twenty with fumbling fingers and leaves it on the table. He stops in the bathroom, listening to the echo of pipes in walls, rubbing his numb hands under the sink water for a long time. Outside, in the alleviating cold, a bald wind blows back on him. The kids are out in the parking lot, romping and frolicking in the freeze. He feels a vanishing stealth as he comes up on them, bouncing pertly on the back bumper of his truck. They've just finished tugging at the handle of the cargo hold.

"You want to go in there?" he says, crossing his arms.

They look at him and then at each other. "Oh, this is your truck?" The girl is instantly submissive and stepping away.

The guy has to peacock a little. "You want me to go in there? Why would you want me to do that?"

"Because the night is young," says Dracula, feeling so much better out here. "And you've had your milk and oats and now you need your honey."

"Uh, what's that supposed to mean?" He glances, almost, at the girl.

"Ew," says the girl. "Let's go."

"You tell me," says Dracula.

"I think maybe it means you're a whackjob." Dracula smirks. The guy seems to be waiting for some insult to give him the volition to get up and walk away. Dracula can feel it. "Nice shirt," he says.

Dracula can't tell if he is insulting his actual shirt or the fact that he's wearing only a shirt in the cold. He shrugs.

"My dad took that shirt to the thrift store last week."

He might have, Dracula thinks. Maybe that was why the kid was staring so incessantly before.

"That's what *I* said," the girl outs him brashly. They both ignore her.

"And do you like your dad?" Dracula asks. It puts just the stitch he hoped for in the kid's expression.

"What? Whatever."

"Can we go?" says the girl. "I'm cold."

Dracula's coat is in the truck and he notices that he's not yet chilled at all. These are both bracing sensations—being out here and badgering these kids. He'll give the waitress thirty minutes to come out for a cigarette and then he'll leave. He could make it happen out here without any effort. He can tell already. He is Dracula. "You could go in there and do whatever you want for thirty minutes."

"Okay. Gross me out. Come on Tim. Let's leave. Let's not give this guy a reason to talk."

"But what are we supposed to do in there?" Tim is really pushing it. Poor Tim. Clearly he can't figure out how else to get on top of this.

"I don't know," Dracula says, spreading his hands. "It's probably your only chance to ever do anything in the back of a UPS truck. You can do whatever you want."

"You mean, like—" Tim is making himself uncomfortable now, with this dimwit craving for explanation.

"Oh please." The girl is going to do it for him. "He wants us to *fuck*, Tim, you fucking idiot. We're just *friends*," she says to Dracula. He didn't mean to imply that. It's just what happened.

Now Tim really can't get up from the truck or get this back in his field of action. The girl just eclipsed him. All he can do now is go all in. Dracula sees it on his face. The flaccid fool's look is there and Tim is out of options. "I don't get it. You want money or something? Why would you want us to do that?"

"I'm leaving. Assholes. I'm going back inside."

"You better go with her."

Tim looks after her. "I didn't say I *wanted* to," he calls out. They watch her pull out her phone.

"Shit."

"Go tell her I said I wanted to watch," says Dracula, lifting lechy brows. "You can both be disgraced by the pervert."

Tim looks at him, seemingly deepening his own disgust.

"It's better than nothing," Dracula says, shrugging.

"You're fucking sick, man." Tim raises his voice. Now Dracula can tell he is going to go a different route.

The kid finds his feet and pounces, torpidly, right as the girl flicks that fated glance over her shoulder. It's a good move, Dracula thinks, but a losing one.

Back at home, he tells Lucinda, "Maybe you should go. Maybe it will help." He doesn't know how he got here.

She's eating sunflower seeds, possibly the only thing he's ever seen her eat. "They're nutritious," she used to say.

"By myself?" she says now. "What would you do? If I went in." She seems oddly complicit, calm with the idea of it. She is not teary and wrung out as he thought she would be.

"I'll find another place," he says, watching her closely. "Nearby." He doesn't like it, her composure. "I'll visit—or not, if you don't want me to at first." After all this, what he needed was the waitress to show him. She's not really eating those seeds.

Lucinda seems to be watching him with some matching but unforthcoming unease. "Don't worry—it's not you, or whatever your... effect is on me," she says, as if reading his mind.

Dracula nods. They both wonder if it is her, and what about her it is, but neither says it. "We can pick back up when you get out." He doesn't want her to think he is trying to dodge her, now that he knows, to slough her off somewhere and leave her there with false promises. "I'll come every day," he says, swinging hard the other way. "I mean—" He is confused by what he's saying. "I want you to get well," he says, pinning it down. "I want you to go so you can come back and be with me." Then the idea of her going so she can be with him disconcerts him. Is that possible? He can't imagine her coming back the same person as the one who is with him now. Is he killing their chances? Suddenly he is terrified. "Never mind," he says. "I don't want to tell you what to do."

Lucinda sighs. "I don't know," she says. "I've always been this way. I'm not dead yet." She shrugs.

Dracula nods. He's relieved, but still distracted by her mild contemplations. What's keeping her so even? He now wants to ask her, what has she been up to tonight?

"Why are you wearing that shirt?" Lucinda asks.

"Oh." He looks down. "I left it on under my uniform," he says, thinking fast. "I wanted to break it in." That was stupid. He should have had a plan for this. Now he's having to scramble back in his mind to the bedroom, when she had him try it on. Had he changed back out of it before or after she left?

"You spilled on it," she says.

He pulls it out into a flat plane, to see. So he did. Right on the pocket.

"Through your uniform," she says.

"Huh," says Dracula, looking up from the stain at her.

"Huh," says Lucinda, looking down from him at the stain.

The Prop (Part I)

Does Lucinda ever get inside his coffin when Dracula's away? Of course she does. Does anything ever happen? Of course it doesn't. It's just a box of wood.

She's schlepping it, all in a rush, out of the apartment and to her theater class as a last-minute substitute, until they find the prop that went missing. Dress rehearsals are the day after tomorrow. They are only a few days from opening night.

Sometimes she thinks Dracula has forgotten all about it.

Her classmate Rory is helping her shoulder the coffin down the stairs. He has a truck and he doesn't mind.

"Why do we have to take it back and forth? Can't we just leave it there through the show?" he asks.

"I told you," Lucinda says breathily. She can barely intonate with the effort. It's not that his casket is heavy, but she's weak. It's a simple cedar box. She's afraid she's having a heart attack right now. Wouldn't that be something? "Where's Seth?" she huffs. Last night Rory had Seth with him.

"Are you saying he actually sleeps in this? For real?" Rory says right over her question, not hearing it. He seems incapable, over and over, of accepting this simple truth.

Lucinda blinks at the horde of insects speckling her vision.

"What does he look like in there? Do you ever look?"

Lucinda finds this question crass. She has never tried to open the lid while he was sleeping. "No," she breathes.

"I wouldn't want to see that. Where is this dude, anyway? I'm never going to meet him." Lucinda has some idea why Rory doesn't mind helping her with this.

"At work."

"Where does he work?"

She doesn't answer. Dracula is, as always, at work. And if he knew what she was doing he would kill her.

"It's so light," Rory says, pumping his end effortlessly. "He actually sleeps in it?"

"Stop," she says. How many times is he going to ask?

Something in her tone must have alerted him to her physical predicament because he cranes his head and says, "You want to put it down for a minute?"

In answer she sloughs the coffin and watches it clatter down the steps.

"Whoa. Is somebody mad at her boyfriend?"

Lucinda is too faint to answer. Rory suggests that she sit down after she is already on her way. "Do you need something? I have Gatorade in the car," he says. "Are you sure you're okay?"

Lucinda shakes her head.

"I'm getting the Gatorade." He leaves. The apartment manager looks out through the blinds of his window. It's the first time she's seen him since he refused them a rent extension. She can see the stiff crimp in the vinyl and she wonders if he's deciding about coming out to say something. She thinks about their plan for their new rent predicament. She wonders what will come of it. Rory returns, holding a bottle out with his hand. Inside is a slosh of foaming blue that is likely slimed with his spit. Lucinda takes it and pretends to swallow.

"I can't do it." She gestures limply.

Rory looks down at the coffin. "Yeah, that's not a problem— I can do it myself. It's really easier that way." She watches him bend down and lift with the knees. He is like some meathead bodybuilder. How did he find his way into her acting class? She lets him lug it away and succumbs to the feeling of impending disaster. She knows that what she's doing is some kind of double sacrilege, a sacrilege upon the sacrilege that Dracula is committing to begin with.

Why does she want to do this? Ever since she went to Vanessa's funeral, ever since her East Coast sweetheart gave her eulogy, Lucinda has realized something. People tell the truth. One way or another, they tell the truth.

Lucinda wants to know Dracula's truth. She would rather know hers without having to look.

Rory is back, swiping his hands together, having apparently done that all the way back from his truck until she could see it. The deed is done, he seems to be saying, thanks to his physical aptitude. He really is a man. He really is a ham. That's what he is.

"Ready to go?"

Lucinda stands, refusing the elbow of assistance. She feels fine now.

She can say, with the exception of a few people, that she really likes her theater class. She might be scared stiff of the play, but she has discovered that she appreciates the challenge of acting itself, and she likes that about herself. The class has tested her in ways that nothing else has. Her teacher is a weird guy. He keeps a puppet in a closet and he sometimes does little enigmatic routines with it that are meant to inspire and/or confound them. It is all part of acting, he says, part of disappearing into that onstage space, that black hallowed lack of self, bringing that out under the lights with you. Stay dark, he says. Darkness is your light. Hell is full of light, he says. A fallen angel goes black in perfect opposition to his own lightness. It's a faultless equilibrium. An absolute reversal, an image transfer, direct from life to stage. All this is just part of the play, of course. He's not a raving lunatic. He's getting them into it.

The play is about celebrities dying young and turning into angels, and fallen angels coming to earth from hell to become pop celebrities. The teacher wrote it with one of the students. He made his puppet to look like a pop celebrity who recently died, to everybody's fervent shock and denial. *I can't be dead,* he has his puppet say, tap dancing around the coffin with ringlets bobbing, *everyone told me I was immortal.* The play is called *From Hell to Breakfast* and the coffin is the centerpiece, a portal back and forth between the idolatrous and the arcane, the consecrated and the debased, the destined and the damned. Where are the lines? Where do they get crossed? When does surrender leach its way into servitude? When does salvation plot a path of trespass? When do trumpets turn to shrieks and when do shrieks slip into serenade? The play is about music and it uses music as a metaphor and it is, of course, a musical.

Lucinda likes her role. She plays an angel eating breakfast after ascending to heaven. The first scene is her sitting up inside the coffin. So is the last scene. The coffin is laid flat. She sits up, then stands, beaming and resplendent, and swishes over to a table where a breakfast is laid out for her. Her breakfast is a feast of light. The effect is produced by placing several glass paperweights on a glass table underlit by a bare bulb. Other characters in the play eat various other breakfasts. Breakfast happens a lot in the play as characters follow their journeys in and out of the astral and the corporeal. Lucinda is now so used to getting in and out of the coffin that she feels discomfited using Dracula's. Everybody does, because they all know what the coffin is used for—because she told them, when she was trying to explain why she had a coffin they could use as a substitute. She now thinks they all probably suspect she stole the other one for some deranged purpose— probably so she could show them this one. She has no idea what happened to the other coffin, but that doesn't mean she didn't have something to do with its disappearance. This she doesn't tell them. She is trying to be helpful.

Lucinda's friend Lauren likes to take peeks into the coffin, in a way that makes Lucinda suspicious. She often pinches a sack in her fingers that droops open at the mouth. Lately she has been carrying this sack to class. She calls it a ragamuffin sack and she says it is her mother's handiwork and she keeps taking things out and sharing them with Lucinda, as if they're talismans for life, or for art. Once she had a dirty sock. "This is for the trolls," she said, casting prophetic looks at the guys. "It's so they don't notice me." Lucinda peered at her a moment, wondering if this was a joke and maybe she left the sock in there after a costume change, and she realized, suddenly, that this girl was cunningly gorgeous, beguiling in a wily, chase-down-an-alley urchin way. She is one kind of opposite of Lucinda. Where Lucinda is lank and luminous as ethereal shreds of cloud, Lauren is tawny and alive as a scampering mouse. Her role in the play is a fallen angel who returns to become a pop celebrity. She makes Lucinda feel like acting is some reversion to a runabout childhood—a place of pure and absolute plundering. It seems like Lauren's childhood goes on and on without restraint or reservation, and Lucinda tries to learn what she can from this. It's unnerving and it's inspiring. Sometimes she can't tell when her friend is acting and when she is just being herself.

Lucinda watches closely when Lauren looks into the coffin. She herself also takes furtive peeks, because she knows there's something going on with it. She keeps finding things in there. After Dracula leaves for the night or when she wakes up, she might walk past the closet, and there will be something cast down around the bottom, like a piece of shed accessory or dropped trash. Part of her is afraid that each thing is materializing, on its own, and that it could happen any time and in the middle of class. It's as if Lauren divines this too and is waiting at the lip of fate for something to present itself. She hopes it doesn't happen in the midst of rehearsal. She hopes

Lauren hasn't already taken something. Tonight, before Rory knocked she found a long loop of some supple snake-skin coil, with perforations in one end, like a belt or a strap.

"What do you think this is?" she asked Lauren, testing.

Lauren clicked her tongue. "A garrote? A dominatrix whip?" It seemed like she was playing a game. Lauren always seemed like she was playing a game.

"I'm serious."

"I don't know. It looks like a strap."

Last night, it was the shirt. A whole shirt. She had Dracula try it on and he didn't seem to recognize it at all. The night before it was the velvet bow that she was sure she had seen on Vanessa's big slab of hair at the viewing. She wore it and he didn't even notice. Before that it was a half-eaten packet of sunflower seeds, the kind you buy in bulk to get lots of tiny snack packs. Where are these things coming from? What's he doing in there, or beyond there? There's always the possibility that she finds these things because she herself is doing it—throwing clues to herself in some blackout madness and then waiting to be lured back by her subconscious to find them. Anything is possible. That's the whole problem. The truth exists but it is infinitely big.

In the same manner, Lucinda sometimes thinks of the other mysteries that enfold her. She thinks she might be the one who killed Vanessa. She thinks she might have made Richard's daughter disappear.

She tries to think of the last time she saw Vanessa, and it gets slushy. Was it the time she met her outside the theater? The day she was so upset about the key? Lucinda remembers she was trying to find a way into the Russian's apartment. She was trying to find evidence that would exonerate her. Evidence of some girl other than her. Some girl existing in a separate and parallel space to hers. Anything to tell her she wasn't the girl. She wasn't the one he was talking to.

Sometimes, drifting off to sleep, Lucinda would jolt awake with a hot slosh of adrenaline and know the Russian had just barked something through the wall at her, a hard blot of breath to tell her how intimately he knew she was there. Other times he would actually say something: *I know what you have. Little liar.* And then he began folding out reams of Russian on her, almost as if he were daring her, taunting her with riddles and facsimiles. What was he talking about? At some point it occurred to her that if he was talking to her about anything then it probably was the key.

"What key?" Vanessa had said, trying to parse through Lucinda's blather that day.

"Well—" she squirmed. "My dog ate it."

"What dog?"

"He's—dead now." Lucinda felt her expression crimp and Vanessa scrunched her face in sympathy.

"I'm so sorry," Vanessa said.

The key was the one that the Russian had dropped, when she found him using it on the wrong apartment door.

Whoops, he had said, looking up at her and then at the door. *All of them look the same, don't they?* That had not been the way to ingratiate himself with her.

It was a long time ago. It seems like that now. She remembers how Vlad was always street cleaning the mat at the Russian's feet with his snout, licking at the Russian's shoes. Lucinda was always suspicious. It was like there was something there that the dog was keen to sample. The Russian sometimes bent down to greet him and the dog did the same thing to his hand. What did he have on his hands and his feet? Did he work in a meat factory? Lucinda always wanted to ask.

What she had asked Vanessa that day had not been the most savory thing to ask.

"I just need—" She didn't know why she was doing it.

The dog had died on the way to the vet—the vet specialist. The regular vet had said they couldn't do anything, and it was too dangerous to perform exploratory surgery on a dog that old. And too expensive.

"It's out of town," Lucinda said.

Now Vanessa was making a bad odor face. Lucinda really just needed a car to get there. Vanessa rattled her new car keys. She had a new car. An old new car, but still—Lucinda wondered how she was able to afford that.

Lucinda sipped a gruel of breath. "I don't have a car," she said.

"Oh—you need a ride somewhere?" Vanessa said.

Lucinda felt all the unspoken words churn. Would she bring a shovel? How would she remember the spot? She was planning on having Warren help with the rest.

Now, when she can't help it, she says to Dracula, "I'm nervous."

He looks at her like this disclosure is what makes him nervous. "What are you nervous about?"

Lucinda detonates her eyes, like she wants him to already know. She flounders to cast a net wide enough to catch the feeling. "I don't know." She goes fractal with the effort. "The play," she says finally, by default.

"Oh, yeah," says Dracula. His tone says that the play is the last thing on his mind. "Well, try and think past the play," he says, notching his hat down over his eyes. "Like when you throw a punch at something and you focus on throwing past it. If you do it right you hit the thing you weren't even aiming at with a kind of explosive contact you didn't know was possible." He demonstrates, cheesily. "I learned that in boxing class."

"I don't really want to explode," Lucinda says, sucking air. She is dubious about this boxing class Dracula is pretending to be taking, ever since he came home one night with yeasty, rising knuckles that had no shape. He says it's to help with the unchanneled aggression—at least until they can find a night to do their test. She knows he got the cupcake knuckles trying to do the test without her and once again failing. She wonders if he's really working when he says he is. She wonders how he got that hat. She wonders if he still goes to the bus depot, where that concessions girl used to watch him watch TV. She wonders how he got that food stain on his shirt.

How can they afford a boxing class? she asks. You'll never believe this, he says. I just found five hundred dollars taped under our mailbox. I think the Russian did it by accident. He waits a pregnant pause, probably to see if she'll shuck her gaping face and suddenly remember she forgot to tell him about that. But Lucinda waits a beat too long, and now it's too late. So now we can make rent. Lucinda tries not to look dumbstruck at her own folly. She did that. She knows she did. Dracula says that now she can relax and focus on the play.

She is pretty sure that Dracula wants her to focus on the play because he actually wants her to think past the play. He doesn't think the play matters. She is perturbed that he doesn't think it matters. And now it's not just the play, but also the coffin. They are not going to find the one that went missing—she knows they aren't. Somehow she has to get this one to the theater on the night of the performance without Dracula noticing. How is she supposed to do that? Her mind is spitting and stubbing on broken bits of strategy at all times. Every time Dracula talks to her she tunes out. Right now she is simply agreeing with everything he says until the play is over and she once again has her wits about her.

Lucinda thinks about calling Warren about the coffin— since she didn't yet avail him for the dog she might for this. He's good at all these tricks. She also thinks about asking

Lauren. In her paranoid planning she has realized something. Warren and Lauren would get along really well. She doesn't often try to introduce her brother to somebody she knows. There was one time she brought a girl home to meet him and it didn't go so well. She looked too much like Lucinda, he kept saying. He wouldn't stop commenting on it until they both felt frisked and fed upon by his vociferous scrutiny. But in this case Warren and Lauren have a similar quality, something that makes her think they would just fuse. And Lauren looks nothing like Lucinda.

"Want to come to my mother's for dinner Sunday?" she asks Lauren at rehearsal. She is pretty sure Warren will be there. She feels stark and reckless asking this question, almost indecently assertive. Maybe it's because of her grisly lack of friends right now. Maybe it's her state of brazen desperation. She might just want a buffer. She has no idea what her mother plans for Dracula.

Lauren hardly considers before saying, "Better yet, why don't you come to my mother's for dinner tonight?" It's not actually better—it defeats Lucinda's secret purpose. She watches Lauren flounce her arms inside her black feathered lycra. She looks like an eccentric sack of trash. "It's not a party or anything," she says. "I was just going to ask you after rehearsal. Isn't that funny that you asked me?"

"Ha," says Lucinda. She can't say much more because her throat clots. She is wary of going to anybody else's house for dinner, because she doesn't like to eat. If you do that at home, that's one thing. If you do it at somebody else's house, it's rude.

"Well, I have to take the coffin back," she says. She hopes Lauren won't see it as an excuse and have her feelings hurt.

"Oh, I know. Rory can bring you back to the house in the truck after. He's my brother."

Lucinda gapes. "He is?" Rory looks and acts nothing like her. They don't even really talk at rehearsal. He's just a few feet away from them, in his pop celebrity wig, nodding at some advice from the teacher, frowning and looking like a deranged Fabio.

"You know what you should do?" says Lauren, glancing with her across the room. "You should give him that strap for a headband. That would look so killer."

Lucinda feels like she's been caught in a solicitous trap. Rory has been helping her out with the coffin, Lauren wants her to come to dinner—it's a perfect double-teaming. She can't possibly refuse. She doesn't exactly answer Lauren about the dinner but she assumes it's affirmed. As the night goes on she finds herself wondering if Rory even knows about the invitation. He looks chastened, and throughout the rehearsal he seems hackled and petulant, as if maybe the teacher's advice was really more of a scolding.

When Marty finally trots over to her, she's disconcerted. He's been doing this all night and the play is in three days— what more could he be modifying at this late hour? "And for you, my lithe Lucinda," he says, without any hint of innuendo. "How about—can we do some more hand action? Just a smidge?" As he talks, he's doing his own hand actions, rubbing dry palms together. Are these the ones he wants her to do?

She looks down, dubiously.

"When you're eating breakfast and you say your line, I want you to say 'light of the cross,' and just flick your hand, imagine you have a fork in it, like people do at the table, when they're eating. '*Light of the cross*,'" he demonstrates. "Not that gauche. Very slight and—" he flutters his fingers—"just, small and insensate like you do, with your splendid sense of subtlety." Lucinda likes it when he refers to her splendid sense of subtlety. She is subtle. She has felt it.

Across the stage, Lauren nods and smiles—not at her but at Rory—as she takes sly peeks into the coffin.

Lucinda knows there is something infinitely empowering about her own subtlety, about the intricacies of inflection that fold open when she isn't herself. Her body is something she can wield upon the lines of speech, a pointed chisel that etches in the real meaning of the words.

Lauren looks as if her smile has gone stiff. She looks as if she sees something she shouldn't.

The teacher brings her back with an ecstatic snap. "Yes— that's it! How did you do it so exactly?"

"What?" Did she do it? She guesses that she did.

"So deft," he says, as she tries to extricate herself from Marty's enthusiasm and get over closer to the coffin. Lauren isn't making any moves to verify her finding. Maybe Lucinda imagined it. "You're talking *to* the light of the cross, like it might be a dinner companion, but then also you're talking *about* it, murmuring aloud your approval and satisfaction like it might actually be the meal. That is it. The mythical innuendo, the mystical switch we're always flipping." Marty is verily beaming. He is talking more gibberish. "Flip your switch, Lucinda. Just keep doing that over and over again."

This, Lucinda thinks, is the whole problem. What makes her good at acting seems to be the same thing that makes her bad at living. When in rehearsal she slips into spotlit brilliance, she hardly feels she deserves the credit. When in life she passes behind billowing curtains, she hardly feels she can evade the blame.

Now she is listing her eyes along the empty cavity of the coffin. She smiles at Lauren. There's nothing there.

The Knife

*T*here's a lot of seaweed on the beach tonight. The crash of cold water, the stars and moon, thrown up into the sky's everlasting gamble with the tides, the grim tribulations of the waves—that's about it. Dracula keeps walking, waiting for a few things to make sense. The blood. How it was just suddenly there. And the knife. How it was just suddenly gone. Later—when he got home. He had brought the knife with him, for some ill-conceived extra measure. It was not a smart move. It must have been outside the diner where he lost it.

A whole odious can of worms wants to wriggle out from there, but it's late, and he's killing time, and it's hard to stay focused. The thing about the beach is that it reminds Dracula of his childhood. Except he doesn't remember his childhood.

Dracula turns around. He's always turning around, before he can even catch himself. He adjusts his hat, as if to screw himself back into a pole position. He is coming to hate going out because of how constantly he keeps swiveling out of himself, out of his center of being. Some of it is guilt, he knows, because of what happened. He can't go back to his job anymore. He has to keep a low profile, and he keeps looking over his shoulder. But really, he has to admit this has been going on for longer than that—this feeling of being trailed, sniffed out, almost by an auxiliary part of his own self, limping off to the side of him, a lame appendage he has to attend to over and over, just so he can try and reel it in. He can't shake the sense that somebody else is always with him. He knows enough now to know that it's not Lucinda.

The knife is what concerns him about Lucinda. Lucinda had it hidden in that vent. Not from him, he had to assume. He knows she took it from her mother.

It used to be that Lucinda would leave the knife laying all about, and whenever she wanted to perform some house-keeping novelty she would snag it up and occupy herself— ribboning up old caulk from around the tub, stabbing hazardous icicles off the mailbox to safeguard Vlad, flicking cakes of mud into the breezeway from her boots, peeling bananas he knows now she didn't eat, and impaling her ubiquitous blocks of bubble gum to feed to herself while they were watching a TV show. She'd been living off of nothing but sugary gum for months now, but she hasn't even been chewing gum lately. It just snuck up on Dracula that the knife had faded abruptly from use. She was using a letter opener on mail now. Where had it gone? All of its voluptuous plea-sures and thrifty economies were suddenly missing from their life, dropped down a secret stairwell. Why was she now living without it? Or why was she now performing her secret life with it outside of Dracula's observance?

He didn't mean to find it in the vent. It was just there when he was trying to block the constant billows with a strip of thick insulation. The closet got so hot in the day. It was a quirk of some apartment conversion that there even was one in the closet. Whoever heard of a vent in the closet? It's because, Dracula has heard, these apartments used to be a motel.

Dracula knows that he has lost track of something with Lucinda. He just doesn't know what.

This is partly why he is out here tonight. He is out here to examine and recall, to retrace his lost footsteps in this life.

This is not unlike what Lucinda's father does, stepping over potholes prodigious with seaweed, coming out to comb for some lost and monumental bloat, something that might wash up on shore to return whatever lost part of himself got knocked away on that fateful day. Dracula wonders if the accident is the last thing Lucinda's father remembers. The last thing Dracula remembers, the first and earliest memory, he has to admit, is the night he met Lucinda.

He was out on the beach before going to the library—that he does remember. There was a couple that he saw—he almost stepped on them. They said something. Where are *you* going? They might have even known him, from the braided tone of their voices. Dracula felt rather raked over the coals, that night on the beach. He was walking away from a battlefield strewn with some recent defeat, feeling rather heroic and vastly alone.

Dracula walks, clanking and loaded down with his burdens, until he is tired. He has not found any answers or corpulent carcasses to consult tonight. He goes home. He doesn't feel like doing anything other than the chores he already promised himself he would do. He brings the smell of the beach with him, a wet mongrel smell. Waves of salt air roll out of his coat as he stoops to get the bucket from under the sink. Before he can even get started on his washing, somebody is at the door.

Not somebody. A salesman.

"I don't have time," says Dracula. He had opened the door before the bell buzzed and now he is startled. The man—or upon close observation much less than that—a figure so puny it looks more like a boy shrinking back from manhood—stands cocked in a corndog-colored suit and cowboy hat, both so cheesy that even Dracula knows they must be some kind of jaunty statement about his vocation. He is telling him that a demonstration will only take a moment.

Dracula doesn't want a demonstration. Dracula wants a break. Did Warren send him? What's the gag?

"No," says Dracula, "I have to go. I'm late." He doesn't really have anywhere to go. He has to go downstairs to get the stain out of the shirt.

"Gift for the little lady?" The salesman seems to be trying out an obsequious cowboy repartee. "Does she do most of the cooking around here?"

"What are you selling," says Dracula, looking around as if to signal the ridiculousness of this to an audience. "Who sent you?" How would he even presume there was a little lady?

"Knives," says the salesman. "I heard you were looking for a knife."

Now this is unsettling. Knives? Is this who was following him? Was he talking to himself, out on the beach? Highly likely.

"I don't want a knife," he says, now flustered. "I'm trying to get some work done."

"Are you sure?" His assailant pauses, and catching his peevish glance says, "Okay, no problem, pardner," and hunches forward and rustles something out of his big suit coat.

"Who are you?" says Dracula, now thinking about the knife.

"I didn't mean to tie you up," says the cowboy. He hands over a cheap photocopy brochure, points at a name inked there in pen, and saunters away with briefcase and coat swishing. Kent Wallaby. What a sham. Dracula pauses to watch him go, keenly aware that his sanctum has been singled out for absurd and possibly malicious intent, possibly because of something he said, to himself. He continues downstairs to the utility sink.

On his way, he knocks into a small cabinet and caneback chair, placed obtrusively in a niche of penitentiary-white cinderblock right inside the door which was previously occupied by only a crunchy rug for scraping feet. A handwritten placard atop the cabinet says, *Your Local Library*. Dracula pauses, blocked at the thigh. He creaks open the cabinet doors. Inside, it's trashy public castoffs—offerings you would find slumped in a bin at a thrift shop or waiting room. He can see bits of streamer sticking out of one, and finds it scored and frilled inside, hunked apart in the middle when he opens it, like his girlfriend at one point was still trying to make that perfect pigeonhole for ideal concealment. He wonders if maybe she was using the knife to make its own hiding place and then finally gave up and went for the vent. Dracula thinks again of the vent. He thinks again of the knife, and the knife salesman. He should have let him show his wares.

When he gets downstairs with his bucket and cake of soap he finds a battalion of plastic jugs and bottles oozing fluorescent fluids off a sagging plywood ledge above the sink. He noses among them. On the far side he extricates a spray bottle of stain remover that indicates he should gently spritz the fabric, massage it in, and let it sit for a minimum of one hour before proceeding with machine wash instructions. He looks at his cake of soap. This is for Lucinda. He decides to test his luck with the green chemical sap concocted in the corporate laboratory.

He leaves the shirt basting in the bucket. On his way back up, Dracula opens the door, and something happens. A little frantic parcel streams past his ear and collides with the overhead light and unfurls at the bottom of the basement stairs. He freezes, frisked with sudden wilderness, and looks down after it. The light in the vestibule is soiled and maligned—a bulb must be out. The bat didn't seem to have flown in at all. It almost seemed like a hand had flung it through just when he opened the door, like a live grenade, and his first thought is to step outside and look around. Nobody's there. The air clings like moist breath in an open mouth. It reminds Dracula of spring. Spring will be coming soon. He thinks of the wet splatting snow that floundered down on him last night. He goes back in and looks down the stairs.

The bat is now balled up under the cover of its own wings. This is the first bat he has seen up close and under lights. Is that true? His mind tells him so but his feelings seem to back away fuzzily from any certainty. The bundle is a slurry mud color, like mulched and muddy leaves, soft and quivering. He watches it twitch, almost cozily, like a baby asleep and dreaming under a blanket. It is right there in the middle of the floor, where somebody could step on it. Dracula thinks about shooing it up the stairwell and back out into the night. He doesn't think it will be a quick venture. Prodding wild things into human logic is an inane desecration of wills. Maybe he'll do it if it's still there when he comes back with the load of dirty clothes.

An hour later the bat is now in the corner, huddled up like a clod of dirt that anybody could have kicked there. If he doesn't do anything, what will happen? Will it simply remain there indefinitely, until it calcifies and dies? Will it implode of nervous exhaustion? He thinks now to open the door behind it and scoop it into the blackness of that other room. That would be the easy way. But it might cause problems.

Now he is thinking of Lucinda as he goes to dump his clothes into the empty washer drum. How she had met him that day in the room. She would roll over in her sleep if she knew he'd actually found a key, or what he'd done in there.

Lucinda, however, is not asleep—not right now. She was gone tonight when he came home. He was only pretending to be at work, walking out on the beach, and he came back early. He expected to see her in bed, limbs asunder, face smashed, deep in the underworld lair the way he has been finding her lately. She has been sleeping very soundly. Sometimes he steps from his coffin in the evening and finds her still inextricably asleep. She always says she's just been napping, but the way she looks, as if pried up from a long, lightless trance, makes him doubt it. He thinks she's telling the truth, in the sense that he thinks she thinks she's telling the truth.

If he is Dracula, then his time in that room is not so damaged or deranged. If he isn't—which is what he thinks she thinks—then it is. If he tells her about it he doesn't know which way she will sway.

Tonight she had her rehearsal again and she could have gone out afterward with friends. He knows she has those two friends who sometimes help her get to where she's going. Maybe he is finding Lucinda so tired all the time because she's been doing a lot of social extracurriculars to and from her scheduled events. She has to put things on the calendar or else she'll forget. Dracula has come to wonder how much of a life she has without him, and how okay he is with that. He doesn't want to be a jealous boyfriend.

Is there some explanation, back behind those looks she gives him from the bottom of a well? Where is Lucinda going or coming to? If you don't look into the dark you can't ever see. It's the same thing with that room.

If you don't look close in there you see nothing amiss. There are old mattresses, soiled and fistfulled into knots and tilted up vertically against the walls. There are some chain-link partitions for storing materials like paint and PVC pipes. There is an industrial fan and a gasoline smell. But some of the mattresses, most of them, are not loose on the walls. They are stuck with an industrial-grade adhesive, and sagging down from the ceiling like an old circus tent. Dracula had to pull at them to find this out. When you go in with a flashlight it's like a padded cell, or a makeshift music studio, some room meant to absorb sound and impact. Dracula stood wondering the first time he was in the room. It was right after he found the key inside an open bag of sunflower seeds. He had found the bag of seeds tucked into the hair of the mermaid and a note that said *The door with the window.* The door with the window was the basement door and it was right in front of him.

Now there is a noise behind him. Outside the open laundry in the hall he sees the clod of softness twitch as somebody clambers onto the landing and down the steps. A floating bike wheel comes forward at a sluggish spin, and a man drops its back companion to the floor with a pursed expression. He rolls it vertically through the door with a sidelong glance and hoists it to a rack on the wall where it hangs apart from the others.

"Hi," says Dracula. He recognizes the man, to the extent that he knows he's seen him before.

"Laundry," says the man, without interest. It must be almost midnight. The man's watch beeps and the stairwell erupts as if on cue with some swift commotion, like someone or something hurtling down the stairs, and then a gloved hand plunges into their open doorway and grabs the knob and swings the door closed on them. The bicycle man lunges for it but there's a click in the handle.

"Shit," he says, jiggling it. "Holy shit."

The deadbolt slides over. They look at each other. Dracula has his hand stuffed down the mouth of the washer. "What just happened?" he says.

"*Why* is there a lock on the outside of this door?" the man says in answer. "Let us out!" He is still wearing his white and gold helmet and it clops against the door as he bangs his fist. They both hear the clatter of keys and the creak of the other door opening across the way. It's all done in a hurry and then with a few foragings and frothy abrasions, like somebody's hanging bunting, a muffled scurry slams the far door shut. The man turns to Dracula with a look of assailed accusation. "This is unlawful entrapment."

Dracula absorbs this. He thinks of the bat stuck in the corner. "There's a bat out there."

"What?" says the man, in a fierce, hostile tone.

"A bat. I saw it fly in. I wonder if someone came to trap it. Maybe they didn't want it to fly in here." Even as he says it, he doesn't know why he is making up such a stupid excuse.

"And locked us in?" the man scowls.

"Well—"

"Why wouldn't they have answered us after we yelled at them?"

"Maybe—"

"No. This has happened before."

"It has?"

The man glowers. "This is the second time this has happened to me. There is something going on in that room."

"When were you in here before?" Dracula is curious.

Suddenly, he knows how he recognizes the man. He's the one who came down the steps the first time he unlocked the door, right after finding the key in the bag of seeds. The man didn't say hi—he just stood in the open doorway glowering.

"What is this?" he'd said.

"I don't know," said Dracula. "I just found it open."

That was a lie, and when he said it, he got a look from the man that was familiar. The light in the vestibule was casting his face in shadow and he was pretty sure he'd never seen the guy before. But now tonight he's getting the same look, and he knows exactly where he's seen him before. At the college. He's the one who detained him over Warren's art. He has that distinct chin dimple, and it deepens when he drops it down, like a crude slot for a coin. There's a kind of avarice about it that sets the man off kilter.

The man peers at him. He seems to be rethinking his allegation, or rethinking his choice to share it with Dracula. Maybe he recognizes Dracula too. Dracula can already tell that he likes to slide into this posture of obligated authority, and settles in with a kind of plush indulgence, as if he just has to have that tacit position of dominance. It's unclear what he is implying with the look, except that it seems to be a way to dispense blame. Dracula raises his eyebrows. How is any of this his fault?

In place of an answer the man is now taking off his gloves. "I'm going to get him," he says, almost cartoonishly, as if the perpetrator is a bashful ghoul bumping around in a house-dress outside. "When he opens the door." Or she, Dracula thinks.

"Who knows when that will be," Dracula says.

"Not long." The man sniffs. "Twenty minutes."

"If it's like last time, you mean," Dracula says, jabbing him with his own repeat incarceration. He is seeing that the man could use a little bit of humble dunk-tanking while he's in here. He is actually wishing he hadn't run up on this man again. After that night at the college he had come to rather like him—or his idea of him, tersely toe-tapping his intrinsic dignity into all the rabble out there. Now, he just wants to battle-ram the Scooby villain all the way out of existence.

The man peels his second set of fingers out of his glove and Dracula feasts his eyes upon a bright white band around his finger—a blanched ring of nudity beaming out from his brown standard-issue bicycler knuckles. What does this mean—the man is recently divorced? That could be a reason for what he's doing in this cursed building. He's between living arrangements.

Dracula waits. The man waits. The machine fills and agitates. Dracula takes out the brochure from the knife sales-man and glances through it. The salesman's name is Kent

Wallaby. In Dracula's current disposition, it sounds like something fantastical.

"Did this guy come to visit you?" Dracula says.

His neighbor squints at him.

"Kent Wallaby? Knife salesman?"

He shrugs. "I just got off work. I haven't been to my apartment."

"Oh right." The machine is rinsing now. Dracula picks up a piece of dropped newspaper. He reads about a local celebrity couple that has gone missing. More than twenty minutes have passed now. The man looks gloomy. "Have you read about this?" Dracula says over the top of the paper.

"What?"

"The couple that went missing. This local car dealer and his realtor wife."

"That's old news," he says.

Dracula checks the date. "Oh, yep," he says, though it turns out the date means nothing to him. This he finds disconcerting. "Did they find them?"

The man frowns. "No. Nor did they find the other six missing people. You don't get out much," says the man.

"I guess not," Dracula says.

"They found one girl in the bathtub. Slit her wrists and drowned herself. But they don't think her case is related."

Dracula nods. "Oh wait," he says, snapping his fingers. "I did know her. Vanessa, uh—" he's blanking on the last name. "My girlfriend was her friend." He is trying to assure the cop that he is not a cretinous creature from the cellar and he realizes in his eagerness he sounds exactly like one.

The cop leans on the wall with his arms crossed, not casually. He gives Dracula a beady stare.

Dracula folds up the paper and offers it. The cop shakes his head.

"So, have you lived here long? In the building?"

The man doesn't answer him. Instead he takes out a phone.

"You have a phone?" says Dracula.

The man glances up, as if he thinks the phone is none of Dracula's business.

"Can't you just have called somebody to get us out of here?"

"That's what I'm doing," he says. The man mutters a message into somebody's voicemail. He folds the phone back under his arm. He is keeping a sideways watch on Dracula.

Dracula thinks he understands now—the man had been willing to trap them both in here to catch the perpetrator before Dracula started gabbing at him. For months he's been flexing his social skills, trying to blend in better with his best approximation of geeky affability, which seems to come closest to his demeanor. He wonders how phony it seems, with his jolting smiles and smoked voice and tic-ish neck popping. For some reason he thinks of the knife salesman, flaunting his getup. Behind him the washer is revving into a spin.

Later, when the door finally opens, it's not how either expected it to happen. "Hello?" says a timid voice on the other side. "Why is this door locked?" She seems to be talking to herself, with the hesitation of a person who thinks she's alone but isn't sure.

"We're locked in."

There's a pause, a startled one. "Oh. Okay."

"Can you let us out?"

The woman seems afraid to open the door. It's the middle of the night, after all. "Just a second let me get my husband." They hear her feet going up the steps. A few minutes later a heavier set of feet slog down and a drowsy man in sweats opens the door. "It happened to you too, huh?"

The cop walks up the stairs with him, trading hostage accounts. Dracula's laundry is almost at the end of its second spin so he stays to empty the washer. The woman comes back down with a hamper and seems embarrassed to find him.

"Sorry. I have a baby. I'm up all hours."

"No problem," says Dracula. The shirt comes out of the wash clean. And smelling of flowers. Harsh and virulent. "I'll get out of your way," he says.

Out in the vestibule the bat is gone. Now he wants to know what is in that room that wasn't there before. But Dracula will have to wait. He can hear the woman thumping clothes into the washer. As he goes up the stairs the bookcase looms hazardously. Dracula goes out into the night.

Upstairs in the apartment Lucinda is back in bed. Dracula has a handful of wet clothes to hang. While he is putting them all on the shower rod he thinks of the time he and she met in that other room, by chance. How they stood in there together. How he claimed the door was already open when he came down. Then the cop stood in the doorway glowering. How the next time he went in he found in the corner a bucket of dirty blood. He sipped from it, just to verify. As he stood there he tried to channel a feeling of horror or release, but neither came.

Now he hangs up the shirt, expunged of its evidence. He had experienced more of both of those feelings just last night—horror and release—in the parking lot with those teenagers. He's still thinking about that, erratically and wincingly. How all he did was lift one knee to the gut of the kid and he spurted out a funnel of vomit, the splatter of which had gotten on Dracula's shirt. He hadn't noticed it right away because a moment before a wet snow had begun to dump from the sky, like a flap of wind had opened a pocket on them, and all these sopping hands were suddenly slapping them soggy. The girl had screamed and hurled something at the same time, which hit the pavement with a clack and whacked against the kid's head. It was basic self-defense, Dracula thought, rolling the kid out from behind his back tire. The kid had lunged out like an off-balance baby and Dracula simply lifted his knee. The knife wasn't in the equation at all. Now the kid was gulping air on the pavement right under the truck wheel and Dracula had to heft him out of the way before he could go anywhere, all with the girl screaming at him to stop. This was where he must have dropped it. Then the waitress and a guy in a grubby apron came barging out just as the kid sat up out of a roll and got to his knees.

"Help! He hit him!" the girl cried. Dracula held his palms up in the air and stepped calmly toward the driver's door of his truck. The cook reluctantly trotted out, seemingly unsure if he should approach Dracula or help the kid, and then he decided on helping the kid, who was staggering to his feet and veering over to the back of an old white Dodge. The girl scurried after them.

"Hey—no—stop!" the waitress said to Dracula. "You!"

The cook tried to steady the kid and they both slumped down onto the trunk, then the cook stood back as the girl leaned forward. Dracula jammed the key in the ignition. A dark gush of fluid spewed over the trunk and the kid spasmed in a deep, convulsive silence. Everybody saw it. Everybody stilled. "Oh my God," rasped the girl. "What is that? Is that blood?" The ignition ground up the rest of her words. As he barreled out of the lot the waitress took it upon herself to chase after him, pulling off one of her shoes and tossing it right into his grille. It banged and flopped against the metal for several miles and then seemed to tear free. He drove for a while in silence. It seemed like nothing like that had ever happened to him. He kept tearing in gauzy breaths of labored air. He tried to contemplate the significance of that.

Twenty minutes later he was in the bland illumination of another town and he stopped at an overnight drugstore to collect himself. He was weak-kneed and clayey inside. The kid would end up in a hospital somewhere and he would probably be fine, he told himself. It was mostly his breakfast-for-dinner, or maybe lunch or afternoon snack, that came out. He would convalesce under the scrutiny of anxious adults— his dad who had traded in his outdated fashions—and he would notice his utter lack of virility. Virility would seem like a strange mirage hovering distantly both behind and ahead of where he now was. He would get back to it someday. Dracula thought this because he was not really thinking about the kid. He was looking at the front grille of his truck, where the broken strap was still lodged in the metal. He tugged it out. Sometimes he thought there was some indifferent antagonist making him feel all his ferocity as if it were the sum of all his failure.

Then he remembered the other item in his shirt pocket and fished it out. What the girl had thrown, hitting her friend in the head, was a can of mace. As if she thought it was a funny joke, she had drawn flowers and hearts all over it and written on the lid *Amory's Ammo*. The poor girl had thrown it at him instead of spraying it. It wasn't her fault. She would have had to mace her friend to mace Dracula. Isn't that always the way.

Now in the bathroom hanging his clothes, he feels as if he is being maced, belatedly. His eyes are smarting and his nose is clogging. As if delivering a punch line the bottle comes tumbling out of one of his pockets. It hits the bottom of the tub with a bang. Sucking in a breath he pokes his head out into the hall and peers into the black burrow of the bedroom. Not a stirring from within. The dark is getting thin in a way he can feel. Dracula picks up the mace and sniffs at it. He washed all his clothes in this. No wonder they smell like hazardous fuel. The bottle seems to be ex-panding under some internal pressure and leaking a tiny noxious thread of gas at him. A sad assault. Dracula goes with it out the door. In the faded hearts and flowers he holds a last unconscious prayer to innocence. Probably her dad bought it for her.

Dracula looks at the basement door across the courtyard, which is now showing a black pane of glass. As he stands there it occurs to him that the woman who brought her wash in after him will likely have residual toxins in her rinse water. That is the extent of his menace tonight. Maybe the clothes are for the baby.

The light in the basement window is off. He thinks of the key, stuck there for someone to find. Then he thinks of the knife, lost and irretrievable.

This is how late those two kids were out, he thinks, looking down at the bottle. This is how young they were, he thinks, seeing its flowers. This is how unguarded they were. The bottle, now, is ready to explode. Dracula throws it hard, up above the building and whirling out over the other side, to a place he can't see or hear. Then he goes inside to think about dinner.

The Prop (Part II)

*L*ucinda and Rory are standing at the apartment door. She is lingering just behind, having unlocked it and stepped back, feeling besieged as always by the Russian's big, baleful window. It looms clean and clairvoyant, taunting her like any pane of blackened glass.

She keeps thinking of that last conversation with Vanessa. "I can't believe you quit," Vanessa said. She was wearing her work shirt.

Lucinda didn't tell her why she quit. She still didn't know why she quit.

"What's wrong? You look like shit."

The rehearsal had not gone well. Her mother had come and gone with the cage that day, flicking her spare key duplicate in Lucinda's face. Then the Russian had said something terrible. That was when Lucinda had broken down and told Vanessa about the key.

"You can go in with me if you want." Lucinda clutched her throat.

"Go in where—into this guy's apartment?"

"It's this thing we have." She tried not to sound as stricken as she felt. "It's..." Now she was hardly holding the acid out of her voice. "It's complicated."

"Ooh," said Vanessa, "kinky."

Lucinda winced. She tried not to.

"I don't understand," said Vanessa. "Why do you want to even go in there?"

They were standing in front of the theater. They had run into each other by accident.

"Oh my God," Vanessa said. She flinched her hand up in front of her face. She slanted her eyes drastically down. And that was the end of that conversation. "That's the guy," Vanessa said.

Lucinda looked. "Who? What guy?"

All she saw was Rory, smacking his way out the theater door, the sleeves of his thermal bunched up over his forearms.

Vanessa had lowered her chin and turned away, even though Rory was well on his way in the other direction. "Remember that double date? The one I said I fucked and chucked?"

"Wait," said Lucinda. "The fireman?" That was Rory? Rory was a fireman? Vanessa slept with Rory? Somehow that seemed impossible. All of it.

Vanessa sucked in air. She looked at Lucinda with what seemed a menacing intensity. "I'm not a good person. You shouldn't be friends with me," she said.

Lucinda was thinking of how she herself had not been a good friend. How she had set Vanessa up for some undoing or indecency from Richard and then never looked back. She just kept taking hundred-dollar bills.

Now she thinks of Rory being a victim of Vanessa's wiles as she looks at the mass of his back. "He stalked me for like a week after that," Vanessa had said. "It was a disaster."

Rory has muscled his way through the door, and she finds herself a flood of nerves. He's breathing heavy after hurtling the coffin up the stairs over his head, tottering into rails and risers. He hasn't said anything to her since rehearsal. Lucinda wonders if he knows about the dinner. Is he just going to expect her to get back in the truck with him after they replace the coffin? She wishes he would say something.

"Are you getting nervous?" she asks in the doorway.

Rory gives her a gloomy glance. The coffin is seesawing lightly on his shoulder as he pilots the narrow passage. "What do you mean?"

"You know—about the performance." She feels oddly embarrassed trying to make conversation with him. Usually he's the one talking nonstop at her.

"No," says Rory, stalking ahead of her. He humps straight to the closet and plunks the coffin down.

Lucinda sits back on the bed, letting him make adjustments. Now he has the coffin wedged against the side wall between the clothes rack and the door, where it has to go. Otherwise the lid won't swing open.

"Sometimes Vlad comes out of there sweating bullets," Lucinda says, nibbling her nails, not sure why she's divulging this. She guesses she's trying to be nice. "He gets so hot."

Rory shakes his head brutely. "Bugs should go find himself a different hidey-hole." Under his breath he says, "Preferably in hell," which makes Lucinda feel less friendly. She doesn't mention to Rory that hell would be even hotter, or that perhaps it is where Dracula has been, because she doesn't think Rory is really paying attention.

Rory straightens. His hands hang at his sides. No satisfied hand-swiping tonight, she sees. Lucinda is having mixed feelings. She finds herself sloughing off the bed, wondering what words she will say next.

"You're coming, then?" he asks. It's not exactly a question and not quite an accusation. So he does know. His whole posture is buckled over in a petulant sulk. She's never seen Rory like this. Lucinda still can't be sure if it's because of the dinner invitation or because of what the teacher said to him.

Strangely, his tone has given her no room for last-minute refusal and she follows him meekly out the door, wondering what his problem is, reminded suddenly of what it felt like to be a child walking a step behind her testy and irascible father.

Hadn't he done things like this? She can't really remember. Lucinda almost wants to snicker conspiratorially with somebody but she doesn't have anybody here.

In the truck, Rory puts on The Ronettes. It's one of the bands that gets a musical number in the play.

"Have you been listening to the bands from the play?" says Lucinda. It occurs to her that this is rather academic of him. It's the sort of thing their teacher is always encouraging them to do.

Rory jams the truck into reverse and bucks them out of the lot. She doesn't think he's going to answer. Then he says, "I like oldies," and turns the volume knob up.

The drive is full of the sweet buttery swaths of girl yearning.

Three songs go by and then they come to a stop outside a row of buildings, each one a slightly different variation of brick. "This is my house," he says. He gives her a look and reaches across her to unlock the door. Whatever its intentions, it's an awkward mauling of the space between them. Now he seems embarrassed. "Get out so I can park the car."

Rory has pulled in at a bus stop, and after she's on the curb he swerves out and drives around the nearest corner. She hunches in her parka with a momentary feeling of abandonment, but it's almost better than being in the truck with him. As she waits she turns and faces the buildings, peering from inside her hood and listening to a bus groan slowly up the street behind her. When the sound has gradually crested and faded away again, she turns to look and sees Rory hurrying up the sidewalk. He lumbers past and walks down steps to the garden-level gate at one of the buildings. It's the one right behind the bus stop, with soot wafting up the brick walls. A ceramic glossy yellow face sticks its tongue out at them from the door. It's grimed with diesel exhaust.

"My sister made that," he says.

Lucinda follows him into a low room with a dark, fishy smell. She feels a queasy stirring of dread. Nobody is here. Where is Lauren? The room is lined with tall bookcases topped with dusty vines in white ceramic pots, and a tweed couch faces into the room away from the door. The carpet is a dark amber hue, and there is no noise inside but the subtle churnings of plumbing inside the walls. Rory escorts her past the couch into a little dining alcove and flips on a back porch light at the same time the water cuts off with a clunk. Maybe that's Lauren. Maybe she's taking a shower. Lucinda looks out at a small patio cluttered with pieces of tarp-covered furniture. Various wood and gold wind chimes gong and twinkle in an icy stirring of air, and beyond this a weedy patch appears webbed with clotheslines and their shadows.

Rory goes back to the couch and drops down. Lucinda looks at the wall behind him. It is covered in a random and arresting collection of oil paintings, one of which is a portrait of a horsy-looking woman with a large hooked nose and small eyes set like black pebbles into a deep collar of bone. It appears somehow meant to look both hideous and powerful, and in some unparticular way it reminds Lucinda of her own mother.

Where is Lauren's mother? Where is dinner?

"Lauren's in the shower," Rory says, just as Lauren herself comes out, looking pert as a puppy inside an old white bathrobe.

"Mom's not here," she says to Rory, without greeting Lucinda.

"I know she's not here. I have to go pick her up. Can I go now?" he says, giving her a leering, obsequious grin.

She rolls her eyes at him.

Lucinda is fascinated. This is how they act with each other? She has never really noticed them in class.

Rory stands up. For some reason the low ceilings make him seem gigantic, like some bulging Nordic deity poised for his music cue. The satin pop celebrity shirt adds to the effect.

Lauren sashays back into the narrow hallway off the living area and Lucinda follows, uncertainly. Framed photos blot the walls with glints and gleams but it's too dark to see the people inside them. Lucinda can hear the sound of Rory advancing behind her.

"Is she one of your girlfriends?" This question is bellowed out over her shoulder, and Lucinda turns to find him clogging up the slim hallway, like a blockage in a pipe. She stares for a moment in surprise. What's he talking about? His shoulders are massive and his bulky dump-truck chest tapers down to a pair of bony legs that could belong to a bird or a girl.

Lucinda looks back at Lauren, who merely opens the last door in the hallway and disappears through it.

She turns back to Rory. "Rory," she says, "what are you talking about?"

"What do you think?" His voice is menacing and uncertain. For a moment they watch each other and he shakes his head, then unblocks the hall and disappears.

At the end of the hall Lucinda stands in the doorway Lauren opened. Inside is a bedroom with pastel blue walls and child's bric-a-brac, and Lauren sits on an iron bed in her robe looking blindly down at a bottle of nail polish. "You want to paint your nails?" Her voice is touchy and loud. She claps the bottle down on the dresser. "I'm going to get dressed." She gives Lucinda a stony look. "Don't worry or anything. I'm not going to make out with you. I'll dress in the bathroom."

"I don't understand," says Lucinda. Is Lauren a lesbian? Why would that matter? Why is everybody acting like this?

Lauren sighs. "My brother's not trying to be a dick. He's just mad at me."

"Okay," says Lucinda.

"He's a good person."

"Okay."

"He likes you. He—" Lauren shakes her head.

Lucinda does not know how to take this. He what?

Lauren stands up to riffle clothes in a duffel bag, pulling out undergarments and that thin, floppy brown tunic again. "He works hard," she says, walking to the door. Suddenly Lucinda has a thought. Is Lauren doing with her what she had a mind to do with Lauren? Having her over to play matchmaker, to prod her brother into action? "He's not a loser. That's not why he lives at home. He works odd hours."

Lucinda feels her breath pixelate. Her mind recoils. "What does he do?" she says.

"He's a fireman."

Lucinda hardly hears. She wants to remind Lauren that she has a boyfriend, and he's Dracula.

As Lauren goes into the bathroom Lucinda stands primly, unsure how to occupy herself. Lauren's duffel is tumbled into the narrow space at her feet and everything's coming out of it. Behind the door is another bed, jammed on the opposite wall. Lucinda can see how more than one person might live in here. In the bathroom Lauren is running the hair dryer, and Lucinda picks up a book.

Pages flutter past her—group shots of grinning girls, boys jumping in inexplicable unison, those sucker-punched portraits of teens in their endless grids, all blending together. It's a yearbook. *Most likely to make trouble!* someone had written over a smudged face. *Love you girl!* The face is oval with an apple bulge of cheeks, waxed to a high shine. The mouth is all but mauled by a false sinister grin, and the eyes lost under a scribble of pitched brows. Is it Lauren? Somehow she thinks she's seen her before.

When Lauren comes out she's put the book away, and Lauren fluffs her damp hair, unaware. She doesn't look like the girl. Lauren is wearing her medieval tunic, the Peter Pan thing she wore before. "Come on," she says, slightly more perky. Lucinda follows. Outside, they sit shivering on a frigid covered bench while Lauren paints her nails on a wooden box. It's for the play. For weeks she has been applying layer after layer of the inkiest blue black, so that it looks like lacquered dabs of armor on her fingers. The rest of her is slumped in that grain-bag brown.

"Aren't you cold?" says Lucinda, who is at least wearing her parka over her shifting layers of corn silk. Rory didn't give her a chance to change after rehearsal.

Lauren shrugs. They are facing inside the house where a single lamp spreads a dim amber glow over the silhouetted furniture. It looks like a cozy parlor in hell.

"So, what is that dress?" Lucinda says, trying to put it politely. She doesn't really think it is a dress. She wonders if Lauren's mother made it, just like the sack.

"Oh, it's my other costume," says Lauren, flashing a smile. Lucinda is about to ask what she means when the front door opens and the low light picks up two dim forms. "Rory went to pick up my mom from work," Lauren says. "Now we'll have dinner."

Lucinda was not sure she wanted to have this dinner and now she is quite certain she doesn't. When they come inside she sees that Rory is holding a baby. She perches on his forearm with queenly poise as she gives Lucinda a groggy, hostile stare. The mother is as tall as Rory and looks like the woman in the painting, except she has yellow dyed hair down to her waist. Despite her height she seems withered down and collapsed. Her chest is concave and her shoulders round forward like they are trying to protect it, and her lips are smothered in a shiny, medicinal-looking jelly. She seems to be afflicted with some atrocious malady and Lucinda has trouble looking at her. Rory stands behind her holding the baby and watching Lucinda react. Despite the mother's appearance she moves into the room with a rough and terrible energy. Lucinda finds herself plowed back against the wall as the woman plunks her purse on the couch and moves over to Lauren.

"Are you messing with your brother?" Her voice is dry and husky, like the croak of a long-term smoker.

"Oh please. Did he tell you that?"

"No. I can just tell. I can always tell these things, honey." She clutches Lauren by the arms and presses their foreheads together in an intimate stare-down. "I think you've hurt his feelings," says her mother.

At this Rory mutters something over the head of the baby that sounds very ugly. He rams past them and grabs a piece of plastic crosshatching from the wall and flicks it one-handed into a pen for the baby. The mother looks meaningfully at Lauren and moves off into the kitchen. Cabinets bang open and shut.

"What do you three want for dinner? Eggs?" She sticks her head out and looks at Lucinda. "I don't suppose my daughter is going to introduce us. I'm Deena."

Lucinda manages to produce her name. Eggs for dinner does not sound good to her.

"It's nice to meet you. Lauren could have warned me. I look like shit you know, Lauren."

The baby reaches out for Lauren. Lauren drifts into the kitchen and puts her head on her mother's shoulder. "Hi babe," her mother says. "Where you been?"

Lucinda stands where she is, not sure where to rest her eyes. Rory reaches for the remote and bullies the buttons until the TV is on. He stands over the baby, watching it, but not really. The baby watches Lucinda, with little red-brown eyes buried close to the center of her face, like candied nuts in dough. Lauren murmurs something to her mother. Lauren's mother pets down her hair. "Don't be like that," she says, "I'm not dead yet." She leaves her to open the refrigerator and Lauren murmurs, "You will be."

"Well shut up," her mother says over her shoulder. "You certainly know how to make a woman feel good about herself."

Rory slams down the remote and takes three huge steps toward Lauren and shakes her. "What is your problem?" He looks right at Lucinda and points. "You shouldn't have brought her. Why did you bring her?" He seems on the verge of doing some violence to her, and she gives him a disdainful look through hooded eyes.

Lucinda feels weirdly like she is in a play, watching it unfold from right in the middle of it.

"Oh, come on!" says the mother sharply. She points at Lucinda with the knife in her hand. "She's company! Do you want me to ask her to come in here with me or can you be nice in front of her!" They all stare in silence. The baby lets out a peal of sound that is either enthused or agitated. The mother holds her long hard look a moment longer and clucks at the baby and turns back to the counter. Lauren dips her fingers into the playpen to fondle her hair and walks to the couch and sits. Rory glares and leaves the room. Lucinda wonders what she should do. Lauren nibbles at the sleeve of her dress.

"Should I go?" she says. "I could take the bus. It's not far."

Lauren barely looks at her. "No. I want to show you something."

Reluctantly, Lucinda follows Lauren back into the hallway. Lauren puts her hand on the knob of a closed door and looks at Lucinda with eyes that Lucinda realizes are exactly like the baby's.

"Whose baby is that?" she says.

Lauren appears to be listening through the door. "Rory's," she says, eventually.

She opens the door and Lucinda is not sure she believes her. She is so tired of learning or not learning things. She thought Lauren was somehow incapable of lies—at least the blatant kind.

Now she has a view of the room. It is a black, tiny box that seems completely filled with a medical bed and machinery. In the bed is a long hump. "Mo," says Lauren, crossing into the room. Her voice is stiff and careful and then the curtains part and let in the backyard floodlight. The room is oddly slanted down, with paneled walls that seem to exude a trailer-park flimsiness. Lauren casts a grim look at Lucinda and sinks toward the bed to stroke the hair of its inhabitant, which lifts in brittle clumps and falls back down. A thick, sluggish sound issues from the man's throat. "I know you can hear me." She pushes a button and the top half of the bed begins to elevate. There is the head of a mummy. All the skin is pulled back taut and he doesn't seem able to close his mouth. It dangles stiffly, with one tooth inside of it.

"Mo, it's me. I came to see you."

Mo fumbles at her with his hands. She holds her arm out for him and he puts it in his mouth and bites it. Lucinda steps back. Lauren merely pulls her arm out of his mouth and hoists him to a sitting position, and he sits like a man petrified, his toothless grimace aimed blankly upward. One of his eyes is blinking frantically.

"How do you expect to hurt me? You have no teeth you goose. Now come on. It's Lauren and I'm here to see you because I love you." Her voice is chipper and clear, more like the Lauren Lucinda knows from theater class, and as she speaks the eye becomes less frantic and the mouth clacks with mucus and the man begins to take large, panting breaths broken by one word at a time.

"I-didn't-see-you. I-didn't-know-you. I-was-having-a dream," he mutters.

His voice is a gritty gale.

"It's all right, Mo. Come on, get your breath." She sits next to him and props him up and arranges him at a slant against her body. "Comfortable?" He is breathing in a choked, spastic way, as if she is cutting off his oxygen, and Lucinda finds herself clutching at her throat. His gaze falls somewhere at her knees and his mouth stretches into a slightly wider grimace, as if he is registering something and smiling. She feels her heart swivel and curtsy.

"Oh. Light-of-the-cross," says Mo.

Lucinda's knees buckle. Why is he saying her line? Why has she been brought in here, like a piece of statuary, she is realizing. She hasn't been brought to see him but to be shown to him. Lucinda finds herself backing into the hall, still hearing Lauren speak to him in muffled tones. The baby is making unhappy murmurs on the other side of a door behind her. Rory must have moved her. Lucinda stands in the hall and feels trapped between two extremes of misery. She can hear the mother clattering dishes out in the kitchen. After a few minutes Lauren comes into the hallway and gives her a vacant look and closes the door.

She draws in an audible breath. She stares at a picture on the wall. "I took the coffin from the play," she says. "I just wanted somebody to tell."

Lucinda realizes she's not surprised. She finds herself following Lauren's gaze. It's so simple and bare, the statement. Yet, she struggles to understand. "For—?" she says. "You mean—?" She stops.

"For Mo," Lauren says.

Lucinda nods. She has never seen death before. Not in a live human being. Is the coffin even real enough for that? For actual death? "Where is it?"

Lauren points. "Out there. I painted my nails on it."

"I didn't even notice." Lucinda thinks about Vanessa.

"Yes—I noticed that," Lauren says, smiling. She shrugs. "We can't afford one, or anything. Mom's medicine is really expensive."

Lucinda nods. This is her friend, she thinks. Her friend is confiding in her. The last friend she had is dead now. She has to be careful with this one.

"It's good construction. It's not like we need fancy."

Lucinda finds herself wondering if the funeral industry has rules. If certain materials and dimensions are compulsory. Does it have to be airtight? Chemically treated? Is there an industry-approved half-life for decay? What about a lining? Wouldn't the wrong thing kill the grass or make a sudden garden patch?

"Come get your grub!" says Lauren's mother.

Lucinda and Lauren look at each other. Is that it? Lucinda is still a little stricken by all the input and yet starting to feel a little relieved. It seems like something has been aired out between them, the tension thinned.

When they get out of the hallway, Lauren's mother is putting plates down on the table.

Lucinda feels her stomach go to lava. She realizes that there are a few reasons for her to feel too sick to eat, and yet it would be too rude to use any of them. Better to nibble and say nothing. Rory stalks down the hall and thrusts the baby down in the high chair and goes around the table to sit beside his mother. The mother sits with the portrait of herself on the far wall behind her. A portrait of an ugly dog is beside that, baring its teeth under a grubby rug of fur and balancing on a circus ball. It looks like Vlad, except for the expression. Lauren sits beside the baby and pats it on the back. She seems perkier after her confession. Lucinda thinks about how perky Rory and Lauren usually are, at and after class. She wonders how much of it is a self-sustaining act.

Lucinda is either at the foot of the table or the head of the table, and she can tell that nobody ever sits here.

The configuration produces a certain effect. Lucinda realizes that Rory looks exactly like his mother and the baby looks exactly like Lauren. Family is a strange mangling. Rory picks up his fork and eats his eggs the way a dainty voracious bird would eat eggs. In addition to eggs there are pieces of jellied toast. The only light in the room is the one right above their heads.

"Breakfast for dinner," says the mother, "Rory's favorite."

Rory seems too mortified or too morose to answer. Lucinda still can't help wondering if she's here because of him. Even though Lauren said it was because of the coffin. And Rory said it was because of Lauren.

"Do you want to know who that is?" Lauren asks the baby, and points at Lucinda. "Look over there."

The baby looks. Lauren's eyes glitter. "That's Lucinda. Can you say Lucinda?" The baby gives a little rat-fanged smile and makes a loud nasal eruption that sounds like "Cinder."

Lucinda waves. The baby is dressed in something different now. Lucinda tries to remember what it was wearing that made her think it was a girl. Now it looks like a boy.

"So Lucinda," says the mother, reaching for her fork. "What do you do?"

"Oh," says Lucinda. As she's trying to figure out how to answer this, Rory cuts in. "Let Lauren ask her. She's her date."

"Shut up, Rory." Lauren lofts her eyes at Lucinda in exasperation.

"She has a boyfriend," he says.

It's not clear if this is directed at Lauren or his mother. Lucinda feels a glancing kick under the table. Was that meant for her? Rory and Lauren glare over their forks.

"Oh?" The mother feigns polite, if not perplexed, interest, her eyes ping-ponging between them. Clearly she is trying to figure out who Lucinda is here for. Or why it should matter that she has a boyfriend. So is Lucinda.

Rory smiles. He grits his teeth and his big ham unhinges. "He's Dracula."

Across the table Lauren buckles in silent agony.

Lucinda sits way back, tucking her legs beneath her chair. What is going on here?

"Oh, that's funny," says the mother, taking a bite of eggs. She's smirking, presumably at the show.

Lucinda is looking around at all three of them, trying to get her bearings. What is she supposed to say? Slowly, she is realizing something. Everyone at the table is wearing a costume. Even Lauren's mother. Lauren's mother, she realizes, is wearing a wig.

"I am too," says Lauren's mother, smiling and chewing at the same time. "You are what you eat," she says.

It's what she says and also the way she says it that makes her seem sinister.

The Hat

*D*racula wonders if he should be making himself scarce. If perhaps he should have planned a little camping trip. Make like a tree in the polluted wood, as the saying goes.

Somebody will surely come looking for him. Should he tell Lucinda? Should he present her with a scheme for meeting? He doesn't think she'll go for it. He doesn't think they'd last on the lam.

If somebody came looking for him, who would it be? A liability lawyer from UPS? A law officer? Charges, he knows, would have to be filed. UPS, he knows, would have to oblige. Information he falsified would be divulged. Then indictments and arraignments, whatever that means. That's about as far as his television expertise takes him. He has begun to watch the mail very carefully. And the door.

Tonight, in recompense for his vigil, he found a letter already stashed in the slot. He looked down the breezeway for a mailman who was surely long gone. It was 6:00 P.M. The last mailman Dracula had seen was in late fall, smiling inside a thick strap of beard when he delivered the mail at 4:45. Lucinda hated how dark it got this time of year. She hated how cold and closed in it was. Dracula felt a little bruised by this. Winter should mean more time with him.

Dracula brought the letter in. As always is the case, it is addressed to Lucinda. In big block script. It's been idling beside his foot on the coffee table while Dracula watches TV. Now he picks it up. Inside, signed in the gruel of Richard's hand, is her final paycheck. It seems a little late for such farewell reparations, even by Dracula's sense of timing. He still wonders why she quit.

For a while, Dracula sits folding. The table jams his legs apart as he leans into the abstraction of his thoughts. He likes to fold mail. He doesn't know why, but the tight creases satisfy him, the breaking fibers under his thumb, the planes and pleats bowing to his brute suggestion. He got a calendar for his birthday once—every day a new origami shape. There was a pig, a balloon, a sailboat. Why does he remember? The paper was colored variously and coated with a satin sheen. There was a smell too, a clean, distant plume of it, loose light on morning horizons. Dracula doesn't really know loose light on morning horizons, but the idea slips in nicely like some well-worn trespass, something else learned from television, another false and guilty refuge in the unknown and inapproachable. At times like this, Dracula wonders where his thoughts come from. He is folding without pause, steady and insistent. All this hit and miss. Lucinda isn't here again. He supposes it's possible that he can wait like this forever, pulling tight the rigging of his remaining days in some dumb, perishing act. Somehow, folding takes him way out past his own thinking. Always to that slow, oiled horizon, those watery mirages of dread and mystification. He juts into the dim clairvoyance. The envelope in his hand is tamped down to a thick, unwieldy slab. It's a bird. Some flightless fossil he's left behind.

Then Lucinda comes home.

"Hi."

"Where have you been?" says Dracula.

"Act two rehearsals." She sits like a splash of acid. Dracula senses he was supposed to know this. "Four hours long." Lucinda scrubs her face. "Why haven't you gone out?"

She means for his breakfast. Dinner as she accidentally calls it. Dracula finds himself stabbed with a wicked soreness. Here he has been waiting all this time and she wants him gone. He can tell from the way her tone curls.

"I just—" He almost says that he knows something. He almost lies and says that he knows everything.

A rattle of phlegm startles them both. The Russian is standing in the lamplit darkness of the open doorway. He is in a camouflage hat and under its brim his puffy face looks subdued and contrite. "This came for you," he says. "Under my door." He hands it over. "Whoops."

Dracula looks at it. It's registered mail. Inside is an eviction notice.

"Evicted? For what?" Rent isn't due for another week. Dracula looks at Lucinda. She detonates her eyes, obviously dumbstruck.

"You know," says the Russian in his choppy inflections. "For the railing outside."

Together they gape.

"Up and down with that trunk every night?"

Up and down?

"That casket thing. It looks like a coffin."

Dracula swivels his head. It might as well be creaking like his coffin. Lucinda shakes hers slowly side to side, with grave unknowing.

"The manager's been watching the girl doing it on the security camera." The Russian seems to bend under their attention. He tugs at his hat brim.

"What girl?" Dracula says.

"I—" says Lucinda. She seems to not be able to say something.

"There's damage all up and down," says the Russian, pointing outside.

"There's no damage," says Lucinda, her face stricken.

The Russian's face looks pummeled into fistfuls of flesh, big and haggard. He shuffles in the doorway. "Well, I am going away for a little trip. I guess when I get back I won't see you," he says apologetically. Dracula can't help but notice his accoutrements. Is he planning to drive all night somewhere? Is he trying to get away? For some reason this is what Dracula thinks.

"I guess you have a lot to talk about," he says.

When they are done exchanging a look, the doorway is deserted. Without a goodbye the Russian has stepped off down the outdoor walk. They can hear his equipment or his hand brushing along the banister. Now they are looking at the empty slot of night, and at each other.

"What was that?"

"I can't believe it. Is he the manager's lackey now?" Lucinda looks wild, and wrathful.

Dracula steps outside and gazes after the disappearing form.

Far away, it seems, and deep inside the night, he can hear something else, something muffled and faint, like a staticky reception that's tuned only to his pricked-up ears. He looks at the railing. Stepping back in, he asks, "What does he mean coffin?"

Lucinda stands up, rubbing her hands down her thighs. She doesn't seem mad anymore. "The one we had as a prop. From the play."

"The play? You mean, there's a coffin in your play?" Dracula tries to remember what she's told him about the play.

"Actually," says Lucinda. "I've been." She's looking odd now, her body wavering there like some unstable concoction.

They share a look. On Dracula's end it's uncomprehending doom. On Lucinda's it's guilty retreat.

"Someone stole that coffin," she says. "Not me."

"You mean—" Dracula takes a wild guess. "It's here?" Lucinda's look doesn't explain. "What?" he says.

She seems to twitch her head.

Dracula goes to his closet. It's astonishingly empty. "Where is it?" he says, looking at the raw expanse of wall. "Where is mine?" The question seems to scrape like chains in his throat.

"Outside. It's just outside," says Lucinda behind him.

"Outside?" Dracula swivels to stare at her knitting her hands torturously. "Where?" he says. *Why?* he wants to seethe.

Lucinda looks like one of those chattering teeth toys now. "The parking lot," she says. "I'm sorry." Her voice sounds mauled. "I was careful."

"You were careful?" He doesn't know what more to say. "Jesus." He plunges past her, unable to fathom what is going on. When Dracula gets down to the lot, his whole throat is caving in. He finds the coffin mysteriously leaning against an empty pickup truck. It looks so puny and old, so preposterous. "What?" he looks around and then at Lucinda, who has teetered down here after him. "What is it doing here? Whose truck is this?"

She ekes out a noise, like a wisp of candle smoke, to get her voice going. "Rory's. He's the one giving me rides to the theater. We lost that prop. So we were just—"

"You've got to be kidding me," says Dracula. "This is ridiculous." He still doesn't get it. His hands are cutting through the air in befuddled outrage. He swipes them viciously through his hair.

Lucinda stands there, her face stiffening. Now she's giving him a look that's stuck like glue. "It is," she says. "You're right."

Dracula blows air.

"I'm sorry. I'll go inside." She seems to curl as she turns, like a burnt candle wick. "I can't—" she says. "You're right. I can't do this."

She can't do what? Dracula feels almost sorry for her, watching her go. Wrathfully sorry. Regretfully furious. As if his regret is part of what's making him furious. Is this somehow his fault? His hand, of its own volition, has floated over to his coffin. It feels cold. The veneer ridged and brittle. Dracula almost wants to cry. When he gets inside, setting it gently down and testing the lid, the bathroom fan is rattling behind the closed door. Still, he can hear her retching into the sink. The shower comes on. He supposes it's too late now to ask her to join him for breakfast. Not that he'd want to.

Outside, going for the meal she seemed to want him to already be off on, he's not sure if he's furious at the Russian or her. Or the apartment manager. He should be furious at her but he's also furious at the apartment manager. That much is obvious.

Dracula feels the night air blow up on him. Like a lover's breath, soft and wet, it's all up in his business. It makes him think about Lucinda.

Whatever happened, with or involving his coffin.

She said she was being careful. He doesn't want to pursue what she was being careful about. It was all the way out there, is all he knows.

As he walks, he remembers when he used to come out here to get her, so she didn't have to walk home alone. How differently he thought of her then. It seems so long ago. When this whole thing was reversed. He thought he was the one who would need remaking, sanding down to shape this relationship. Every day he walked all the way to her work because he thought it would help. She'd have him wait outside, and then she would come slinking out that open door, clutching her hood under her chin. He thought he was coming to get her because she didn't feel safe. He used to get stuck all the time talking to people because she was always late coming out. There was that girl Vanessa. Then there were the passersby who went out of their way to talk to him—the men from the bus that asked for a cigarette, the vagrants with clanking parcels that asked for change, couples that asked for directions, the girls, younger than Lucinda, that complimented his hat. Now, peering inside the incandescent cube, Dracula wonders.

Why did she have him come? Why did she quit?

"Bro."

Coming on quick in the dark Dracula sees somebody yank his head back. Is that a smile jerking his cheeks? Dracula feels a familiar pang. Whoever this is stitching along the street is in soft, slouchy attire.

"Still keeping things contagious? Ha ha." He seems to think they know each other. Dracula has no idea who he is.

"I keep waiting to see you when I bring the mail. You're never there anymore."

Dracula is switching slow gears in his mind. He is making the connection that this is a mailman. Except this is not his mailman.

At least Dracula doesn't think so. At least not his current one. The only mailman he can picture has a sketched-in beard and round cheeks and teeth that seemed folded away inside the little cavity of his mouth. This mailman is tall with a pointed face and prominent teeth, a look of oiled buckskin about him. In the streetlights his eyeballs and hair seem the same color yellow.

"Where have you been?" he says to Dracula.

Dracula shakes his head. He's still trailing vestiges of Lucinda in his mind. Was he expected to be somewhere? He only ever saw the mailman when he delivered the mail late in the day. Around this time. When he would leave to get Lucinda. But this wasn't the mailman he saw. "I—" he is too flummoxed to address the confusion. "Here?" he says. And the mailman looks at the shop.

"What—you work here? What is this place?"

Dracula doesn't know where to begin. "Health drinks. But—" He is going to say he doesn't work here. Then he is going to say he doesn't know the mailman.

"Wheatgrass." The mailman's cigarette bucks over his lip like a coin-fed bronco. "That stuff is fucking good."

"Uh," says Dracula.

"You've never had that? Wheatgrass?"

In the liberty he's given the mailman by not saying his bit soon enough, Dracula feels like he has somehow become roped into an old, devoted friendship. "What is wheatgrass?" he stammers obligingly.

The mailman plucks the cigarette down from his lips. "It's like grass that you grind up and drink the juice. You don't have it?" He's now scanning the shop's sign overhead. Dracula has never looked at it. "Yeah. You're not a health shop. This is some bullshit commercial fad outlet that stocks pesticides to the masses. And probably offers all those powder supplements in a bullshit way that perpetuates herbal ignorance in a world that is getting fucked over by criminal corporate medicine. We need real herbal education. Jesus man." It's as if Dracula is doing something criminal himself. "You actually work here. Here."

"I—I don't," says Dracula, trying to decide where to begin.

"I mean you've got practically an imperialist, racist logo up there dude. Fruits dancing the conga? What the fuck are you thinking?" The mailman doesn't wait for an answer. "I guess you can't always—I mean if you need the money, but still do some shit that matters, or at least doesn't hurt anybody, like deliver mail. A civilization always needs a mail service. Brutal historical antics aside. I mean—you gotta have mail. It's just simple. Anyways," says the mailman, and now he stands back as Richard comes to the door and pulls the heater inside, baring his teeth like a beaver. "What the fuck is your asshole neighbor up to all the time now?

I keep seeing him everywhere I go. It's like he's following me."

Dracula balks. What asshole neighbor? There's only one of those. But this is not his mailman. "I think he's out of town," he says, thinking of just now, when he went. The whole obscure plot is getting away from him.

"No he's not. The only time I don't see him is if I deliver in the afternoon. There's at least one place he always goes." The Russian? His companion snorts. "The theater."

Why is this funny? It makes Dracula nervous. It's just this—something that Lucinda is not telling him about the theater.

"I—don't know," says Dracula. Or did she just tell him and he didn't get it?

"Are you seriously here all the time? You're never home anymore."

It was about a prop.

"Oh shit," says the mailman, his eyes blasting wide, and he laughs. "Oh my fucking shit. Never mind, dude, never mind. I just—wait a second."

This is when Dracula assumes he has finally recognized his mistake. His coffin? Was that the prop? The mailman is pitching forward into the shadows that Dracula is standing in, peering up the brim of Dracula's hat like an animal sniffing out a burrow. "Is that Warren's?" he says. "I thought he got that—dude, whoever you are, you're wearing Warren's hat."

Dracula brings his hand up. This is Warren's hat? This is Warren's mailman? This is the end of Dracula's confusion but also the deepening of his disbelief, because what a coincidence, and also it seems incomprehensible that someone would actually mistake him for Warren, even in the dark. Richard is swiping a dry, milky smudge off the window. They gaze at him as the mailman sheepishly says his goodbyes. Now Richard has squeaked away, the sound loud through the glass. The next thing Dracula knows, clasping his brim, is that the mailman is dodging down the street.

Dracula looks inside. When he tries the door it's still unlocked. Far down the mausoleum stillness he hears a voice. "Hi."

"Hi," says Dracula. He doesn't know yet what he's doing.

"Just about to close." Richard lifts his hat and swipes at a few invisible wisps of hair. He must be working up a sweat.

In answer, Dracula shucks off his own hat. He's trying to get his bearings. So Lucinda was duping him. Has he been duping her? All this feels rehearsed, like they're cueing each other for their next lines. Richard looks at Dracula's hat. So it's Warren's.

"What can I—" his eyes skid politely up to the eyes of Dracula.

"Oh—" The hat is herringbone. With a big red spade on it. It reminds Dracula of a drop of beaded blood. It does seem like something Warren would wear. "No I'm not—" says Dracula. It seems like Richard wants him to order something.

Richard has now just cast a glance at the bag at Dracula's feet. It's the birds he hasn't yet discarded. Dracula looks down too. His own breath seems to break through him like static. "I'm Lucinda's boyfriend."

Richard oddly seems splatted with the tomato of Dracula's words. "Wait, I—" his hand flinches up to his jaw, as if to wipe them off.

Dracula didn't know if he'd been planning to say that, but now he has.

He pulls the cinch handle of the bag. Has he given himself away? "She quit," he says, as if Richard doesn't know.

"I uh—" Richard gives him an ugly squint, like he's trying to make him come into focus. "I don't—are you—is she out of that apartment?"

That seems completely askew of any conversation they might be about to have.

"Apartment?" Dracula crimps his brows and hairline down. He flips the hat on the counter, and it skids across and the man tucks up his knee and flinches, like he's dodging a Frisbee. "Whoops," says Dracula. Why is he looking at him like that? Dracula's gaze is beginning to feel a bit seared by all the reflective surfaces he's used to seeing from the outside of the shop. Richard stands a little punctured at the register, hands gripping its sides, his face now slack with uncertainty. It still looks like Richard thinks he's going to make an order. Dracula looks at the menu board. "I'm not going to—" He sees something. "Vampire Juice?"

Richard chucks up his chin. "Oh yeah." He gives a stiff, uneasy grin. "I can do that with ginger or not if you want."

That doesn't—"What?" he says. That doesn't make sense.

Richard pushes up his glasses, his jaw sinking into his neck. He keeps looking between Dracula and the menu board. "So she's done with that other guy then."

Other guy? "She's—" What guy? "I'm—" he was going to say the guy.

Richard pulls on his nose. "I actually just sent her paycheck there."

Dracula wants to say, nodding, that he got that, but Richard seems to regret having done it from the tone of his voice. "I can just cancel it and she can give me wherever she's living now." He seems to peter out at Dracula's puckered face. It's like he's not computing. Or Dracula's not.

"With me. She's living with me." Still, he wants to say.

"Oh, with you?" Richard lifts his hat in bald surprise. "Well, I guess she was trying to move." He rubs his face, all the un-shaven folds blackening. "Glad she got out of that. I was help-ing her with money and then—" Now he stops himself, wiping sweat onto his jeans, and looks off behind him. That seems to be mostly where Dracula's gaze has gone.

"Not a nice guy, if you know what I mean."

Dracula doesn't even know what to ask. He was giving her money? Is there someone else? But isn't it him? He thinks of that empty pickup truck.

"Where did you—did she—did she tell you?"

"Eh, last month. Her coworker—Vanessa, said she was trying to get out of there. Said the guy was an idiot and acted like Dracula."

Dracula's stomach glugs like a drain. Now he is the guy.

"Yeah. Some big—" Richard holds his hat in the air. Dracula squeezes his own hat. Warren's. Does that mean he's not the guy? "I don't know him," says Richard. "I met him when he dated my daughter."

Now Dracula's words are jammed in his throat. Where had all these entanglements come from? He knows he never dated Richard's daughter. Richard has gotten a wrong idea. There has to be some reason why he thinks Lucinda is dating somebody other than Dracula. And who acts like Dracula.

Dracula swallows. He seems to be unable to say anything more. He is still grinding his thoughts over this intractable other guy. He can't be. But of course, he has to be. "I don't know." He sees Richard's hitch of lip.

They both look at the menu board.

"Vampire juice?" asks Richard.

Dracula squirms his mouth. Is his relationship crumbling out from under him right now? He keels his head back in grim suspicion. "Ah," he says. He seems to be nodding a dank foreboding.

Now Richard's plugging in the order. Had Dracula just said yes? Dracula has to pay him $3.75.

While Richard makes the drink, Dracula grips the cinch handle. Up and down. Tense and release. She had just said it tonight. *I can't do this.* What was she supposed to be *getting out of*? Even though he asks it he knows it's obvious. It should be. He's Dracula. That's the problem. That will always be the

problem, whether or not she's also doing something unseemly on the side. Or was. Is she now? Dracula can't stand
the stab of his own thoughts. He lets the handle go as Richard
hands him the drink. The bag slumps at Dracula's feet, sad
and soft. Dracula thinks of what he could do, turn it upside
down and let all the birds flop out, in a dusty landslide of
warmed plumage. What good would it do?

"Hey, don't forget this."

Richard is holding the hat. Dracula stares, looking daggers
unaware.

"Tell Lucinda I said hi."

Nodding, Dracula grips his own fist as he swishes out the
door. The drink in the other sloshes under its plastic lid.

Some oncoming pedestrian skims up from his other side.
"Nice hat." For a moment, he thinks of the mailman, coming
back the other way, but it isn't. Dracula reaches for the hat.
He can't even tell if it's there. His head right now feels like a
chunk of freezer frost.

Is he speaking to the man? He seems to have already said
something. "It isn't my hat," he just said.

The Puppet

*L*ucinda senses a winking atmosphere at rehearsal today. Marty is dancing the puppet around the coffin. "You are what you eat," says Marty's puppet, in the voice of a pop celebrity. Lauren is actually winking. Lucinda is realizing something. The puppet looks an awful lot like Dracula. And her teacher looks an awful lot like Lauren's mother.

Lauren seems any second about to laugh with Rory over something. Lucinda finds all this disconcerting, all things considered.

"Hey—remember the playbill I put up at your work?" Lauren flaps the new stack in her hand. "Somebody took it down."

"I don't work there anymore," Lucinda says.

Lauren tilts a look at her—playful, like a puppy. "What are you so afraid of?"

Lucinda's heart opens like a mouth. It's as if the question has never been asked of her before. It's as if the question consumes her as it forms her. It's as if the question is all there is.

"It's okay. I'm here," says Lauren, mocking her with a patting hand. Lucinda sometimes thinks that Lauren knows all there is to know and has already foreseen Lucinda's improbable truth—whatever that is. Lucinda hopes this is not in her head. She doesn't know if it's good or bad. Either way, there is some magic talisman that she clasps whenever she's with Lauren.

"Sorry," she says, not knowing what she's sorry for. Suddenly Lucinda wonders what Lauren thinks of her, what she believes about her and what she doesn't. *You are what you eat*—were they all just making fun of her?

Last night on the way home, Lauren made a point of bringing it up. "I noticed you didn't eat any food at dinner."

"Oh," said Lucinda, taken momentarily off guard. Lauren leaned pertly into the steering wheel—the one Lucinda usually saw Rory steering. Lucinda brushed at the suggestion. "I never really eat." Was that okay to admit? As she said it she realized that she didn't, at all. She hadn't eaten anything in quite a long time. Those sunflower seeds the other day were just for show, to see if Vlad would notice the bag after she found it in the coffin. *You are what you eat.* As she looked at Lauren she felt her blood run colder.

"You know what you need?" Lauren was looking back at the road.

"What?" said Lucinda.

"A sheath."

"A sheath?"

"You're always shivering like that."

Lucinda was already wearing a parka. And how did Lauren even see her shivering?

"I'm surprised Marty hasn't said anything. It's not very angelic."

"Oh," said Lucinda. "You mean—for my costume?" Marty liked the air to be *cold as a brisk beach wind* in the theater, and she was always shivering through rehearsal.

That's when Lauren gasped out a big smile. "I just thought of something." Her eyes frolicked over Lucinda's face.

"What?"

Lauren leaned forward. "It's nine fifty. Can I take you? They're still open."

Lucinda felt a familiar slamming of dread. "Where?"

"It's this shop. It would be so perfect for your costume."

"You mean—like something to wear?" She felt a moment's relief realizing it was an item of wardrobe. Still, she was inclined to conjure a refusal. "Is it expensive?"

"Oh, don't worry about that," said Lauren. She winked. "I do this thing."

Lucinda watched her put on the turn signal.

"You'll see. Or maybe you won't," Lauren said, as if to answer a question Lucinda hadn't asked. And that was how they ended up in Lucinda's mother's shop.

As ever it had been, the pawn shop was in piss-poor condition. Lucinda's mother presided over it like a cave of plundered loot, keeping sporadic hours and discouraging all but the most desperate specimens from bringing in their wares. It all looked the same—dodgy and picked over and random as a pimply face. Lucinda remembered when she was a child, having to go with her back and forth between the pawn shop and the bank and listening to those infinitely cryptic exchanges about money transfer and debt and accrual. Standing insensate under the hot and cold ozone of voices she would stare down at the waxed linoleum and will herself to pass into that skin of light where some other lost, insoluble version of herself welcomed her forever away from the adult world.

"Well well well," her mother said.

Now Lucinda wasn't even allowed in the shop.

"Here you are," her mother said.

Lucinda crinkled her lip, as if at a bad smell. She couldn't help herself. Not only was she unabashedly disgraced to be standing in the caged yellow light that had lately been a welcome forbiddance, but she was rankled by Lauren's arms and elbows further jostling her from behind. "No," she said, "I'm not—" Lucinda turned, trying to deflect both forces at once and ending up even more before her mother. She realized she was still angry. And inexplicably guilty. "I didn't know Lauren was bringing me here."

She turned for Lauren and saw nothing but the playbill on a corkboard. Lauren had disappeared from sight.

"Oh my God," said Lucinda.

Her mother put up her hands in a pantomime of confusion. "Who?" she said, "What?", and her look stayed deliberately on Lucinda. She continued to smile. "How's that boyfriend of yours?"

Lucinda crossed her arms, shivering. "Fine," she said.

"Is he getting his exercise these days?"

Lucinda knew when she was being needled.

"You should get a birdfeeder," her mother said. Then her mother thought this was very funny. "So, what are you eating these days?"

Lucinda could feel the playbill behind her. She could feel its poster-weight heft curling out, its whiteness consuming all the space on the corkboard. "Nothing," she said.

"Well, why not, don't you want to live?" It was such a direct question that Lucinda took it like a punch. "Who's telling you not to eat?" said her mother.

Lucinda shrugged. She didn't think her mother really believed she wasn't eating. She thought of the Russian, telling her over and over to eat, as if he was looking at her through a series of spy holes and just wanted to say it so she would know he saw everything. That was as good as telling her not to eat. She still doesn't know why her not eating should be killing him, as he so cloyingly puts it.

"Well—as long as you're around," her mother said into Lucinda's silence, and it seemed like she was insinuating more than that with her phrasing. A little man with a cowl of dark hair was coming down the long counter with a box in his hand. "Meet Bruno. My new assistant."

Bruno gave her a tight nod. "Howdy ho."

Lucinda looked back over her shoulder. "Hi." She felt like she was forgetting her manners. Was Lauren still here?

"He's coming to dinner Sunday."

"Yepsiree." His little pipe-cleaner mustache on his serious face seemed like a joke. His brown suit was farcically big. Lucinda was losing her bearings. Was that actually a girl?

"I have to go." She was sure that Lauren had just left her in here. When she turned, the playbill lifted a coy corner.

"So soon?" her mother said, but her tone had the familiar flint of eviction in it. "Why don't you invite your friend to dinner?" she called after her. "The one with the granny sack and those sticky fingers?"

Uh oh. Lucinda plucked the playbill down.

"That's pawn shop property now."

Outside Lucinda was barely relieved. The idea of these two variations of herself, somehow alighting in mixed company, seemed swiftly obliterating. She'd be the bug at the lip of a flytrap. Her mother had an actual flytrap. It was one of those gruesome plants Lucinda liked to pluck the petals off of.

Now Lucinda had pulled the playbill down twice—once at work and once here. It was satiny and fibrous, much like one of those predatory pods dangling over the clay pot—and then not.

The keys and bill were now bunched in her pocket.

She found Lauren waiting in the truck, her smile a big wet slice of triumph. Lucinda still didn't know what joke had just blindsided her, or whether it was at her expense. Lauren tossed her ragamuffin sack in Lucinda's lap and pulled into traffic. "Ha," she said. Lucinda had forgotten what they had come in there for. Now looking at the ragamuffin sack she tried to still the spokes of spinning confusion. "Look inside," said Lauren.

Lucinda groped at the bag's opening. "You took something?"

"That's my thing," Lauren said. "There's these two shops I love. Nobody ever notices me."

"That was my mother's shop." Lucinda wondered whether she felt disgraced or somehow vindicated by this—Lauren stealing from her mother.

"Oh my gosh," said Lauren, her eyes turning to black swarms in the streetlight. She was openly aghast and laughing. Was she actually? "I'm sorry. That's so—the one you hate?"

"I don't"—Lucinda let a look of distaste bloom on her face and hoped it seemed more offended than that—"actually hate her."

"Oh, I'm sorry—I didn't mean—"

Lucinda brushed her off. She still wasn't sure how convinced she was by Lauren's performance. It somehow had her mother's wiles written all over it. She opened the sack and pulled something out—a shawl—and watched it beam back the light of the street. "She invited you to dinner Sunday," she said, her heart tolling. The shawl was slithery and warm. Or else the whirring pulse of her suspicions had heated her through. It was such a perfect seesaw of intrusion and dispensation, the conniving weave of her mother's chaos. The air was now so temperate Lucinda couldn't feel it. "I have a feeling you should come."

"If I can," Lauren said. Her voice seemed to be dimming. "There's going to be a lot of cleanup after the play and I signed up."

Lucinda's eyelids began to droop. "Signed up?"

"Marty passed around a sheet before you got there."

She should take the shawl off. Her mother often had this effect on her. Or maybe it was the shawl. She should take the shawl off.

She couldn't help thinking of her mother. The day she came barging in with Lucinda's mail.

"Okay missy," she said. "Sit."

That was when Lucinda sat.

Lucinda always cooperated when her mother told her to sit. Her mother told her to sit and then she tied Lucinda up. Lucinda has been tied up two or maybe three times. It was for her own good, her mother has said.

She went looking through the apartment. Lucinda was pretty sure she knew for what.

After a minute her mother scuffed across the hall. "That girl went missing," she said, pointing to the mail she had plopped in Lucinda's lap. There was a name there, *Amory Sinclair or Current Resident*. "I knew I recognized that name."

Lucinda stared at it. Recognized that name? Did she mean from Lucinda's mail or somewhere else? She went missing? Did she mean from here?

"You should be careful," her mother said.

What did that mean? Then her mother was in the bedroom for a while, riffling books.

Lucinda couldn't help thinking of Richard's daughter. She didn't like that he had said just the same thing to her the day before. *She's really missing.*

"Aha." The startled spray of feathers had followed her mother's invading footsteps. She had come to the bathroom. "You should keep this door closed."

Lucinda rolled her eyes.

"It's not healthy. Birds have germs."

"I know."

Her mother came out and looked at her. "I'm so mad at you," she said. She sniffed. Either it was the birds or something else. "You can just untie yourself," she finally said. "That dumb boy-friend will do it. Or I'll let the neighbor in to help you."

"No," said Lucinda.

"He likes to hear himself talk, doesn't he? Do you know him?" Her mother had gone to the window and was aiming a grimace out through the crack in the curtains now.

"I don't like him."

Her mother of course heard her. But she pretended not to.

"Lucinda?"

That was the last thing Lucinda heard in the car. The next thing she knew she was waking up in her own bed, a smell of burned rug around her. Lucinda slammed back the covers. What had just happened? The sound was atrocious, like a fish hitting linoleum. She'd heard that sound many times in her mother's kitchen. Oh God. She stared across the room, her eyes landing right where Vlad, supposedly behind that closet door, was sitting like a corpse waiting to fall out on her. This was life.

Now she went creeping from the bed on crackling feet, every bone popping. She was still wearing her flimsy costume. When she got to the hall door she was so severely swabbed by fear she went out like that, at a terrible slovenly slouch, frisking lights and slipsliding through an undisturbed apartment, looking for anything amiss or awry. How had she gotten here? It looked like dawn was gloaming through the curtains, cloudy and sepulchral. Lucinda went into the bathroom and found a half dozen stiff garments hanging on the fixtures and smelling of turpentine. She thought strickenly of the shawl. None of them was the shawl. A note on the mirror said, *My bad. I'll fix.* She didn't like it, but it was his handwriting. Fix what?

In a slice of uncanny quiet, Lucinda opened the apartment door. Outside, she tried simply to breathe, hoping no one would see her.

Of course, two surveillance cameras saw her plenty, giving dusty blinks from under the eaves. There were two others on her side of the courtyard, looking out just as she was. And, she knew, one vultured over the basement door on the ground floor, and one stared dumbly at the dumpster like a mute raccoon. Why so many? What was there to see? Nobody would have an inch to steal anything around here, she thought.

Then she thought of her mother. Then the Russian had walked by. Then he was whistling.

He made a big production in front of Lucinda of unlocking his door. She went back inside.

The clock in front of her said three P.M. So that cloudy light outside was not dawn, she thought. She had slept through morning and much of the day.

When it was time to go to rehearsal she put a note on the lampshade for Vlad and then went down to the parking lot to wait for Rory. The note told Vlad to take his shower right after he woke up, the excuse being that his four A.M. showers always woke her. Vlad's four A.M. showers never woke her, and they both knew it. It was getting just that finite, her feints and calculations, the inane sliver of window she had for this deception. Lucinda was so sick of deception. She'd be so glad when the play was over.

She stood slumped in the parking lot, shivering, like a girl who had to stand at the bus stop before dawn, hating the slow, leeching world. She didn't even know if Rory was coming—considering the way things ended at his house. Then, he did, and she started to feel the scrim on that pane of misgiving vanish, like a fist rubbing out a breath of steam, the distance between her and the world smudging away, everything coloring slightly in the rosy flush of his cheeks as he puffed her a smile to tilt the coffin quietly, because they were doing it with only a rush and tumble of water between them and Dracula.

"I'm that burly guy in a heist," Rory muttered to her. He seemed oafishly sneaky and gleeful tonight. "He never notices it's gone?" His lip curled in a babyish way.

"No," said Lucinda, looking away. "He keeps the closet closed." Though she herself liked to open it.

Outside Rory clipped the coffin around corners and strutted it down the steps. They went out to the truck. "You left this in here." He held up a handful of cloth when she hoisted herself into the cab. "Lauren said it was yours."

"Oh, sorry," said Lucinda, putting it on her lap, feeling a raw buzz in all her bones.

"Act two rehearsals," said Rory.

"Here we come," she said.

"We're almost there, people," said Marty by way of greeting them. Then Lauren was arriving, just as it was starting.

Now, while Marty performs his salutary antics with the puppet, Lauren answers Lucinda's query: "I *did* carry you," she whispers from behind her hand. "You were literally weightless."

Lucinda gawks at her. "*You are what you eat*," says Marty's puppet. Can she believe that?

Lauren cracks a wider smile. "Just kidding. Rory helped," she says. "I called him."

"Oh." Lucinda doesn't like that. It makes Rory's giddiness tonight seem dodgy at best. Sitting a few people over in the circle, he has a dazed look of mirth on his face, like he wants to laugh at some joke he keeps retelling in his mind. "Were you there?" she implores. "What happened?"

Lauren leans in. "Your boyfriend came home."

"What?" Lucinda says, too loudly. A few eyes dart her way. "*Excuse me*," says Marty, but still in the voice of the puppet. "*Aren't I the only one here? I thought I was the only one here.*"

Lucinda can't tell if it's aimed at her or not. She gives Lauren a prodding look.

"Rory had to park in the manager's spot, so he brought you in and then went down again." Lauren speaks behind her hand.

"With my key?" Lucinda interrupts.

"Then I was getting your shoes off and he came home."

"What time was this?" Lucinda says. What was he doing at home?

"I don't know. Like maybe eleven?"

Lucinda can feel her heart sagging with each new detail. He was supposed to be at work last night. So he has been lying.

"He was doing laundry. He went into the bathroom and I snuck out." Lauren cringes. "I'm sorry. I didn't know what to do. You seemed fine or else I would have called an ambulance. Should I have told him?"

Lucinda can't imagine either of those things being preferable, even though they would probably have been more appropriate.

"You know, I just didn't know, if he's Dracula—I didn't want him to attack me or anything."

Lucinda tries to notice her own expression. She tries to put on a look of sober appreciation. "No, that's okay," she says. She's barely remembering her manners. "Thanks for your help. I don't know what happened to me."

"It's because you're not eating." Lauren doesn't seem to say this with concern so much as authority, like it's a textbook fact she just knows.

Lucinda nods. She can't decide if Lauren's attitude toward her eating is presumptuous or invasive or just oddly blasé. Neither can she tell if Lauren is serious or only humoring her about the Dracula thing. There's an elephant in the room but Lucinda can't decide what it is. Lauren either knows something she won't say or doesn't know something she won't ask. Same with Rory, meeting her eye right now, as if she's in on his chuckling thoughts. Who are these two? How friendly are they? And by what design? Lucinda never asks this question soon enough.

"Hey," Lauren asks, eyeing her. "Did you bring the shawl in from the car? You're chattering."

"Oops," says Lucinda.

They pause to watch the puppet tumble into the *pit of immolation and self-regard*.

Tonight, and every night, the puppet is dancing its antics along the edge of their coffin. Her coffin, but it's theirs too. It's not only just Dracula's anymore. Lucinda can't tell if this makes her sorry or afraid.

"What are you doing after the opening show on Friday?" Lauren asks.

Lucinda scissors out a sigh. She is barely able to turn her thoughts over to this. "I have to go to my brother's." Warren is having his party on Friday. It's the last thing she feels like doing.

"I didn't know you had a brother." Lauren makes a sympathetic face. "Too bad. I was going to ask you to come to a party with me."

Lucinda opens her mouth, finds herself raked clean of words, and shuts it with a thin smile. Lauren winks. It must just be a coincidence.

For some reason, looking at the coffin, she feels like everyone is looking at her.

The Play

Dracula is walking to the pharmacy. He needs Tylenol, for his headache. He's heard that's what you take.

Lucinda is walking up ahead, because she can't deal with him right now. Apparently.

They'd been having a fine enough dinner. At least somebody had been having dinner.

"How did we get here?" he asked at the restaurant. Somehow he felt like one of them was an invention of somebody else's mind.

Lucinda cranked her upper lip. It was more of a quiver. "You came to the door and said you were hungry. You asked me," she said.

Was it all over? "Ha. Like when we were dating."

"Where are your keys by the way? Were you locked out?"

Dracula had seen the truck again, pulling out when he was coming in. When he got upstairs, for some reason he knocked.

Now he looks at her. She doesn't look exactly happy. But she doesn't look like she's in the midst of betraying him.

"Have you ever looked into my coffin?"

"No, of course not. It creeps me out."

Dracula remembers the first time she saw it in the closet. How Vlad went sniffing around it. How she kept pulling at his leash, embarrassed. "Vlad," she said, "Vlad," with uneasy admonishment. He didn't like how it sounded.

Dracula thinks of how it was at first, when they were dating. It would always have to be something outside, with all three of them. The dog would be always with her. Waiting on the steps whenever he came, both of them like two trammeled daisies. The dog would wheeze as they climbed the path to the light rail. They would crumble biscuits into water while the trains whistled by. Lucinda had her newspaper out. *We could do Kites at Night. Mead making. Laser light show.* That's what Dracula remembers. None of those options sounded appealing to him. Lucinda didn't like to leave the dog tied up outside, so they would sit on the train one way, only to find out they couldn't bring the dog with them and go the other way, only to get somewhere else right as it was over. Dracula got so he could hear the dog, all the time. Taking wet open breaths at his side. He never looked down. He could almost hear it right now.

"Are you okay?" Lucinda follows his gaze while he looks around.

He's eating a pork belly BLT. A man in a kimono serves them.

Dracula lets his tongue out like a tide. He stares off into the distance.

"The play is tomorrow," Lucinda says. "You don't have to come. I mean, I don't expect you to come."

Dracula feels his stomach lurch, and then somehow senses a repeated refrain. Is this something she's said before?

"I—why—" he clears his throat.

"It's not like—" Lucinda cuts herself off.

Why is there a geyser of hot lava stinging the inside of Dracula? Does this actually terrify him? He hasn't been able to say so to her. It seems like such a brash and sacrificial entrapment. Anything could go wrong in a play. The actors and the audience all stuck there like so many flies. What if somebody bombs? Dracula at least wants his art to be over and done with before he observes it. "No, that's silly," he says, clinging to the table's edge. "Of course I'm coming. I'll come."

"I don't want you to come."

Dracula rolls a raw sample of air across his palate. Is this a test? Is it because of what happened?

"But, what if I want to?" He stumbles over the right thrust of insistence. Relief, he notices, is flooding through him.

"No," she says.

How long should he keep up the protest?

"Are you done?" she says. He's not sure if she means with the meal or the act.

That's when Dracula senses the waiter's hand, floating surreptitiously into view. The man seems to query Dracula with a smile. Dracula looks down at his plate. He is not sure if he is done. He feels like he hasn't even begun. The waiter defers with a murmur.

"I think we should stop seeing each other," Lucinda says. Dracula is not entirely sure that he isn't dreaming this.

"I think I need something." He reaches down somewhere. He unfolds his napkin.

"I'm going home," Lucinda says, standing. A dog barks. It's warm for a winter night but still the patio is chilly.

"Wait," says Dracula. He is now aware of a squinting sensation in his heart. "Is there anything you should tell me?" he asks.

Lucinda subsides into a look of grim scrutiny.

"Are you dating someone else? Did you?"

"What?"

"You want to leave the apartment," Dracula says.

Lucinda screws her brow. "We are leaving the apartment. Next Monday. We've been evicted." There's a billow of silence between them, like a sheet hovering in air. "And I didn't do it," she says, as if maybe that's what he's still trying to talk about. "The damage I mean."

"No," says Dracula. He can't figure out what he really wants to say to her. His words feel ruffled up inside him like cloth.

"What's your play about anyway?" He's thinking about the coffin.

"I don't know," she says. "It's hard to explain."

"I think I need a bathroom," Dracula says. "I'm going to throw up."

When he comes out of the bathroom, Lucinda is unsurprisingly no longer there. "Did you see her?" he asks the waiter.

The waiter looks around.

"Maybe she went to the bathroom. Is there more than one?"

"More than one bathroom? Yes," he says, and he nods with his chin where Dracula just came from.

Dracula lowers himself into the chair. For some reason he can barely recall his own recent digression in the bathroom.

"I couldn't help overhearing," the waiter says, in an undertone. "You were talking about The Play. Are you involved?"

"Oh." Dracula tries to pry open his throat. "My girlfriend is. She's in a play." With his coffin.

The waiter's head faintly tilts. The gas heater hisses behind them. "So," the waiter hesitates, "you mean... it's called... ?"

"It's called," Dracula studies the waffle weave of the table. "Something, I can't remember."

"*The Play*?"

"Yes, the play." Dracula's getting a little turned around by the reverb.

"Is it now?" The man holds his neck stiffly. "I hear it's very experimental."

"Now?" says Dracula, wanting to check a watch he doesn't have. "No."

"The Play? It isn't tonight?"

"Her play," says Dracula, squinting. His head is starting to throb. "It's tomorrow."

"Her Play?" The man looks perplexed.

"Wait. Are you saying that's what the play is called?"

The man shakes his head. Whether he's confused now or withholding, Dracula can't tell.

"It's not called *Her Play*," Dracula says, for extra clarification. "Or *The Play*. It's something else."

"Something Else?"

It seems like Lucinda has been gone for a while. Dracula drums his fingers on the metal, then he gets up to give the waiter room and wanders out the back patio gate and leans under a tree. She did say tomorrow. He looks up at the rectangle at the back of the restaurant where he's imagined she has vanished. It seems like a long time has already passed. It seems like Lucinda is not coming back through that corridor of mist.

"I'm exhausted," Lucinda says. She is right by his side.

"Did you just break up with me?" he asks.

"When? I was paying the bill."

"When you said that about not seeing each other."

"What?" she says. She is looking at the receipt.

What was her reason for them to stop seeing each other? Did she really mean that? Those are the questions he should ask now. "I need some pills," he says. She nods. "I have a headache." They are way beyond not seeing each other. It seems that phrasing would have belonged better to those nights on the train. *I think we should stop seeing each other*. No more round-trip rides to nowhere.

Lucinda starts walking. "I'm going home," she says.

As Dracula walks, he thinks he can hear other people's murmurs perforating the night nearby, and his nausea, like bubbles popping in rank puddles, festers and subsides. Lucinda has outpaced him. That's how it mostly seems to him. The pharmacy is on the other side of the street, and Dracula detours in that direction. He looks absently for any sign of her.

He has barely stepped up onto the curb when a single yelp of a car horn warns him. "Oops," he says. He waves, veering into the parking lot.

Another bleat and a sudden light revolves in the dash of the car. It's a cop, pulling him over.

"What?" says Dracula, looking at the unmarked car.

The cop leans closer to the side window. "Okay. Yep," he says.

Dracula looks down at himself.

"Come on. Let's go," says the cop, getting out.

"Go where? For what?" Dracula wants to be sure he isn't misunderstanding. When he sees the divot in the chin, his eyes roll to heaven. "I should have known," he says.

"Jaywalking," says his neighbor.

"Excuse me? I was just looking for my girlfriend."

"Your girlfriend was the woman who ran up to my patrol car just now?"

Dracula looks around, disoriented. He is especially disoriented now.

"What happened to your shirt?"

Dracula looks down at his shirt. "I threw up," he says, holding the bundle out. "It was making me cold."

The man is squinting at his shirt. Then he looks down pointedly at his pad. "Are you intoxicated?"

"Am I intoxicated?"

The man has been standing by the driver's-side door and now he steps pertly up on the curb. He seems about to pluck at Dracula like loose trash.

"What happened?"

"I'm just going to the drugstore," Dracula says wearily, watching the officer work his pen over the pad.

"That doesn't answer my question." The officer stabs a look up.

"I hit my head." Dracula holds his head. It's still pounding. Did he really?

The officer isn't looking again. "We've found more of your bird genocide around town."

"I didn't do that. I told you."

His neighbor sneers. "Of course you didn't."

For some reason, Dracula feels a stab of wrath at this.

"You know, I could have arrested you with probable cause that day, but I let you off," says the officer. After a moment he rips a paper and flutters it at him. "I'm assuming it was just an innocent mistake."

Dracula takes the citation, utterly flummoxed. What was an innocent mistake?

"I just did you a second favor. Now," says the officer. He seems to be savoring this pause, in a showy way that Dracula is supposed to tolerate. "Under the circumstances I have to give you a ride home." He taps his head with grim censure.

"What? But—" Dracula squints, swiveling his head to take in the drugstore. "I need—"

"You need what?"

"I'm—my—"

The officer puffs a dissatisfied breath. "Your girlfriend isn't here. Come on. Let's go." He flicks his fingers as if he can't stand the chitchat.

It's just as well. On the way home Dracula shuts his eyes. He doesn't know how the night slid away from him like this. It occurs to him that he's not used to being a passenger in a car. The cold upholstery smell and the rocking motions are forcing his breath into queasy spurts. He remembers the last time he was in one of these cars was with Warren. It was someone else's car and Warren was borrowing it. Wasn't that tonight? They were on their way to dig up the dog.

"It's not my fault," he says. He remembers jarringly that he's in a cop car.

"What'd you do?" says the officer.

"Nothing." Dracula cuts the confession short.

The officer breathes an idle whistle, like one you might give in response to an unwanted overture. After a while, Dracula remembers something. "Did you ever get a visit from that Kent Wallaby? Knife salesman?"

"Listen," says the cop. "Right now I am not your neighbor. I never have been and never will be your friend."

Dracula feels a little like laughing at this. It's more of a bothersome feeling than a bracing one. "Okay," he says, going for flip. "Fine by me."

For a while, they don't speak. Dracula notices it slowly creeping up on him, the sound, like a slight break in atmosphere. Is it crying? Just like that time he was waking up. When Lucinda was outside his door. But Lucinda isn't here. Perhaps she never was. Dracula has no idea how many nights he's spent with some facsimile of what he thought was her, what he thought was real. He looks out the window, headlights smearing past in slow motion. Coronas of buzzing neon and brash spotlights in a sudden stretch of construction.

There's a big hole in the ground that he knows wasn't there two days ago. He wonders, when he gets home, if he'll be there before Lucinda.

The Note

Sometimes somebody is there that you don't see. Vlad told her that. Just as much, and at the same time, sometimes somebody you see is not there.

As a child, Lucinda had a lot of nightmares. The one she remembers most was about a man putting on brick-red lipstick in a bathroom mirror and then smiling at his reflection. It was a devious smile. It was imprinted on her from a scene in a television show she saw passing through her living room one night. In the show, the man left the bathroom and walked with sinister bearing across a crowded lobby, took an elevator down three floors, stepped off into a dim corridor, lifted aside a grate in the ceiling and climbed up into the ductwork and disappeared. That's all she remembers.

She wonders occasionally now what he was doing. She doesn't want to pursue it. It would have been better had she not seen the inexplicable sequence. In the same way, she thinks it would be better to avoid seeing this new infringement—this one upon her established reality. The security footage. Anything that might instill the depravities of daily life into her unsteady equilibrium is best avoided. She knows she has a right to see the security footage, she knows the apartment manager is legally obligated to avail her of it, but she doesn't want to test his willingness. She knows she didn't do the damage. She's allowed to carry things up and down the stairs. But it doesn't matter. Either way it will feel like seeing a shudder of her own wickedness, a glitch in her own personal being, playing out before her. It's always been this way. When people do inexplicable things she feels inexplicably involved, sliding in on them from some enigmatic lie that gets uttered just beyond her. What's to say she isn't doing more damage than she thinks? The only thing she can do is not watch. And not watch is what she will do. When she was a child, she didn't know she had that control. She probably did watch the rest of the show. She knows she did. But it's impossible to remember now.

Lucinda thinks of this as she stands outside her apartment door. The cameras take their slow underwater gulps. She imagines how she must look, undisturbed, private as a koi pond, with a light gray mist hanging above her. That's not how she feels. They're just on their way out and a shout has stopped them. Lucinda is stuck on profound pause, seized and struck dumb by the manager's voice.

In the corner of her eye, the coffin still seesaws on Rory's shoulder.

"Excuse me!" he says again.

They both turn.

"I'm going to have to take that."

Lucinda glances back. What? When she looks again, the apartment manager's lip is curled in a feisty snag.

"Who are you?" says Rory, bloating.

"I manage these apartments." The manager's nimbus of hair has grown to a fertile fungus. He has sprouted a short goatee.

"I hardly recognized you," Lucinda says, almost as if this can stop him.

"Yeah," he says vaguely, pointing. "I need that."

She opens her mouth. She looks back. She feels her breath blow out in flimsy tatters.

"You can't have *this*," Rory is already saying. "This is hers. His. Her boyfriend's—"

The apartment manager is shaking his head. "She's damaging apartment property."

"What?" says Lucinda.

"I can't have you taking that up and down like that." The manager peels his eyes at her. Then at Rory.

"What?" she tries again. Lucinda is clutching her throat. It doesn't make any sense. He can't do this now.

"It's going into storage until Monday. You can check it out with me through the business office. We have a rule here about hauling equipment up and down the steps." The manager plucks a paper from somewhere behind his ear—or in his hair. Suddenly he's handing it to her.

"Are you kidding?" Rory says. "What equipment? It's not equipment."

"It's in the lease."

Her fingers fumble to unfold the paper, and when they do she sees heavy black lead scrawled over its yellow surface. It's a repair estimate, filled out by a business called Icon Ironworks, for two thousand dollars.

"That wrought iron is fucked," the apartment manager's arm flings out. "It all has to be redone. Also, noise matters."

Beside her, Rory has begun to blow out battle-axes of breath, just like her father used to do, his raised elbow as he steadies the coffin brandished like a battering ram. "No way," he says. "You can't prove we damaged property."

"I can," says the manager. He doesn't elaborate.

Lucinda, raising her eyes, sensing her great, everlasting futility, cannot seem to stir herself into the debate. It's all over. Her heart swishes on some great pendulum, blowing vast distances in her chest. She can't get her voice. It's all her fault.

"Oh come on," Rory says, like it's all a mad, elaborate scam.

The manager tilts himself back. There's a pause, a gritty shoe-scuffing silence, during which he seems to be ready for something to happen, and that is when Lucinda sees his dolly parked down the breezeway at the top of the stairs.

"We won't move it from the apartment." She barely murmurs, wanting nothing more than to put it back.

The manager shakes his head. "Too late. You already cost me money."

Lucinda looks at Rory. Rory's face is a red, swarming gas, very small and dense. He is having trouble keeping the coffin steady. He looks floridly at both of them.

"Time to move," says the manager.

Then Rory seems to step into a weightlifter's stance, to peer cruelly over the edge of the railing.

"Stop," says Lucinda, thinking the worst.

"I'll call the cops," says the apartment manager.

Rory scuffs a brute breath. "I'm not helping you," he says. He drops the coffin down.

They watch the manager sidle up and carefully put his shoulder into the dinged buttery wood. He hefts the wobbling coffin to his own shoulder and stands for a moment, calibrating, his face caged in a look of concentration. Then he teeters over to his dolly. As he eases it onto the carpeted ledge and bungees it, Lucinda feels the need to reach out for the wrought-iron railing. The manager bumps his way down the stairs, hair sagging like a soaked sponge. Lucinda wants to wretch.

Rory makes immediate haste to leave, and before Lucinda knows it he is lobbing out threats over the manager's head, riding the sails of a last spat promise to her as he blunders down the other staircase. Lucinda can hardly keep up with him. He's going home. He'll confer with Lauren. There's another one and he can use it. For a moment, watching him dash away, she feels lost. How will she get to the play? It's starting in under two hours. Fumbling with the cold metal foliage in her hand, she can see the ugly hump of the couch through a crack in her curtains. He'll be back.

Now, reopening the door, Lucinda's thoughts are guttering in and out. Just like that. It had passed before her with the incantations of a spell. Yet another craven nosedive into meekness. Each new circumstance seems to slap her more insensate than the last. Now what will she say to Dracula? Could another coffin even work? Lucinda wavers in the darkness. When she turns on the light is when she finds herself back once more in the wreckage of another ambush.

First her knife on the table, a shiny wet blot in the light of the lamp. How did it get there? All day, she's stayed away from it. Dracula was sealed in like a mummy, but then, abruptly, when she had come up from the parking lot with Rory he had not been taking his shower—he was simply gone. It both did and didn't surprise her, after their last exchange. What was here, in abundance, was the paper plumage he kept folding and leaving behind. Lucinda picks one of the pieces up. When she unfolds it, she realizes it's mail. The envelope is marked *FINAL PAYCHECK*, adamantly, as if to get somebody to open it. On the other side she finds her name, printed in wet black pen. There's no stamp.

Lucinda is all the way inside now. She wonders if Richard delivered this here himself, while she was out. She wonders if Dracula had been here to take it.

"I thought you'd be here."

That was what he'd said to her the last time she saw him, when he'd tried to give her an envelope just like this. It was at Vanessa's funeral.

She had been shocked to see him, and to be there at all. Her friend was somehow dead, and here she was standing in death's dim foyer. Richard was sniffing intimately at her, eyes red. She couldn't tell, looking at his face, what exactly he was feeling.

"What happened?" she said, not knowing what she meant. Then she regretted it. Richard was stuffed into his green shirt like an olive, his face a blue cheese oozing out the top. His coat was turned open at the zipper and his hand pulled at something that wanted to stay in the inside pocket. He got it out and jerked his head around before jabbing it at her. She had just barely gotten herself in the door.

"You're living with him," he said, but she wouldn't take the envelope. "The same thing happened to my daughter," he said. "You need to get out of there."

Lucinda found her mouth too stiff to move.

"Put it away." Richard pushed up his glasses, grimly expecting something. "I don't want him to see it."

Even as she felt her thoughts open to utter darkness, unable to croak out a question of any kind, a blot of shadow was softly beckoning for her, some peripheral swishing like leaves silent behind the window. She turned and saw that they were being summoned by a tall, spruced-up usher. Obligingly, they staggered into a room of milling people, lit by long, cloud-coated windows. Lucinda pushed the envelope back at Richard's maroon tie and heard it dropping through his hands as she teetered in. She didn't know why. He didn't follow her at first. There were chair arrangements, little pats and strokes of speech everywhere, people smiling their hooks of humble greeting. Someone touched her arm.

The lady smiled as if they'd already known each other.

Lucinda smiled back then, holding her sleeves down over her wrists. There was some jam-up in her throat.

"Are you a friend?" said the woman, nodding with a great big swish of perfume. She had a head of flaky brown hair.

"Yes," Lucinda managed to warble out.

The woman's smile was rather blank and flummoxed. "Good, I invited as many..." She nodded off into the room. "I'm sure you knew," the woman said, "Vanessa was..." She continued to nod and smile as if her head were trembling on a spring.

Lucinda nodded back.

Now the woman seemed to have gotten her head stuck at a somewhat savage tilt. "So, you're... ?"

Lucinda stared at the gazing face.

"What's your name?"

"Oh. Lucinda."

Richard was pacing the room's periphery and periodically aiming a snout into the air, as if to keep her scent in range. Then he looked at something.

"I'm—" said Lucinda. "I don't know what to do."

Or at someone.

"To do?" The woman crimped her mouth in confusion.

"I've never been to a funeral before." Lucinda tried to follow his gaze.

"Oh, well," the woman broke into a thistled look of sympathy. "They're all—you know," said the woman's plunging voice.

Lucinda nodded. The woman, as it turned out, was Vanessa's aunt. Lucinda had hung off her left side, like an unwanted umbrella, until it was time to go in for the service—getting put down here and there behind chair legs and on windowsills, the woman's look less and less tolerant of her own accessory miscalculation even as she resigned herself to carrying it around.

Inside, she didn't see anybody. There were heads and sniffs, and they had played that song, and Vanessa's voice had greased the aisles like a dirty diesel glow, all the right words, slathering all of them. It was almost unbearable, the density of that voice. In the reception hall, digital copies were available to all attendees. Lucinda had skidded past them and now she was heading for the door.

That was when Richard found her again.

"Here. Now don't," he said, grabbing her at the wrist, down at her side, by the reception room door. This was a different room. There were tables of food inside. "I want to talk to you about this." Lucinda had almost been feeling a quivery improvement in herself, like a bad stomach settling.

"Listen," Richard said.

It was that song. That song was just a terrible coincidence.

Lucinda yanked at her clamped hand and dodged into the foyer.

She hadn't been planning to go to rehearsal after the funeral. But sitting in the crusty quiet of her living room, imagining another bungled melodic interjection, she had turned on the TV, and the glib stream of images, that irksome buzz that only got louder the longer the TV was on, was even worse on her nerves. She decided to go to rehearsal. She arrived late and slipped in at the back during breathing exercises. It was so much better. Here was living flesh that looked just as pallid and immaterial under the lights, ready to be sloughed off. She was not sure why this soothed her.

Maybe Rory noticed her, sitting there in her peaked gloom. But suddenly he was tilting back and clutching his pectoral with a brawny hand. "Do you need a ride home?"

"Oh," said Lucinda. She looked at the hand. That was the first time Rory had taken her to the apartment. He brought her all the way up to the door and paused, as if unsure of something.

"Did you just move in?" he asked, doing a hollow sweep of the room.

"With my boyfriend," she said, doing a tin rendering of her voice.

Lucinda remembers standing shivering in her apartment with Rory looking around. Lucinda is still shivering in her apartment as she looks around now.

Lucinda is in the bedroom, yanking on double sets of leggings and cinching a bathrobe over her turtleneck sweater over her costume. The empty closet gapes at her like a gouged-out eye. She's still not warm. Lucinda hugs her arms.

Homelessly dressed and waiting, she goes twitching around the apartment like a bug with two broken antennae, unable to decide what to do or where to go. When will Rory come back? She needs to let Dracula know what happened to his coffin. She herself doesn't know what happened. She keeps repeating her lines for the play.

She thinks she might go open the front door, but instead, she finds herself tripping druggily the other way, to the bathroom. It seems so quiet here now. What had the Russian said to her, that other day?

Go home, little girl. Does your daddy miss you? Does your daddy know where you are? Who puts the key in, you or your daddy? It was through the wall as it always was.

Lucinda looks in the mirror. She sees the gray stretch of lips, the plum paste of her skin. *My bad. I'll fix.* The note is still there. She pulls it down. Then, twisting and gagging, she is suddenly swinging off her own string, tingling again and too stiffly astringent for feeling. It only lasts a minute. You need to get out of there. That's what Richard said. *Go home.* That's what the Russian said. Rory said, *Did you just move in?*

With my boyfriend. That was what Lucinda said.

Lucinda spits in the sink. She has a feeling she is right now looking at something she doesn't see. All she knows is she can't stay here. That's what Richard seemed to be saying. Under the running water is a sound like knocking. Is it pipes or him at the door? When she runs to it there's nobody there. It occurs to her then, staring out, that before she leaves for the play she should really write Dracula a note.

The Keys

*T*his is interesting. Dracula is turning into a dribble of mist. Pretty soon, if he continues at this rate, he'll have to be kept in a jar. He's sitting in the Russian's apartment. His fingers tendril out beyond him, his nose drifts up in front of his eyes. Will he soon do the movie rendition of himself—his signature blast of steam? What will be left of him when he's gone? It's not an unfunny thought. To think that all his many eons are just about to end right here, in a bummy slouch on a stranger's couch. He's not even showered. Maybe it's just the light in here. Maybe it's his imagination.

The Russian's apartment is much different from his. Everything in his own is rickety and collapsed, like the battered props of an overused set. The one dining room chair. The lumpy couch, a mealy patchwork brown. That lamp that looks like an empty bottle, the kind you toss off a ship with a note inside. The Russian's apartment has big, bovine chairs, burnished frames, leather tables stretched taut under ashtrays and magazines. There is an actual plant—some kind of spineless cactus. Dracula dabbles his forgotten fingers in the pot.

The girl at the bus depot had asked him to come here.

It turned out to be a good idea.

At the bus depot she had said to him, "You're some kind of spy." She had come up to him and said this.

Dracula was standing at the bulletin board, patting his pockets. He was looking for Lucinda's play like her play was a lost dog. Where was the play? Was it tonight? Wasn't it? There was not a flyer in sight. He knew he used to see them here.

All the information he needed was at home on the fridge. But he couldn't get in. Where were his keys? Dracula can't seem to think at all anymore. He feels like he's swirling in a slow, broken drain. His thoughts are caught in the clog. He can actually smell them.

The girl can too. She makes an egg face. "I know what you're doing here. You don't have to pretend." She has brown short hair, blown back in a swoop, and now she's noticing his shirt.

"I don't think—" Dracula is thinking of Lucinda. He looks at the bulletin board. He's not pretending anything. When he woke up tonight she was gone without her stuff. Then when he came back from the trash she didn't answer his knock. Was it his fault? Had she left already? *I think we should stop seeing each other.* He is beginning to take this literally.

"I've seen you," the girl says.

Well, who hasn't. Except of course himself. He peels his lips. "I'm not following."

The girl shakes her head, as if to reprimand that expression away. Dracula can hardly stand it. His head has been hammering all the way since yesterday. "I know you live right over there. You're following me. And he's following you."

"Right over where?" he scoffs, "Who's following me?" He knows at least that's true.

"Dracula," she says.

It's the closest corroboration he's gotten yet of who he is. And yet it's not.

"I'm Dracula," he says.

Now, it seems she was talking about the Russian.

It's funny. When the cop had walked Dracula to his door last night, he had peered pointedly at the next-door window, black as a boxed ocean. Dracula wondered if he'd heard something about the Russian's accessorized departure. There was gossip here like everywhere.

Now, he is in the Russian's apartment, looking through the glass darkly.

The rest of the conversation with that girl had been even worse.

She shook her head. "You can't leave me alone. You're not letting me get away."

"I don't know what you're talking about."

"Why were you there all those times?"

"I was where all those times? Maybe it was you who was there all those times," he countered recklessly into the void. The girl's cheeks looked swollen, rolled into biscuits right under her eyes.

"I mean you—"

"Maybe *you* were following me." Suddenly he wondered— is this who'd been following him? Or was it Dracula? Or the Russian. It was impossible to make any sense of it.

The girl looked at him. "I need to get into my old apartment," she said, cutting through the confusion. "I need something."

Dracula didn't understand. It was odd. That's exactly what he needed.

"Your apartment," she said.

"Wait a second," Dracula said.

She almost rolled her eyes. "I—no, I need to get in. Can you let me in?"

Seriously? She wanted to get into his apartment? After accusing him of following her and spying for somebody she wanted personal access now to his private domicile? Dracula skipped the incredulous questions of why and what and went straight for the cinch. "Actually," he said, patting his pants. "I don't have keys."

She scuffed a breath, like she didn't have time for him or his lame excuses.

Dracula put up his hands. "That's what I'm doing here. I'm locked out."

He had gone to take the trash to the bin. The shirt that he put on in the dark was the stale vomit one from the night before. He left it—he was about to take his shower anyway. Lucinda, when he came out, was nowhere to be seen. Her bag for going to the theater was packed and on the arm of the couch. He walked to the dumpsters and then on the way back he saw the truck. Idling.

Dracula looked up at his window. His ears were suddenly fuming. Were they up there? His hand fit right into the crevice of the cracked window, and he pulled the lock. That's when the door opened. That's when he got in and jerked into place and pushed the metal clutch and yanked the gearshift into reverse. It was like driving for UPS. He gave the gas a nasty stomp. The engine roared and he jolted forward. He gritted his teeth, thinking of Lucinda sitting in here, thinking of her taking his coffin with whoever it was. Then, when he was drifting toward the exit, whoever it was was flailing after him. Dracula plowed the beast out on the road and for several blocks floored the gas. When he was done doing what he was doing he swerved into the gateway for the cemetery. There was a pylon in the way. Then his head hit the wheel and he looked, stunned, out the cracked windshield. Again, in the same spot. His head detonated. He got out with the keys and threw them in a slovenly manner. Then, with some onlooker laying on their horn, he scurried across the street and walked home. That was how he'd gotten locked out.

In the depot, standing at the bulletin board, he said, "You don't know anything about a play, do you?"

"A play?"

If only he remembered the name of the place. "It's in my apartment. I can't remember where it is."

She looked at him like he was crazy. He rather did feel crazy. Then she said, "I know. I know what we can do."

Now they are here, doing something. Dracula is willing to be in the Russian's apartment as long as it means he'll shortly end up in his and eventually—soon—be at the play. It's worth a shot. His fingers, dangling in the cactus, have stubbed into something. Maybe they're not disintegrating after all. He pulls it out.

"Why does he have a pacifier in his plant?" he says into the bland air behind him. Other things the Russian has that Dracula has just noticed—a slitted wooden block full of knives. Some jug of oil with frilly ferns embalmed in it. His kitchen is clean. The girl comes scuttling out.

"That's mine."

"It's yours?"

"I have a baby." She swishes her hand as if this is irrelevant. Her face is stitched into a look he can't read.

"What—with *him*?"

"He has a name," she says. Her hair got slightly flattened by the hat she wore over here. She's not wearing it now. Dracula thinks she's going to say the name but she doesn't.

Whatever, he thinks. "So he's *not* the guy that's following you? That's somebody else?" He gets up and follows her into the bathroom, where an arachnid of wires crawls from the corner of the ceiling. He cringes slightly back. "What is that?" Dracula says.

He's not even sure she knows what he's asking about, because she's running her hands through open drawers of calcified hygiene products, sniffing with sneezy eyes. "It's not—we used to do this thing—my roommate. When I lived over there. Never mind." She had explained that riddle of living arrangements as they were walking from the depot.

"Excuse me," Dracula had said, "but how do you know where my keys are?" The pale mushroom face was still chewing its lip.

"No, it's a spare." She flicked her hand. "I have to get dressed," she said, and disappeared. She came back in her cowboy outfit.

"You've got to be kidding." Dracula had a feeling he wasn't being very nice, but why should he? He was getting what he needed in the most upending way.

"Do you have the knife?" he said to the knife salesman. "Can I get it back?"

"I'll give it to you," she said. "It's in there."

"In there? Are we talking about the same knife? My knife is in his apartment? Why?"

"Because. Just—I know where to find it."

What does that mean? Why does she have it?

"You were following me," he says. "Out on the beach. I knew it."

"I only did that because I wanted to make sure. It is you. You're the one who's been following me."

"I have not been following you!" Now they are back to this again.

Even as he chafes, he is realizing something. He does recognize her. From the diner, yes, and from the beach.

Dracula gives his knuckles a crack. "So how do you have keys to his apartment? Do you live there or something?" He's suddenly ablaze with suspicion. "Wait—are you the girl? You're not the girl, are you?" He's thinking of the girl who lives with the Russian. Lived.

Dracula never got corroboration on whether or not she was the girl because she seemed to think a cinching of her brow was adequate response.

Now the girl is rummaging around in the apartment to find his keys. Or some keys that might go to his apartment. Not his exactly.

"So the Russian used to live in my apartment?" Dracula asks.

"No, I did," she says.

"You did."

"Well he did too. After my roommate left. With me. Then I left."

"You had a roommate."

"Before I lived with him. Over there," she says.

"Where I live."

"Then he moved here."

"After you left there," Dracula says, disoriented. Was that the day he was moving boxes? They were both moving in somewhere.

She's running her hand along the bottom of the cabinet, like a crime detective. Dracula notices he is steaming up the bathroom mirror, all by himself. "Do you see that?" It seems by his orientation that the mirror is exactly affixed to the opposite side of the same wall in his apartment that holds his mirror.

"Where would he put it?"

"You know where I'd put it?" he says, staring. "In the vent." He's joking, but away she goes. That's when he knows. These apartments are mirror images.

"You're the girl," he says, "aren't you?"

But the girl is gone, jimmying screws on the vent. She knew just which one to go to.

Dracula kills the light in the bathroom. He turns it back on. Now he seems to have drawn her image in steam, a very specific but filmy rendition. Lucinda's. Right on the bathroom mirror. She's there, raising her arm just like his. The reflection is something, but still it isn't him. The mirror is showing him a vision of Lucinda. And now the him that was her is already gone.

The girl comes in with a ring of two keys.

Dracula looks at them. "So the Russian had a key to your apartment when you lived there."

"I gave him a spare."

Now it is finally hitting him. The Russian has a key to his apartment. The Russian can get into his apartment. "But hey," he says. "We changed the locks."

"You did?" She drops her arm. "I thought—the manager never does. I figured that out when we moved. You changed the locks?"

"Me and her did." After her mother let herself in.

She drops the ring, right on the floor, like a dumbbell she wants to rebuke him with.

"Let's just try it," Dracula says.

Outside, her hat back on, she hands him the flashlight that she brought for looking around the living room. Then she locks the Russian's door with her keys, the spare he gave her when she lived where Dracula does. The portcullis squeaks open below and the apartment manager comes through with a brown paper bag. Is that his dinner? Is it dinnertime? Why didn't Dracula look at a clock while he was in there? The girl seems to duck her head down as the manager looks up, then lets his gaze go opaque, as if he might actually be peering at a bug on his nose and not all the way up at them. It's the first time Dracula's seen him since the eviction. The girl hovers behind while he walks to his door. There's a note there now. *It's downstairs. Go look in the closet. Come to the play and I'll explain.* The closet. Dracula looks downstairs, where the manager is going inside his apartment. He feels a crinkling of dread. The girl is all hat brim now, trying the key. One of the keys.

"What does the other one go to?" Dracula asks.

"Downstairs," she says. "Storage." Now she's trying the other one.

"I didn't get a key for storage," he says. "You mean the room down there? In the basement?"

"You have to sign a contract." She drops her arm.

Dracula looks at her leaden face. "Let me try." He wants to be sure. While he jiggles the keys she stands there crumpled over in the cage of her arms, looking dully down.

"I don't know what else to do," she says. "I have to get in there."

"Does it have to be tonight? There's not a bomb in there is there?" says Dracula.

She shakes her head. "When is your girlfriend going to be home?"

"She's at a play," says Dracula, then corrects himself, "in a play. I don't know." She might never come home. That is entirely feasible.

Dracula is pretty sure now that he's not going to get to her play. He may have already missed the whole thing. And now he's pretty sure that she does want him to come. Even though she said before she didn't. If that even happened. He's still unclear on that night, or whether he's even still in it or in another. All he knows is that he is doomed. The note says downstairs. This whole thing makes him crawl with dread.

The girl is clamping her hand over her mouth, looking down at the manager's door. "I can't stay here. I have to go." She has forgotten all about the keys. She leaves without the flashlight too.

Dracula goes down to the courtyard. He begins the process of resigning himself to his own absence, whatever that might mean. His hands seem to be back to normal. They're not disintegrating anymore. Up close, the hedges all appear to genuflect at him, in accordance with their own personal anatomies. It's as if he's being invited into some rare and final festivity, everyone halted and enamored by his unexpected presence. The butterfly tilts its deferential wing. The mermaid rushes up in an effusion of joy. The centaur blocks off a fanatical crowd that apparently followed him. Or else it knows something the others don't about Dracula himself.

Dracula imagines the ensemble cast of his story. The manager hasn't answered his knock. He's being just that blatant.

Is it late? It must be late. Is that a stadium glow in the sky? Dracula can't tell if things are beginning or ending. His head feels dry and full of that same loose powder overhead. He works the keys in his hand, thinking. He's got nowhere else to go but down.

He might as well. Down the stairs, everything grimed in linty light, Dracula seems to hold his breath for something. It isn't until he has groped his way into the dark, a dark much deeper than the one outside, and the door locked behind him, that he thinks to flick on the flashlight. The mattresses are all vertical and lank, ghosts lamenting their ugly garments. His light is like a police beam, narrow and accusatory. Dracula teases out a tangle of metal legs—two stacks of chairs along one wall. But now he sees what he must be looking for. Over in the corner, long and dour, a tumbled crate beached on the uneven concrete. Dracula's heart bobs and blots out his entire breath. He ekes himself forward. How can this be? How can this possibly be? He knocks on the wood. He opens the lid. It's his.

The Parts

O ne of the things her mother has told Lucinda is that she didn't even know she was pregnant with her.

One day, she just went into labor.

"It happens," said her mother.

Apparently this is why Lucinda's father eventually ran off. By then he had met another woman.

"He was cheating on me," her mother said, with an over-seasoned grin, "because *I* was cheating on him."

Lucinda couldn't tell if her mother was rubbing in her father's suspicions or actually coming clean of her own misdeeds. Her mother was always that hard to read.

All she knows is that her mother did marry the pawn shop owner, and either she met him before or after Lucinda was born. Lucinda's impression is that her mother likes to call him Lucinda's father because she seems to think that Lucinda has no real father.

"I made a baby with fate," says her mother.

When she thinks about this, Lucinda sometimes feels like she herself is contaminated by fate, as if fate were a named progenitor, or else maybe she is the byproduct of the fate that severed her parents. Or perhaps, oppositely, she is a contaminant sent by fate to pry her parents apart on the seam of their betrayal. Whichever way, there was a day her parents' marriage ended. It is also the anniversary of Lucinda's seventh birthday. Every year her mother commemorates that day with a gift for Lucinda. This year, her mother had brandished a book. "I couldn't resist," she said. It was a book about dead celebrities. "You'll like it. Your father's in there."

It was like a lost instruction in tongues. Lucinda choked. "My father?" she said.

Her mother winked. "When you're done with it you should show it to him. He'll love it."

Lucinda looked for her father's name in the book. But the one whose name she knew, her second father, obviously wouldn't be in there because he was still alive. Her other father's name, her first one, she didn't even know.

Lucinda sat on the steps. First, her father came down— the second one. Lucinda watched him walk away, the door batting behind him. One or the other of her father's voices was all up in her ear at the moment. She didn't know which.

She knew where her father was going. To hear him talk, dead animals were a rare gift, a surprise discovery that brought close the emphatic mysteries of the universe. Such encounters could make a man's heart beat with vigorous wonder and trepidation, and they gave him reason to get off the couch and walk along the beach, scouring the sand at the horizon for any telltale lumps or areas of darkness. Lucinda remembers all this now as she remembers the bits and pieces her father used to rattle around in his tin cans, pinching out and inspecting, filling his ledgers with drawings and diagrams of bodily infrastructure, hinge and phalange and ledge and lever, recording all angles of connection, conjuring the absent musculature, consulting his reference books and extrapolating whole beasts from these bitty parts.

Lucinda stopped and thought, that day and this, that perhaps she also just wanted to put something together. After looking at that book. After thinking of her father.

Lucinda went to the library. She wrote a note. *Going to the library. See you after dinner.* She left it on the door.

Now, looking back, walking away, she thinks that's what made her write the play.

Lucinda seems to be taking the bus. She used to ride the bus all the time, before Rory was coming to pick her up. The driver is a big man with his chin hoisted high in the air, as if to outstretch his indigestion. Lucinda listens to him from the seat behind as the bus squeals and hisses through the streets. It stops at three traffic lights, one beside a fire station. She wonders why Rory didn't come back to pick her up. How did he think she would get to the play?

At the next stop Lucinda wanders off the bus, floating like a lost spore, and finds herself strewn by the winds of fate to the theater doors. Will anybody be here? It almost seems like the whole world is deserted.

Inside, it's a different story.

She is whipped into the lather of last-minute preparations, flung along a wheel that is now slipping her forward into swift, obliterating tableau, no time to waste. Lucinda looks around. Frantically, it seems, things are clattering into their slots, all the props and players, their fervor winding them up like a clock about to spring forth its furious cuckoo. That's what it feels like, especially so to Lucinda when Lauren comes scurrying up, billowing all in blousy black. Lucinda had expected her to say good luck. Break a leg. Lauren pinches a paper in her hand. "Did you hear Marty's going to close with a curtain speech?" She says this with a stinging blink.

Lucinda shakes her head. "Are you okay? What is that?"

Lauren looks at it, distracted. "Oh in the coffin. I found it." Her voice has plunged as if tripping into a ditch. It's the note Lucinda wrote for Dracula. So, how did it get here?

"I hear he's going to do it with the other writer."

The other writer? The other writer was everybody's biggest question. Nobody knew who the other writer was. "Really?" says Lucinda.

She'd never heard Marty make mention of this.

On that first day of rehearsal, she had looked around as the rest of them wondered who it was that wished to remain anonymous. She remembers the fiendish urge to write, and then seeing the stabs of desperate reverie all down the sides of the book. The rantings of a deranged mind. Then she saw Vlad, watching her in the window.

There was the backwash of light that meant anybody could be looking in from the outside. She was up on the second floor. Vlad was howling on the steps below. She could still hear him. Vlad didn't like to be left alone. She wouldn't like to be tethered to someone else's predicament either. She didn't like it now.

When Vlad came out to meet her on the steps, she'd thought he was talking about the play. "You're like me," he said, holding the book. No no no, she said. She'd thought he meant that he was a writer.

All this time, she's had no inkling that Marty would expose her with a curtain speech. Not even in his backstage speech, which he had just given to the cast in the back corridors, in an alcove of painted plywood, all of them squatting over sound wires.

"I have said that the other writer of this play has asked to remain anonymous. That's because the body tells the spirit what it knows—" Marty held up a distracting finger. "But it always keeps some secrets. And the spirit tells the body what it doesn't know. But it always scatters some truths." They all looked around. They all had their humoring faces on. Did they all know it was her? Her anonymity was part of the play by this time. She and everyone else had gotten used to it.

Sometimes Lucinda thinks Dracula is simply another part of her, one that was there in the glass when she looked up, expecting to see her own reflection and instead finding his. Sometimes, because of how she wrote the play, she thinks that he is the play. She thinks that he is the play inside of which she has prepared a part for herself, and that part is also her because she wrote the play. The play is the presence of her absence and Dracula is the play and out of the play emerges her.

Lucinda doesn't know.

All she knows is that she's in the play she wrote.

In the play, a coffin opens, and Lucinda steps into an unlit room. She is in the play right now. She wants to clear her mind—to swipe out all the webby tremors and inflections of her life, everything that swept her here and stuck her fast. She thinks of what the audience sees, which is nothing.

Sometimes somebody is there that you don't see. Just as much, and at the same time, sometimes somebody that you see is not there. This is the part she likes best.

Now Lucinda steps through the false door into a vortex of black. She has the distinct impression that she is going to a place she's never been before.

"Hello?" she calls out. "Mrs.... ?" She knows she has no name for this person. That's how it was written from the beginning.

"Not Mrs. anymore," says the voice pertly, or shrilly— it's right in between and hard to tell. "Come on back, babe." She hears the soft *flump* of a book, closing itself or hitting a table, and a light seems to ignite from the sound, like a struck match. "I'm just reading."

Lucinda conveys her unease on her face.

"Hon, don't let the whole night inside. This place is a horror to heat." There's some of Marty's signature kitsch. She knows she didn't write that line.

Lucinda has been coached to cringe imperceptibly at these endearments, to shudder as she shuts the door. She finds the lady sitting deep inside the long room with a reading lamp behind her, shadowing her face, like one of those anonymous interview subjects. Lucinda steps in, as if to an interrogation, or a play. As always, and again.

"Listen, babe. I need you to help me," says the voice.

Then Lucinda says the line that harkens back to the previous scene, when her predecessor emerged from the coffin. Lauren was her predecessor. Her scenes are right before Lucinda's. "Cocoa?" she says.

Suddenly she's aglow in a pool of chilled light.

"This is my only illumination right now," says the woman. It's the fridge shining the light. "The whole fuse box is blown. All except the fuse that the fridge is on. Odd isn't it?" She brushes at horsehair bangs. They remind Lucinda of Vanessa. "The last one couldn't do it." Lucinda glances back into the living room, partitioned now from the kitchen by a pane of lowering glass, and is reminded more of the smoothie shop and Vanessa. Cables reach to the rafters. She might herself be standing behind the ubiquitous splash guard, watching her friend go out the doors. Which doors did she go out, the last time Lucinda saw her? She's supposed to stammer a look now like how did she get here, in a kitchen, so far from where she just was? Her face churns with the unasked question, a swirl of steam sliding off a test tube. She thinks it does that. It does not betray her awareness of the mechanical marvels of the set, in action beneath her, the stage swiveling out on its rotation of wheels and belts, iron and oiled rubber, making an orbit as old as the world itself. It juts smugly over the auditorium void.

"Modern convenience is such a sham," the woman says, and gives Lucinda a sideways smile. "Anyway, let's get that cocoa!"

The milk comes out. A pot. Powdered granules in an unmarked Tupperware bin. "Is this cocoa?" says Lucinda, picking it up and sniffing it.

"I've been waiting all day for this," the woman says. "Now." She closes the refrigerator door. "Let's light the stove."

The auditorium fills with the click-click-clicking of the dial turning and the woman says, "Here, you do it."

A box of matches finds its way into her hand. The audience can hear it. "Open the fridge so I can see," Lucinda bleats in haste. "Turn the dial off."

"I can't," says the woman's voice, which seems to be coming now from somewhere in the dining room. More machinations of mystic proportion: a table and chairs conjured in the umbrella gloom. "Unh," says the woman, "be quick."

The dial clicks like a bomb. Lucinda strikes a match in a hurry, before the gas can spread, and holds it into a dreadful emptiness. A ring of flame jumps out in famished bloom. The heat slides off Lucinda's hand. "Okay," she says, relieved again that the pyrotechnics have gone off without a hitch. That's only the second time they've tried them. Her leftover adrenaline propels her to the pot to plunk it on the stove. The audience seems to sit in a blight of burdened silence.

"Phew," says the woman. "You know I hate that." The glow of the burner is now smothered under cast iron. "Here's what I need, babe." Lucinda peers after the voice, the motions of the stage unfolding her gaze out over the audience as it retracts back like the wing of a wounded insect. Lucinda can see heads in the dark. She makes her face plaintive. It speaks her question in soundless clarity: didn't she already do what the woman needed?

"What I need is for you to read this book to me." Some sort of holdover from the book she had read, cover to cover, from her mother. A hand, just visible, pats the hefty volume now—a different binding. The woman has resumed her place in the living room.

"In the dark?" says Lucinda. This is only the most formable of her questions, Marty has told her. This is the question she can ask.

"You'll find you have the light. That's what I need. It won't take as long as you think," the woman adds, as if to answer for the book's bulk.

The woman gives a cozy gesture to a spot in the dark, and Lucinda flicks her eyes to the outline of another upholstered arm. She can just see the color. A pink wingback.

"I thought you wanted me to help you fix cocoa," Lucinda insists, stubbornly, from the kitchen. Her hand is quietly searching around in the contents of an open drawer.

"You won't find it in there," says the woman.

Lucinda doesn't like this. The dovetailing, her mind alight with oily recall. Didn't her mother do just this in Lucinda's kitchen drawer that day? She can't help thinking of the knife.

"Why do you have it?" she says, not knowing what it is.

"Come sit," the woman says, "and I'll tell you."

Lucinda hesitates. She's supposed to. This bit of the play has always slipped inexplicably through her grasp. What does the dispute mean? Why didn't Marty cut it? She doesn't know when and how their collaborations were actually taking place, and here is where the loose stitching snarls. She can't remember what she wrote. What's left behind seems to be the inexplicable correlations of their partnership, currents of some obscure collusion. She's always tried to ride this moment lightly, to skip the surface of its enigma. She can feel herself sag under her own scrutiny.

The woman seems to have fallen into a sanguine silence, like she senses a hitch but can't let on. The woman is another actress that Lucinda knows. Tonight though she's being played by Marty—or somebody that looks like Marty. Lucinda is suspicious. She sounds a lot like Lauren's mother. It's a mystifying last-minute substitution that has Lucinda all up in twists and burls. She can barely see the woman's hands, busy with a button on her jacket. The pumps the woman kicked off earlier are strewn on the rug, plain beige casings. "Come sit down," she says, as Lucinda lowers herself on the edge of the chair. Is the woman adjusting a microphone on her lapel? Lucinda assumes the tensile posture she's been taught and then actually feels herself ready, at any moment, to spring.

The woman smiles and picks up the book. "I don't have what you have. You have all the light. All I have? Famine and plague. All these pills. Deadly tonics and poison tinctures." She sniffs. "I have to eat them. They're keeping me alive."

The phrasing smacks her with a literal chill. Because she sees, they are. This is Lauren's mother, filling in, and Lucinda has written her a part. Lucinda utters her line, as she should, and wonders if Marty really is going to do a curtain speech.

"Am I going crazy?" Lucinda asked the dog once, before writing the play.

"No," said the dog.

"Of course you would say that."

They were on the steps in front of her apartment. Lucinda had just written a note and put it on her door. *Going to the library. See you after dinner.*

That was when Lucinda went to the library. That was when Lucinda met Vlad.

When she looked up, at that exact moment, the dog outside was howling. There was always some inscrutable synchrony between them, as if they were two notes paired to make a full chord, without need of the third note. Sometimes she thought that the third note was thrumming quietly somewhere between them, like a missing voice speaking in another tongue. Once she thought it could be the dog that was speaking to her. Now she thinks it was Vlad.

"You know, you named me after a dog that you love more than me," he said once, the night they came home without the dog.

Lucinda frowned. She felt caved in.

"I tried to tell you not to leave it there," he said, as she sat collapsed on the couch.

Why had she done that? "Vlad is not an *it*, Vlad," she said in hassled monotone.

He put his hand on her leg and patted. He was sorry.

"What did you say he swallowed again?"

"A key." She noticed he didn't ask what key. "I didn't name you," she said, putting her hand on his hand. For a while, sitting, they couldn't seem to bother with the gaps and chasms of that impasse. And later, they couldn't seem to find a good time to go back to where they had buried it.

Now the woman has reached over and shut the book. Lucinda looks down at the cover. "Well babe, I hate to break it to you." Lucinda recognizes the book. "It's time."

That is the last drifting tendril. The arm that goes into the void unpossessed. Just like the woman's arm, dangling limp over the chair. She gets that she is the woman's spirit, but what does that final summons mean? That's why it's a musical, Marty has said. That's when the music cues.

Lucinda watches the woman's eyes glimmer and gutter out. She stifles a gasp. She's supposed to. It is time, now, to walk to her breakfast.

She finds that with an audience watching, the play seems to fetch too far, to speculate way outside of what really matters. Marty had never so much as hinted at how or why he salvaged it.

"The body tells the spirit what it knows," Marty had said, during his backstage speech. "The spirit tells the body what it doesn't." He was so fervent. He went on to say, with his arms outstretched and looking around, "There are doors all around that open and close." Was he talking about here, the theater? "How do we know that heaven and hell aren't here, or right through those doors?" He must have been talking about the stage. Or more precisely, acting. "The search for salvation is always through an open door. But it is always a study in trespass," he said. "Sometimes," he lifted his finger as if to a group of guilty pupils, "we don't search for salvation. We go through the door and come out somewhere else." Lucinda wondered, as she always does, why this wasn't something she could talk to Marty about. It just doesn't seem like it could ever have been her play, from the way he carries on.

When the scene ends, the play ends. Lucinda notices that it takes the audience a long, laden pause. She looks sidelong at Marty, in the wings. The woman does not stir. Marty's chin is cocked back, holding on to these final moments. She's pretty sure the rumors are wrong. There will be no curtain speech tonight.

The lights blatt off. There's a sound, like a scattered flapping of wings. She thinks of a bat caught in the eaves. It's Dracula. No, it's applause. Unsure and insincere. Lucinda feels it all the way down to her hollow bones.

The Room

*D*racula has had dreams. He dreams of waking up and being without this weird, festering urge, this unsatisfied thing he can't even explain. He dreams of walking ruthlessly into daylight, of seeing great bright distances that outlast the eye, of tacking along under winsome white clouds. He dreams of the cherry blooms of birdsong, so different from the mad claustrophobia of every hacking magpie. He dreams of bumblebees slowly blimping over flowers, stewed open in sultry sunlight. Some of these dreams he has in the daytime, when he's sleeping, and some he has at night, when he's awake. He would call the dreams he has at night daydreams, except technically they're not. Often the TV sets him off. Sometimes he falls asleep in front of it and then he has real dreams. One of them he has over and over.

This recurring dream is of plunging deep into water and continuing to breathe. He floats around, past expiration, wondering what to do with himself. If this were a story being told it would be anticlimactic. As a dream it feels suspenseful and invigorating, as if he's stuck somewhere but also unhindered, endlessly sifting the unnatural waters of himself. He only hates the sensation after he wakes up. He gets out of his coffin grayly, shaking a leg, letting it stream off him and sensing he's already drifting back, swimming around in something that doesn't have any vital provisions to give him, and yet here he is.

Like right now for instance. He thinks he's woken up, but he's not sure. He can't get out of the box. He's awake inside the coffin and this never happens. He has no memory of falling asleep or dreaming at all, which might make this a dream, and he has no clear sense of where he is. His coffin for all he knows could be tossed into a rented dumpster trundling off to a landfill, or stabbed sideways on a spit and roasting like a slow pig, or sliding through the ageless maw of a whale sifting its freezing leagues of uncharted water. Wherever he is, he can feel movement. He can also hear breath and exertion, chopping through some steady gush of unrelenting sound, a slurpy drone like a helicopter or a boat engine. Is he in the room?

Dracula feels stiff and reluctant to find out. He has never been stretched this way from sleep, tugged like a string of gum from the sole of an unsuspecting shoe. Neither is he used to this much resistance on his lid, being accustomed to pushing it out like a door in an upright position. Is someone sitting on it? It feels like someone is sitting on it.

Now there's a knocking. Nowhere, ever, in his long and legendary history, can he remember this sound of knocking on his lid. Not even living with Lucinda.

"I have a letter for you," says a voice. A letter? "Special delivery." The way it wings up like bent aluminum is oddly familiar. *"Dear Dad."*

Oh boy.

Now the voice is quoting the letter, and it seems to be condemning him, Dracula, for something that he sewed in his own home. Sewed or sowed? What has Dracula ever sowed? He has done a lot of sewing—all those patches, and that one fur muff. Somehow he doesn't think that's what the voice is talking about. It's very lordly, the voice, and full of itself. Now it's complaining about an insatiable sensation that craves only itself. It sounds like a suicide note written for an audience. The voice is really projecting, stirring the soup of this person's pain. *"It's pain,"* admits the letter now, as if it just read his mind. *"I can't stand the pain."* Now this is getting a bit syrupy. Are suicide notes really like this? Why is he hearing it? Obviously he didn't write it. Obviously he doesn't know who did.

Dracula pushes peevishly at his coffin as the letter bucks into a rant about how unreachable he is. Or this *Dad* person. Dracula is not a dad. "You suck. Why did you have to fuck up so bad?" The voice seems to trip unexpectedly into that outburst. It sounds like it's talking to itself.

If the lid did anything at all it gave a puny lurch that went entirely unnoticed. Dracula shoves harder. A creak in the wood gets the attention of his messenger clearly because the voice stops in the middle of a word. It feels oddly as if the voice is now absolutely vanished, like it belonged to the coffin itself, so crisp it was in its disappearance. Dracula tries the lid again. It swings right up, so fast he had to have help. Dracula sits up.

A single light illuminates the blackness, like a spotlight. Or—it's his flashlight. Turned on its end and aimed up, barely denting the darkness. Some shadow or waxwork is right there not turning around. This is chilling. It feels like it's supposed to be chilling and it is. The figure is hiding by holding still. Is it? Dracula's making enough noise now—catching his breath, scuffling up from the wood, holding on like a drunk in a dinghy. Is this who was reading to him? At first it seems to be drawing its very powers of disregard from Dracula's panic. Then it looks like it's going through some letters. Reading them. It's doing it mightily and with a knotted intake of breath. Something conks Dracula's head.

Somehow he hadn't noticed a boot hanging in his periphery. He flinches back, looking up into the recesses of the ceiling, wondering if that too is part of this performance. That is how it feels. It's hanging right beside his coffin, just like a grunt's duffel in a barracks. A body.

"Christ," says Dracula, reeling away. It looks real.

"You missed the play," says the hulking mass, in a voice surprisingly reedy.

Does he recognize it? The body? All he can see are the feet.

Dracula suddenly has the feeling that something terrible is happening. Obviously one terrible thing has already happened. "Who is that?" he says, looking up.

The figure smacks its mail on the ground. "I don't think we've met."

"Is it real?"

The figure lunges from the shadows as if to answer him with violence. Seeing him in full bloom almost makes Dracula belch a stunned laugh. He's like a big turkey drumstick, protruding over Dracula's head. "What did you do to her?"

"Do—what?" Dracula recoils. "To who?"

"She left before I could take her home." This person has incomprehensibly just assumed a gunslinger posture, peeling the flaps of his coat to reveal a tool belt full of—what? A gold cross. Before Dracula has reacted he has jutted it into the air with a look of fierce embarrassment.

"You mean—" Dracula is trying to put two and two together. "From the play?" Is this Rory? The one who was giving her rides? "Are you Rory?"

There's an actual rope of garlic knotted down his thigh and assorted wooden stakes. "It doesn't matter. Forget the play," says Rory.

Forget the play? Wasn't he just harping on the play? Dracula already feels bad enough about the play. "What are you doing?" he says. "What time is it?"

Rory loosens a stake and flicks it, so it cartwheels hard at Dracula. And what is that—a spray bottle? "How did you get down here?" says Rory. "Why don't you die?"

"How did *I* get down here?" Dracula feels a helpless bloom of confusion, even though he is bruised and affronted. "This is a joke," Dracula manages, raising his hands. It has to be. Such a football concentration on Rory's face. So this is Rory. He's seen him, he realizes, all over town.

"You've been following me." Is this who the girl was talking about? He's anything but Dracula. Especially with his tool belt for killing Dracula.

"I came to lock up. What are you doing here?"

"How long have I been down here?" Dracula asks.

Rory points his finger. "You were not in that coffin when I carried it down. I put it here myself."

"You put it here?" Dracula wonders why. As he looks around he's completely without a clue, but the tiny snowball of light is enough to show him the door to back toward.

According to Rory's bad choreography, he can still get out. Why would Rory back him toward the door?

"Do you have a key?" says Rory. The room feels smaller now, with them inside.

Dracula realizes he wants to know the same thing about Rory. "Did you do the blood? That bucket? What are you doing?" Dracula asks.

Rory bites into a knob of garlic and throws it at Dracula's face. Does he think it's a hand grenade? "How does it work?" says Rory, spitting.

"How does what work?"

"Your thing, how you do it."

"I don't do anything," says Dracula, because he doesn't, and that makes him feel just now like a very lame excuse for who he is.

"You killed Vanessa," says Rory.

"That—" is confusing. "I didn't," says Dracula, because he knows he didn't kill anybody. He knows he's never seen death now. Looking up, he knows.

"You were there that day on the beach. I saw you."

On the beach—everybody was on the beach, it seems.

"Where were you?" says Dracula. Now he's at the door.

"You're going to do the same thing to Lucinda." Rory has stopped advancing now. "Let her go," says Rory. "I actually love her. *I* do." What's that supposed to mean? Somehow, Dracula can't believe it. He hurls a chair at Rory. Dracula has no space really to speak and he doesn't know what he'd say if he did.

Now Rory holds up something. He jingles them at Dracula.

"My keys. How did you—"

"You wrecked my truck, you tool."

"Oh—" says Dracula.

With a squeak of sneaker Rory lunges.

Dracula finds himself with all the time in the world to deflect Rory's advancing jabs. He seems to be wielding a stake. Badly. It's as if he's picked the wrong grip and can't find the proper stabbing posture. Maybe he came too close. They grapple half-heartedly, because Rory is now trying something else. "Shit." Rory fishes in his belt, his hand or weapon snagged. It's hard to tell what Rory's actually mad about. There's a body overhead and he's talking about his truck. Dracula has been bullying him off with one chair and now he's practically cleared the door for himself. He decides to put another chair between them, pushing Rory back like a cautionary snowplow. He heaves into Rory's flank until he stumbles and sits on the coffin lid. Suddenly, and completely, it seems like Rory is drunk. He has to be drunk. Now, not to be deterred, Rory is unfastening the spray bottle and pointing it.

The body is teasing Rory's halo of hair with its toe.

"Marguerite Green, 1491. Abner Mullins, 1702. Felicia Rhodes, 1636. Robert Mann, driving his betrothed home from an evening of dancing. Dolorous Potts, in the middle of wet-nursing a newborn babe." Rory seems to be reciting these scenarios with a dull ire, each new register accompanied unevenly by a squirt from the bottle. He reaches back and scratches his head. "Does that hurt?" Then he looks behind him and jolts forward. "What did you do to Vanessa? Where is my sister?"

"I didn't do anything." The boot is now hanging further behind Rory's deadpan head.

"You better not have done something to Lucinda."

"Why would I do something to Lucinda?"

"Because you're Dracula."

Dracula, though he is, has never felt less like Dracula.

Rory is now bulging his eyes and blinking. The stinging jabs of water he squirts are freezing cold. He does not appear to notice what he's doing.

"This is what my mother uses to water her plants." His face crushes in.

Dracula, for some reason, can't seem to leave though he's at the door.

"I gave up girlfriends," says Rory, on his own wavelength now. "I moved back home. I'm raising a baby all alone."

"I—" Dracula finds himself ready to grimace out some lame dime-store encouragement, some magnet-rack inspiration. Can Rory focus on what's important here? "You can—"

Rory stares at him, pig-eyed.

"I was going to kill you but I can't even—even though you're Dracula and—" He smashes the heel of his hand into his nose and rubs. For a while. "Just—" His face is blotching. His body sags. "She doesn't even like me anyway."

Rory's slouch is now complete. It's the saddest thing. Pitiful Rory. Pitiful in a way that makes Dracula suspicious.

Dracula shakes his head. He thinks of Lucinda, where she might be. "She might have broken up with me," he says, for no reason at all.

Rory looks at him.

"Let's—" Dracula goes for the flashlight. "Just—you want... ?" Dracula has no template for this. He points the butt of the light over Rory's head. "I'll do it."

Rory turns and stares, blank-faced. "Why did you show up here at all? You killed all my chances." He's looking hard at the body. "I can't keep being by myself," Rory says at the body.

Dracula, suddenly unsure, floats the light over him. He wonders if Rory killed this body. Maybe this was all about Rory doing something to himself. Because of Dracula? Now Rory does the worst thing. He pushes at the body. Swings it out like a heavy bag. "I sure as hell didn't carry you in here," he says and stands.

As Dracula keels back, the light falls upward and hits the waterlogged face, and suddenly there it is, ejecting its secrets, its tongue like a big brute snake. Dracula squishes in on himself.

"That's not—" It's not her. It's not Lucinda but it looks like her.

"Lucinda," says Rory.

He slugs it with dumb indifference. "That's for the play."

That's when a door outside slams. And Dracula hears it—from outside their cage of confidences the boulder comes rolling down the stairs, just like that other night, when he was leaning elbow-deep in the mouth of the washer: the raucous slamming of one door, and then, as he predicted, the hurtling open of this. It hits him in the elbow and he's blasted by a supernova of nerve pain, his whole funny bone gone cripplingly haywire.

Rory's voice says, "What the—" before muffling.

It's the knife salesman, or something like him, pesky and preternatural in gardening gloves and a beard, reaching down to scoop up the loose letters. A little bundle that Rory had teased apart. The golem takes one look at them and flinches back and runs.

"That was—oh my God," says Rory, turning his smacked expression at Dracula. "That was my sister. My fucking little—" And up the stairs he goes.

Dracula is left standing in the silence. He's left staring at the body. Why does it look like Lucinda but not? When he touches it, it's hard as molded wax. This, he thinks, was not a great way to wake up. There's a tall set of lockers. Where are the mattresses? There's his coffin. It isn't even his coffin.

When he goes outside, he's in a hallway he doesn't recognize. Speckled linoleum and gasping furnace. The corridor stretches in front of him.

Behind him, the plaque on the door says PROP ROOM.

The TV

*T*his could all almost be a sequel to her childhood, Lucinda thinks. It is a sequel to her childhood. Everything is still here, or here again, in variation. Waiting on the steps. Knocking with no answer. Walking through these rooms, lurid with TV illumination. When she got back to the apartment, the TV was on. Dark corridors on the screen, cables snarling. Just like the play. Nobody was there to pick her up from the play. She had to walk home all alone.

A man trips as he bursts out a service door. An empty lot. Much like the one she had stood in behind the theater. The TV flickers its candlelight of images. She doesn't blame Dracula. She knows it's her fault he doesn't have a coffin. She knows he has no reason to trust her or do what she asks. Some men come running into a building, the wind peeling their coats. Stairwells of clattering footsteps. One man stands on a rooftop, panting. Another finds a patch of suspicious black in the ceiling, a tile skewed out of place. Now cut to the man of her nightmares ducking out of a car that he just swerved to the side of the road. Here he is climbing the hill. Was he chasing the woman up the hill? The one she just saw? Or was that actually him the first time? Perhaps the plot has just looped itself back to the scene where she first walked in. She didn't expect to be coming back here tonight. She only came back to look for Dracula.

As the man climbs, the wig slides back on his head like a block of melting chocolate. He looks absurd but no less sinister. The man is the woman. She sees that now. "You're not supposed to be here." The man puffs and pants beneath the wig.

It was her father who said that.

You're not supposed to be here. His hand flushed her out of the room.

This was one of the shows Vlad liked to watch. She can recognize all the characters now. It's just hitting her this instant like a mallet in the knees. On this television, passing through rooms muted to Vlad's nightly entertainment, without knowing it, she has been commuting back and forth across the very bedlam of her childhood. Now it is finally back to the same episode, on repeat.

"Vlad?" Lucinda can't help it. Her voice comes out in a corroded whisper, afraid to stir some sleeping intruder. Why is the TV on? He never leaves the TV on.

Lucinda knows he must be somewhere—she knows it because of the clues he keeps leaving, little bland crumbs he has dropped here and there, declaring his continued existence. First the note that Lauren found, now the TV.

She wonders, what wild fangs of fate might he be snagged on right now. With her coffin tomfoolery, her adolescent gambling of his eternal constraints, Lucinda wonders if she killed him.

She looks down at the note. She doesn't know how she can possibly keep thinking like this. About Dracula. She doesn't know what suspends her in its cruel allure. It's like something she can't look away from.

Without the sound, cars swarm the screen and the room turns red and blue. Dracula had a thing about cop shows. Her father did too. She remembers that. Now the credits are rolling. It's already over.

Her father would have left the TV going. He always got up and walked away when his show was over. It was up to somebody else to change the channel or turn it off. Vlad was different. He never did that. He always turned the TV off, with prompt intention. That's why this was so strange. It was like her father was here tonight in place of him.

"You're not supposed to be here." That's what her father had said. Lucinda had heard him and then she had ignored him.

That night, getting up from the TV, he was answering a knock on the door. She remembers following him. And the voice of the salesman, the way his drawl came drilling into the house like it was bringing with it some emergency. The knock on the door had been that way too. "Lemme ask you something," she heard his voice say. She hears it now. "You got problems with vermin, contamination, plague? Something inside that's got to be got rid of?"

It makes Lucinda think of the dog now. And of Dracula. Though this happened years ago.

"This can get it out," the salesman said.

Her father had looked back at her. Then he had bought the knife.

Her mother seemed to think there was something special about the knife too. Whatever it was, they both wanted it when he was gone. When the knife had been his no one ever touched it.

Where is Dad? she remembers saying to her mother. Or maybe Daddy was what she had said. On that day, bright gray light was drifting down on them like a silent movie—or like surveillance footage. A clutch of birds galloped through the sky without a sound. Or else this was a dream. One of her childhood nightmares. In her dreams, her father always came out of the ductwork. He came out of the ductwork in her room and said if you want to do that, then go outside. I have work to do, said her mother, this time from behind the hedge. She was holding the knife. This was all in the dream.

What does the dream mean? Lucinda doesn't know. Just like the play, it clings in scary little bits that she can't shake off. She doesn't know what these things are telling her about herself.

By now, the people have all left the play. Lauren said she was going straight to the party. Rory, when Lucinda left, was lost somewhere in the theater, putting away the props. She had no idea where he had gone to put the coffin. Had he brought it down there? It was not out here anymore. Lucinda needed that coffin, if she was going to have it for Dracula. It seemed like Rory had forgotten all about this. Or else he didn't want to help her. It seemed like every person in the world had deserted her.

Lucinda clasps her coat. She looks around the shabby apartment. She often thinks that these things—these things inside her apartment, these thoughts and dreams inside her—are not really hers. They have always been just the set dressing of her life, plugged in and switched out and substituted. None of this is who she really is. Just like in the play she is not the woman but the woman's spirit. Just like in the play they are all here to clutter around and tell her something. What they tell her is she shouldn't be here.

Lucinda knows that already. She is ready to leave. She really is this time.

Outside, walking, she can't decide where to go. She could go anywhere. But there is here, and there is where she just came from. Those places are real. The air stirs. It carries a mild mildew scent, a deep cellar chill into which she gropes along, down the damp cement, her shoes like tired tongues lapping and smacking. She can feel the fur of her parka going sticky on her neck. It seems like the clouds are moving too quickly, shredding apart and swishing off, half dissolved in their cosmic rush. Where to? That's what Lucinda asks. She doesn't blame him, but she can't believe he didn't come.

"Hi."

He says it before she even looks. There he is walking up just like her but from the other way. She's in front of the bus depot. She was just looking in the yellow vats of window, trying to see if the concessions girl was there. The one who used to stare at Dracula.

Lucinda's a little surprised. What's he doing here? Rory botches his smile. "Where were you?" he asks. She doesn't know how to answer.

She used to come here to spy on Vlad. Why was Lucinda always spying? Her mother used to say—go your own way, steer your own ship. But it always seemed like she was joking, making fun of her. Lucinda never went her own way, steered her own ship. She should. That's what she was thinking right now. She didn't blame him, but she couldn't wait for him.

Rory takes a big sniff of the cold. "It seemed like you—I thought maybe you were mad."

"Oh," says Lucinda. She realizes, dimly, what he's talking about. The missed ride? "No," she says. She does feel a soreness in her chest. She doesn't want to leave Dracula. It seems so obvious now. He was never there.

"He took my car."

She almost doesn't hear him. "What?"

"I was really late for the play. Did you see me whiff my first lines?"

First lines? Why are they talking about this? Lucinda shakes her head. She can't tell where Rory has really come from. He doesn't seem to know what he's saying.

"Anyway." Rory leans back and looks over her head, as if hair might be floating up there. Lucinda realizes how bad he feels. He really does feel bad for stranding her. Rory's not so awful. He's fine. She has to remember that. "So are you going in there? Gonna jump town?"

Lucinda looks in the window. She shakes her head. Maybe to get warm. She probably was going in there. Maybe.

Lucinda feels a little strange. "TV," says Rory, following her gaze to the window. "Family court." He leans back and grins. "Fun. My sister used to work here."

"Really?" Lauren didn't seem the type. Not for public drudgework.

"I ran into your boyfriend," says Rory.

Lucinda looks from the TV. She feels a gaping rush. She feels a space that starts to fall.

"He was sleeping in the prop room," says Rory, looking slightly fake amused. "He was just there in the coffin when I went to lock up."

Lucinda can't tell what Rory's face is doing right now. She can't tell what it's telling her. "Are you serious?" she says.

"That guy sleeps like a corpse," says Rory.

Now Lucinda is waiting for him to tell her he's dead.

He's not quite looking at her. "I read my lines over him. I even locked him in and left and came back. He would not wake up."

"You locked him in?"

"I mean, isn't he supposed to get up at night? Does Dracula like to sleep in or something?"

Lucinda feels a little bit banged around by Rory's words. They seem like they're turning into some kind of joke, by accident or on purpose. She can't exactly tell.

"I had to lock him in."

Lucinda feels so utterly unsure right now.

"I didn't know what he was going to do. I mean, he's Dracula. And I couldn't find you. I thought—" he cuts himself off, now looking just as hurt by his own blunt force. He sips at the stinging air.

Lucinda really wants to ask a question.

"You know that effigy?"

Yes. She could only blame herself for that effigy. She was the one after all who wrote the play.

"Yeah he saw that."

She gapes. "You mean—he woke up?" He did?

Rory winces out a smile.

"What?" She's relieved.

"I think he thought it was real."

"Wait—what?" says Lucinda. She looks at Rory's shrugged-up face. "You mean, he saw the dummy." She has a new bad feeling. "So he thinks I'm dead?"

"I didn't realize—hopefully after I left he touched it or something."

That is the opposite of what she would find herself hoping. "My boyfriend thinks I'm dead," says Lucinda.

"Yeah, well, if he touched it he would know. "I think he did," says Rory. "He would, if he thought it was you." This is how he's trying to make her feel better. "Unless he doesn't know what a dead body feels like."

Lucinda does not like this, not at all. "What was he doing there? You were in the room? You talked to him?"

Rory airplanes his hand nervously. "Eh." What does that mean? They talked a little? Maybe Rory's embarrassed. Maybe Rory ran away after seeing him and now he's out of breath.

"Is he still there? What happened?"

"I don't know," says Rory. "I had to chase my sister."

"You had to chase your sister?"

"That's another story," says Rory, swiping a hand out. He's looking really on edge now.

"What is going on?" says Lucinda. "I don't understand." Why is this getting so totally inane? "Lauren came in? While you were in there?"

He jimmies his head back and forth. "So, she's my other sister. Half sister. It's not important. You want to go back? Let's go back and see. I have to lock it up again. I'm just—he might still be there."

Lucinda looks at him, suddenly afraid. "How long ago was this?"

Rory looks back at her. He seems just as lost for time as she is. Why did he chase his sister? What happened to Dracula? "I'm really freaked out," she says. She's surprised to hear herself say it. Or to say it to anybody other than Dracula.

Rory looks at her, in the way he keeps doing, like he's found her now and needs something slightly unspeakable. "Yeah," he says. What can't he say? "I am too."

The Party

*A*t the party, everyone talks about the play. This Dracula manages to surmise murkily, through shale clouds that haven't yet cleared. He can't believe he's here.

"What the hell?" he says, when Warren answers the door. They were supposed to meet here. He and Lucinda. He had gathered this from the shirt she set out. It was strewn beside some other items of clothing on the bed, as if maybe she was dressing for the party. Dracula had had to call Warren for the address. But when he got here she was nowhere.

"I'm glad you came," Warren says, with extravagant courtesy. His hat is on backwards.

Dracula feels all his questions shoulder in at once. Warren's hat is herringbone. With a big red spade on it. Just like a bead of blood.

"So then it was a suicide?"

Dracula swivels around after the errant voice.

When he turns back, Warren's arm is around somebody Dracula's never seen before. Dracula drops his bag.

"Is that your hat?" he says to Warren.

Warren looks at the sack Dracula brought, his brow rippled. "This is Lauren," he says, as if he hadn't heard. He motions with his drink hand.

"Nobody even knew it was for real."

"I mean, did *you* give that hat to me?" Dracula turns again, partway, catching himself in the zipper of the other conversation.

Warren's face is now stuck in a gooey grin. "She's in the play with Lucinda," he says.

The girl tries to smile. Her attempt is a wavering chalk line in a slop of black. "I like your shirt," she says. Her eyes blister with an ice of artificial white.

Warren is wearing black-on-black stripes and like a primped, impassive panther, he's perched at her primordial shore.

Dracula looks between them. He thinks maybe he smiles into their arranged obscene faces. The girl seems to be all painted. Is Lucinda also painted?

"Where is Lucinda?"

Lauren murmurs a rejoinder, and like a slow slime moves off, a pair of bare black lobes swelling abruptly out over her legs. Dracula looks at Warren, realizing that he has just been looking at her naked body. Warren is opening the sack Dracula brought. With his fingerless gloves he paws through it.

"I hear they're still arresting people," someone says.

Dracula stares. The bag Warren is plundering was supposed to be a gift. It was supposed to entice him into letting Dracula stay with him for a few days. And Lucinda too, of course. Until they can find a new apartment.

"The theater got *mobbed*," says another voice.

Dracula finally turns. "What happened?" he cuts in.

"Oh it's just this play."

"Somebody hanged herself."

"For real."

In a slurpee of pink landsliding out of the corner behind the woman's head, Dracula can see lumps and sharp points, slow avian slicks of oil as they cascade to the floor. She peers at him through a bale of yellow hair.

"What?" That cannot be. He knows that was a fake. "Which play?"

"It's not just the actors. *Every*body's in trouble."

He stares, his nerves firing afresh, his heart jigsawing into big bristly pieces. Dracula is in trouble. He knows that.

"All of them disappeared."

"All of who?"

"Here. I have something for you." Warren keels back and hands Dracula the hat off his head.

Dracula, nervy and incensed, bats it away, and less effectively the ugly chitchat. He's never felt more like he wants to duck and cover. What is this conversation telling him? He feels more and more urgently like he should be asking about Lucinda. And about Lucinda's play.

"Where is she?" he asks, as if Warren should already know who he means. He does.

Warren has paused with the hat lofted in the air, ostentatiously overhead, and then he makes a show of looking around. "She hasn't come," he says. "You can actually help me."

This is not what Dracula wants to hear. He tries to brace himself for some inevitable entanglement. When he got here, everyone was going up to a door. He thought he saw a sizzle of Grecian hair, a smidge of bronze myth disappearing. It was her. Was it her? He thought he heard someone mention *art at the party*. Now he is here at the party.

Dracula fans his shirt. Lucinda put it out for him. That much he knows.

"Here's the thing." Warren is looking around, still too set on unveiling his own request. "I followed you," he says, settling his gaze.

Dracula jerks his chin. He looks at the hat. He realizes he can't even parse this confession out. Not from all the others that are following him.

"I have been," says Warren.

"What is that smell?" someone asks.

"Birds, man," says Warren, as Dracula fans his shirt.

Dracula is confused, watching him clench the neck of the sack. Is Warren blaming the birds for the smell? Because it's not them.

"...why they would put on a play like that?" someone says.

"I had to," says Warren. "You won't ever *give* me any."

Dracula tries to focus. He looks at Warren's face. The hat is back on Warren's head.

"Isn't it, like, if you saw it you're implicated," someone ventures.

"Really, I'm just a witness," says Warren, casting a tight look over his shoulder. He seems to notice the interweaving too.

"Is that how you got my hat?"

"I'm out on bail," Warren says.

Dracula jerks his head. "You're out on bail?"

"They caught me." Warren pinches the brim of the hat.

Dracula tilts back, then can't help blasting a breath.

"It's all still happening right now," says someone. "It's all over the news."

"I know you really think you're Dracula," says Warren.

"Jesus," says Dracula, not expecting that.

Warren looks over his shoulder. "I just need you to back me up," he says. "You owe me."

Dracula clamps his mouth in a noncommittal rage. Now he knows Warren is waving the oily banner of blackmail.

Warren tips his hat, dismissing everything left unspoken. "The thing is, I have a record. You can get off easy. Just say you did the birds."

"Excuse me?" Dracula can't help it. He butts the air with his chin, like an angry goat.

"That's the only thing they can get me on," says Warren.

"I did not do the birds," he says.

"Yes you did!" Warren scoffs. "I just picked them up."

Dracula looks at the lava of pink corpses. Somehow Warren also got more birds, besides the ones that got him caught. "I'm not your scapegoat," says Dracula, pointing.

Warren lifts only a finger and puts his whole hand down on Dracula's shoulder. "I'm going to tell them anyway."

"Brutal. You know who did that?" someone says.

They both turn.

They are looking along Dracula's pointed finger to the pink concoction.

"Amory." It was Warren who said this.

He takes off his hat.

Everyone rotates. Someone is still pointing at the upturned slushee. Dracula whips a look at Warren.

"You're talking to us?" The woman stares, one rubber chunk of black hair shaved into a curl on her cheek. Now her voice is lost in the loud trill of a schoolhouse bell. Some jarring sound effect from the living room.

"It was her?" someone says.

"Her who?" says Dracula, before he can help himself. Who is Amory?

"No, she's not here. She's already gone," someone says, a man running his hands down his chest as if to pet his own sweater.

"She's not even coming," is the inexplicable retort. It makes Dracula think again inanely of Lucinda.

"Hmm," says Warren, darting his gaze around.

"Wait—who did that?" says Dracula, not even asking the question he wants to ask. Why should he care who did that?

"This is her room." They all spin to take in a painting— of a hanged man in oil. A figure dangles in a heavy gas-lamp gravy, thick and smudging all the way up to his wooden post, with its little puny lantern, like a trickle of shower water over his roped ankle. It's huge. It reminds Dracula of something.

"Well that's dark."

"She's the artist in relief. Each room is a different artist." Warren's nodding all over.

"It's—can I say this is a tragedy?" offers a short, biscuity girl, patting her lips. "I'm normally not that hysterical. It feels like a tragedy."

"But, how did she do it?" someone asks.

"Do what? What did she do?" They all look at Dracula, who is irate with incomprehension, with somewhat smacked faces. It's as if he's just gone way out of emotional range.

"I thought she hanged herself," the petting man muffles a woolly whisper.

"Not *her*."

"No," says somebody, "she didn't hang herself."

"It was an injection. She was sitting in a chair." They all look sedately aghast.

"I hear the audience was horrified. It must have been bloody."

"It wasn't bloody. How could it have been bloody?"

"She went crashing through a mirror."

Oh God, thinks Dracula. Who was this?

"Which play are you talking about?" someone asks.

"I heard she's not dead. She's in the hospital right now."

"She's not even in the hospital. She was *here* tonight."

"Who?"

"That girl."

"No," someone says, "not—"

"Do you mind?" A stub of hand, mostly cigarillo fingers, hooks into Dracula's shoulder. Warren's voice is thin and prickly. It's as if Dracula is his ward, and suddenly they should have all known it and spared him something. They stop talking.

"What?" says Dracula, but Warren, like a wise caretaker after a disaster has faded to gossip, signals something with his eyes. "Peace," he says.

"Uh." Dracula feels utterly compromised, driven to some debilitating sanatorium state. He looks at Warren. Dracula is now being clawed from the conversation like meat from a bone—in a quick little feisty tug.

He yields, uncomprehending and unnerved, and unable to think of anything but Lucinda, as Warren leans in and says confidentially, "I think those people are in the play."

His confusion is all hurtling forward into horror. "The play?" he says, grappling with the obvious. "Right now?"

He can still hear them talking.

"I don't think the play is over," says Warren, smiling with such slick innuendo that Dracula feels like he's taken a nosedive into a well, right off that dry hill of propriety and preservation Warren had just pulled him up to. He feels tricked.

"She's not just an *idea*," the thick one still quarrels. "She's been here for how long? She's a whole part of this—what do you think will happen if a big hole just—"

"It's not going to be a hole—"

Warren tethers out a smile. "On your toes," he says, coyly.

The air accordions out of Dracula. What is he talking about now?

He looks, vacant with unease, unsure what he's meant to be imbibing or avoiding, as Warren spreads his arms in a showy way. "There's a lot happening tonight."

Dracula doesn't like it. All he sees are people and what appears to be taxidermy—scattered all over the apartment. In fact, the painted people look just like taxidermy, now that he thinks of it. More of them are milling around. One has a hide of putrefied fur skimming the ground at his feet. One of them is that girl who walked off, biting the rim of her cup as she stands in a doorway. She looks like a roasted lizard. Dracula flaps at his shirt, trying to ventilate his skin.

"What's that?" says Warren, leaning in with a sour expression. "Some cologne you spilled on yourself?"

Dracula is blasting out the bitter brew of his shirt. *Amory's Ammo*. Wait a second—is she the artist? "I don't understand," he says. He still has to ask Warren if he can move in. It's the last thing he wants to do right now, and be embroiled with this. He really just needs to get out of here. He really just needs to find Lucinda and go somewhere else.

"The Grannies," says Warren, flapping his hands happily in his pockets. His gold tassel shimmies down from his ear.

"What?"

"What those people were doing. They're doing some recruiting for their theater group. Impromptu performance. It's like those flashmobs but with plays."

"Recruiting?" says Dracula, his eyes skipping like pebbles off the other partygoers. People seem to be adorned in the color spectrum of chemical spills—steamy blues and greens, rabid and festering pinks. The pink at the entry was just the beginning. One girl is shrouded in glowing green leaves, like an extraterrestrial hedge. The only thing natural here is the art, and that's debatable. Over shoulders and under elbows are effigies of grubby gray and brown, snarling and sniffing with hesitating noses.

"Actually"—Warren tilts his head down to him—"I always thought you were one of them."

Dracula has to trawl back to get to this.

"Oh come to the light, man," Warren says, snapping at him. He flogs at his arm with his hand.

"Ouch."

"I mean, who *are* you, man? What's your story? You just show up here—"

"I've always been here." And by always he means always.

"Who were your parents? Who was your father, your mother?"

"My mother?" Dracula says, still looking for Lucinda. "I remember a beach." He didn't mean to say that.

"A beach?" It doesn't seem to interest Warren.

Dracula senses they're drifting someplace, uncharted and impenetrable. It's too late. He already knows he's missed her.

"Were you happy?"

"Happy?" Somehow she has slipped back out without him seeing. Or she was never here.

"Where's the snake?" A sudden voice jolts Warren's head out of its speculating tilt. It seems to be originating from behind Warren's shoulder. Without looking around at the voice Warren searches.

"Maybe she ate herself," says the funny guest.

"Ha," says Warren. "Ha ha." He looks down at Dracula as the man comes into view.

He dabbles his fingers in his patchy beard and smiles. Warren introduces him as Marty.

Marty? Dracula has heard that name before.

"I was saying," Warren says, gesturing at Dracula. "The Grannies. I was telling him he might be one of them."

"You were?" The man seems to be taking this as philosophical conjecture. "Hmm." He leans forward to stare with his chin cocked out.

"You know they pick people at random, from a lottery," he says to Marty and Dracula. "But you have to have entered the lottery. You have to have said you want to be part of it."

Warren waits for Dracula to say something. The man nods crisply. "Yes, yes, it's an aesthetic movement," he says. "Very experimental."

"He thinks he's Dracula." Warren points unceremoniously at Dracula.

It's once again as if a big stake has been driven in. "Ugh." Dracula's air is dully deflating.

Marty veers back, awfully surprised and fascinated. "What does that mean? Renfield syndrome? Do you—I mean—I guess I shouldn't ask? I don't know." He peers at Warren, belatedly confounded by the way this was just sprung on him.

"Never mind," says Dracula, putting up a blunt palm to push the conversation away.

The man sniffs. "Didn't mean to pry. What's that smell?" he says.

Warren points. "It's him."

Dracula is close to being done with this. He feels like such a loser. Such a terrible, grody loser. It's not just poison in his shirt. It's puke on his skin. He hasn't even showered since forever. He's an embarrassment to the world and himself. He should be locked away and sanitized, in every meaning of the word.

The man, as Warren tips his cup, averts his eyes with a polite nod and backs away. "Well," he says. He washes back into the slow foam of guests.

Dracula looks down the hallway, his chest a cracked karate board.

He can still feel Warren's blue eyes, dissolving him like solvent. The idiot has been following him all this time. Everyone has. Why can't they all just leave him alone? That girl is going into the bathroom. She might know where Lucinda is. She was in the play. "Excuse me," says Dracula.

This is what Dracula knows: something has ruined him, upended him irredeemably. He is not Dracula anymore. Some back-alley warren or subway catacomb or construction impasse has misguided and rerouted him to this. A crappy roadwork detour, one that doesn't bring you back. A stairwell traffic jam or hallway holdup of everyone ever, coming and going around him and over him. He is on his ass and awaiting redirection and everyone wants it that way. He stands at the door and waits.

When it opens, he says, "I need to find my girlfriend."

She jumps a little back from him. "What?"

"Where is she?"

She casts a furtive glance into the hall.

That's right, he thinks, something is all amiss.

She tilts her head to indicate that he follow her into the bathroom. "In here." The all-white interior has a luxury asylum feel, and Dracula is immediately seared by the light of the mirror. It's nothing like the soothing blown smoke at home. He feels weird going into a bathroom with a girl he doesn't know.

"She hasn't been here," Lauren says.

Dracula casts his eyes aside in the laboratory lighting and almost doesn't see it—so preoccupied he is in his effort not to stare at her naked body that he just accidentally ogled her in the mirror and looked away before his gaze had registered—the little porcelain dish, aloft and proffering some soggy rolled towelettes and silver prongs like an incomplete surgeon's set, balanced over a peculiar fur perch you could almost take for a bit of chintz.

It's the dog. He doesn't believe it. It's Vlad. Not only that, but around him coils the body of a snake, head raised and jaw flexed, the whole mouth drastically unhinged, the throat hideously distended around the wasted hindquarters. The dog's mouth is caught in a gory rictus of revelation.

"Oh my God." Dracula is struck violently with an impulse to spring forward and to shrink back. But he and Warren didn't find the dog.

"Oh," says the girl. "That. I know. It's the ugliest one." She seems to be commiserating with him over his dismay. One of her false fangs plinks on the floor. "Oops."

It occurs to Dracula then that she is a snake.

The door opens and two men—one tall and the other short—come in talking together, as if they might just be entering a kitchen for more booze. "Oops," the men say, chuckling in embarrassment. Is this an ambush? "You never saw us," says the short one, turning back to the door. The tall one is Marty. "Excuse me," says Warren, popping his head in before they can even leave. "I need to do something in here."

Dracula finds himself squeezed in to make room for Warren as everyone rearranges.

"Hey," he says. The girl, who Dracula swivels around to look for, is somehow gone. He checks inside the shower stall. Warren is now dumping the dead birds into the jacuzzi bathtub.

"Where is she?" says Dracula. "I was just talking to her."

"I need you to do something for me," says Warren, shaking two spray cans.

Dracula's heart feels like that pressurized liquid. He suddenly has an urge to spit venom.

"Where is she? Where is the fucking girl?"

Warren hesitates, looking briefly alarmed and glancing out the door. He bends and starts to lacquer the birds. "I figured I'd ask first." Ask first? Before what? Now the door is closed.

Dracula tenses, ready to spring, his head pinging around for some sense of rigging, some hidden snare he is sure is here. He finds himself looking again at the horrid effigy. It's atrociously incompetent—the snake's tail is lopped off in a big meaty hunk and its eyes sit in ruffles of dried flesh. One of its fangs is broken. The poor dog. It occurs to Dracula that it's not really eating the dog at all, only arranged against the will of rigor mortis to look so.

He can't believe the dog is here. That night, Warren had said he needed help. Dracula had asked Warren, when they got there, one more time to clarify. "What exactly did Lucinda say?"

Warren hacked at the ground. "She needs to get something out of it. It ate something—"

"And she wanted me to help you find it?" The smell of this was going to roll up on him any minute, like bad trash.

"She couldn't remember where it was buried. Ack. Do you see something?" Dracula leaned down. The shovel jerked through a root and jabbed forward into his head.

"It's not going to hurt, man," Warren is saying now over his spray, as if Dracula is just being a bratty baby. He pops a cap off another can. "It's just my first *effect*. If you're not going to back me up with the cops you can at least do this." As if the two even correlate remotely.

Dracula is suddenly in a wicked wrath. He can feel it—how beyond long Lucinda has been missing. The dog and the snake caught in this grisly false nuptial. Warren had gone back out and found the dog. Yes, an ambush awaits, indecipherable and impermissible. In Dracula's head is collecting a torrential static, a vast unhinging wind. He sees, just in time, Warren dart out an arm. Before he knows it his hand is on Warren's face, pushing him back into the sound of clacking tiles. He doesn't know why but he grabs for the dog. A yelp and a mist of colored spray shower the air, and Dracula ducks and casts a flinching look at Warren. Some sticking nozzle whirs out a shower of speckled neon over them. The window above the tub now gapes like a busted mouth, the night asunder in some feral disarray. Through the open hole comes a brawl of black, and before Dracula knows it, something is slathering the air with confetti hues, dicing and splicing the sterile chamber into a pandemonium spray of sherbet until a brittle smack tells him it has gone shattering past and through the mirror.

Dumbly, Dracula gapes into the hole, this new one. It's birds. The birds founder forward. Are these—they can't be the ones from the tub. There's none in here anymore. They look, from behind this odd partition, like puppets on strings, passed through into some appalling and profound sentience. He and Warren are standing just watching. What's weirdest of all is they seem to cross a stage-lit chamber toward a collection of human forms on the other side. An audience? Some dummy strung from the ceiling gets mangled in the ambush and now pigeons tilt and careen as heavy red syrup dumps them out of flight. This is insane. It's just what those people described. All of them.

More bodies come pouring past now, over his shoulders. The room or auditorium is parceled out with more plague. Dracula watches people gasping and tumbling from their metal folding chairs, the dead pigeons fumbling into the throng, battering various hair in avaricious descent. The people seem to be scattering and crab-walking the floor. A ghastly gladiatorial glee erupts from every mouth.

"What the... ?" Dracula swallows the rest of his words. He has to work hard not to crush the rigid parcel in his arms. He can't help noticing the bucket, swinging down from its string, dribbling blood.

"Two-way mirror," says Warren, spluttering reverently into his suit coat. It's as if he's reporting into a hidden microphone in his inside pocket. He hunches the flimsy coat further up over his head like a protective hood, elbows pinging birds away.

Dracula sees the woman with the sticky curl, tilted off her face now like a false mustache. That man Marty bares his rickrack teeth.

Are those birds baring back? Are those fangs?

They turn to look at each other through the passage, all the people, faces dappled with wet confetti. Dracula feels far away from Warren's voice, swimming in cold belts of unending silver.

A two-way mirror. So it is. So it was.

Lucinda had been looking right at him. Then she was gone. That was the last time he saw her.

Dracula has to gasp his way back to the thin and finite moment, extract his own heavy resolve out of his limbs as they grip too hard on the frail artifact, nestled like a frozen lunch in a paper sack. "I'm taking this," he says, or he thinks he says, in an echoless voice.

"Whatever," says Warren, looking down at the dog. "Be my guest."

The other door beyond the mirror slams shut. A latch falls and clicks. All the people are out of the room now. All the birds are in. Here I am, thinks Dracula. He turns to Warren. Here he is.

The Mirror

*E*verybody is just trying to help Lucinda get out.

It used to be, not long ago, that they all wanted her to stay *in*, especially the ones who had something to lose.

This is all according to Lauren. Lauren is painted blue-black and dungeon-thick. She is at Warren's party. Lucinda has accidentally come here. Rory brought her.

It had occurred to Lucinda, driving home under the influence of Rory's music, that it was all just like the song. She cannot live with or without Dracula. She is forever stuck, just like he is, on this lofted seesaw of fear and forgetting. She doesn't know who he is. She doesn't know where he is. Somehow she is okay with this—all their mysteries and secrets. As Rory escorted them both home in the truck—her and the coffin—this is how it suddenly seemed. Simple. In the way that Dracula is.

It used to agitate her, how simple he was. Trying to talk to him, getting past his television attention span, his flabby lack of guile and into something that made sense—some sharpened point of sensitivity or ire, some acuity for what he was doing and who he was—it used to make her feel so alone. As if not even he was really there. He reminded her of her own father, the one who hit his head. It was living all over again with disability. But now, that is just what seems necessary—to both who they are and where they're going. She likes how it acts as a balm on her—how dumbly trusting it feels to have Dracula look up at her from their living room couch without a lick of ulterior motive. She stands in the doorway, thinking, *is this really Dracula?* and it makes her feel special, privy to something no one else is.

Even the secrets Dracula keeps—his not going to work, his headaches, his scraped knuckles—seem like minor inflections on the part of him that matters, superficial things that happen to him more than things he determines. She knows the coffin is another one of these. She knows something happened with that coffin. She suspects Rory knows more about it than he's saying.

"Can I just—?" Rory had said after they were driving away from the theater. They didn't find him. "He doesn't seem—" He never finished, but Lucinda knew what he meant.

Now she's upstairs with Lauren. "He was trying," Lauren is saying, parsing the words into unsure bits. "I had no idea that would be his plan." She's talking about Rory.

Lucinda feels herself fissure. She doesn't know what Lauren means. Does she really want to know?

"I need to give you this," Lauren says. Lauren is hardly recognizable. Her paint is some phosphorescent underwater color, a sea-serpent bruise. She reaches into her sack and pulls out something. A key. "And you forgot this again." Lauren takes out the shawl. "I don't know what you want to do with it." What is she doing? What are these things she happens to have, as if compelled to some obscure preparation for tonight?

"I don't—what is this?"

Lauren's eyes fester doubtfully.

Lucinda can now feel all the inconsequential darting looks from people passing in the hall, peering in at them or else at the room, murmurs mittened behind hands. There are some gross photos on the wall. What kind of party is this? Are people actually talking about them, or about the room? There is a puppet hanging in the room that looks like Marty's.

Not to mention Warren's whole new apartment is right on top of Lauren and Rory's. What a place for it to be.

Lauren swipes at a phantom hair. "I'm sorry," she says. Lucinda doesn't like the sorry, the way it twangs out through the rubber band of her mouth.

Here she is trying to decide what scheme she might be standing in. One thing Lucinda can say about Dracula. He doesn't scheme. His secrets never sting. Not in the end. It's always some accident or coincidence by which he gathers them. It's his own sheer obliviousness. And then he seems as much a victim to them as her or anyone. When she finds out, there's not so much a sharp discovery as just a slow erosion of unknowing, or a soft burgeoning of truth. It almost makes it seem okay.

"You know the night you came over? For dinner?"

Lucinda nods. She wants to stop her.

"He made an extra key."

"What?" Lucinda can't even quite believe this. "To what?"

"When he left to get my mom. He took yours and made a copy. I had no idea," says Lauren, waving her hands drastically. Her black palms seem like chunks of broken asphalt. "I found out and made him stop. He only did it twice, but still. I know," she says, folding up her face for Lucinda's benefit, as if they are commiserating over heinous acts just discovered. As if they are together on this instead of very far apart.

"Did what?" Lucinda manages to rasp out. What did he do?

"He just went in there. Your apartment. He was looking for something." Lauren flits a hand up to her forehead. It trembles slightly. "From my sister."

Lucinda feels her mind stumble. "You have a sister?" she says, feeling fierce fibrillations in her voice. But she already knows.

"Half sister," Lauren says. Lauren looks at her with that skin of spoiled milk on her eyes. They look upset, but mostly they look like kitchen catastrophes, poached and jellied and larded cries for help. They seem to jiggle under the light, like gelatin fish in tins. Abruptly Lauren flutters her fingers in front of her eyes. "These are killing me," she says, bending. "I have to get them out." She comes up in her normal eyes. "I'll put them back in," she says, looking blearily around the room, trying to focus. "It was all just getting worse." She stares away from Lucinda.

Now Lucinda wonders if Lauren is talking about her sister or her eyes. Lauren blinks at her moronically.

"She used to live in your place, and she hid some letters."

"Letters?" The word seems fake. What letters? It's the idea of letters that seems unnatural, like something no one does.

"A guy she wrote to is stalking her and she won't tell anyone who he is. That's why she's hiding." Lauren has her hands splayed up on either side of her head, as if her eyes might be rabid animals that any moment might spring.

Lucinda wonders if these letters are love letters. Could that be? This is something she has seen in books and movies, but always with that dirty smidge of disbelief. Who would really write love letters?

"At first we thought it was our mailman but now we think it's someone else."

Dracula. That's her second thought. She's still thinking about the love letters.

"Then we thought it was her ex—that guy who used to live next door—but we figured out it wasn't. She had him taking care of the baby for a while. It's the guy she had the baby with but we don't know who it is."

The baby. Lucinda can hardly tumble a baby into this. She almost forgot. "Rory's?" She never thought it was Rory's.

"It's not Rory's. It's our sister's. Half sister's."

The baby, whose beady eyes sat in a fistful of kneaded flesh? She can't help thinking about who the baby looks like. It looks like Dracula.

"She was trying to keep him away from the baby."

For a second Lucinda thinks *him* and Dracula are the same. But that makes no sense.

"It's complicated," says Lauren, putting on a face as if to brace herself. "There was a double date." Her mouth seems rigid, unable to finish. "And then she just—" she blows her new eyes wide. "That was it. She just disappeared."

Lucinda knows about the double date. Vanessa had mentioned it. She had gone on it herself, with Rory and Richard's daughter. Lauren wipes up and down her face now, as if to revivify herself, or satisfy an all-over itch.

Lucinda is realizing something. It's about to make sense. "Who's her father? Your sister," she blurts.

Lauren scuds out a disgusted sigh. "You know—from where you work. He's never even met me. That's how attentive of a father he is to his own daughter who *lived* with us. He doesn't even know who she is. And he would never understand," she says.

Lucinda is now uneasily remembering what Richard said. *The same thing happened to my daughter. You need to get out of there.* He does understand something.

"Something bad happened on that date," Lauren swallows her words. "I just don't know what."

It occurs to Lucinda that maybe she knows. She does know one thing about that date. *I slept with the other guy instead,* Vanessa had said, that day in front of the theater. Her gaze was trailing after Rory. *I'm a terrible friend. I just went off and slept with him.* Leaving the other two on the beach. Rory and his sister.

"Where's the snake?" an obtrusive voice barges in from the hall, blaring a bugle through their conversation. "Maybe she ate herself," he says merrily. The voice sounds unnervingly like Marty.

Lauren's face looks slightly botched.

"Ha ha," says another voice that sounds like Warren's.

Lucinda realizes she needs to get out of here. She didn't even mean to stay.

Lauren, as if sensing this, reaches out for her arm. Her fingers are dried and raspy. "Hey," she says.

Lucinda finds herself searching her face.

"He should have just asked you. I doubt he'll come," Lauren says. "I haven't seen him. He hates Warren."

Lucinda knows she's talking about Rory. Rory does hate Warren. That's exactly what he said to her in the car. He told her to say it too. To Lauren, when Lucinda explained why he wasn't coming to the party. Lucinda is here to deliver a message.

Lauren heaves out a shaky sigh, squints an apologetic look, seems to sink into hesitating reverie. She wants to say something. Lucinda is sinking into reverie too. Is she mad about this? Furious? She can't believe what she's just heard. But is she mad? Why isn't she more mad?

"It's just been a rough year. My sister wouldn't even talk to me about any of it. She just—" Lauren lifts a hand to her eyes. "My mom is—she's got this autoimmune disease. Mo—he's our stepfather—went septic after someone stabbed him. Out of the blue. Rory—it's just—" she can't finish. "And then Marty." That's an odd addendum. Lauren's face squishes in. Lucinda, who unconsciously follows her dissolving gaze, finds herself looking back at the puppet. It is Marty's, and it's wearing a shirt that looks awfully like Vlad's. It's hanging from an open hole in the ceiling. She wants to say something to Lauren.

As much as she feels it, Lucinda finds her throat a dry canal, unable to cough up the wanted words. She repeats that name in her head. Amory. Is that the name of the sister? It's the name on her mail, of the person who used to live there.

That's when Warren comes in. "Here," he says. He hands her a heavy rectangle.

"What is that?"

A mirror.

"It's your piece of the party," says Warren, tipping his head until his tassel touches his shoulder. He is all aglow with unknown antics. "You can have it. Carry it around," he says like this is her special treat.

"Carry it around?"

Warren seems to notice her tone. He seems to notice she isn't thrilled. "You can take it home after," he says, as if this is her compensation. "Is your boyfriend around? I need him."

"No," Lucinda says, with certainty. There is no way Vlad would come here. He wouldn't even know how to begin.

Lucinda looks at the mirror, its beveled edge that she tucks and clasps at her side, like a book. Lauren is sniffling, trying to smother herself into polite silence. She's naked and painted at a party. Lucinda gets the wax of her hand to move toward Lauren. She does get a scrabble of fingers barely on her arm, cold and crumbly as a thornbush. Lauren flicks a lost smile. Is their friendship over? Lucinda wonders, but not in any pressing way. Maybe that means it isn't.

It's when Warren looks at Lauren that Lucinda decides to leave. She doesn't like her brother in this moment. She doesn't know why she'd ever introduce a friend to him. He's a fish in the sink, smiling its dead eye at you.

While he and Lauren talk, Lucinda recedes, out of the room and down the hall, past some gory photos of Warren doing his art, to the entry with its fading vapor smell like the stale gasp off a test tube, and then outside. The night lusters up around her, dips her in its deep distilling eons. Rory cups his hands in the truck, right exactly where she left him. He's grim and brimming.

"What's that?" he says, when she gets in.

"Nothing," says Lucinda. She puts the mirror between them. She forgot she had it.

Lucinda knows, from experience, that if she holds a certain look long enough she can stir the silence of another person. Tease them into speech. She did this with Richard all the time. She didn't have to do it with Vanessa. It only works on certain people and she can usually tell, when she wants to, when and how. It's one of the ways in which she is subtle. Just like Marty has said. Keep doing that over and over. She does do it over and over. It's her only power.

She does it to Rory now. Perhaps she wants to punish him, to fault him unflinchingly, to make him dredge it up from his own self. Rory, though, looks like he's being unspooled into a mess of different expressions. He looks afraid and overeager. He looks like he might be about to confess something else.

Lucinda looks away.

"Let's go," she says. She hears but doesn't see him put the key in. She thinks but doesn't say she can't forgive him.

The Voice

*T*here's a bullhorn on the beach tonight, or else the voice is in his head. Dracula can't tell.

At the party, Warren had given him a drink. "It's reconstituted," he said, not unkindly. This was after what happened with the birds.

Dracula wasn't hearing the voice then. His ears then were full of the dull discoursing of waves, rushing through him as if he were Dracula but with the echoing head of a conch. Maybe a conch is what they're using on the beach tonight.

"Excuse me?" Dracula swivels around.

He did the same thing at Warren's. It was when Warren had given him the drink.

"I said it's *grape* juice." It was Lucinda's mother who said it. Yelled it, mightily, over the kitchen counter and his vast internal expanse. Because Dracula wasn't hearing anything. His shock came just as much from seeing her there. What was she doing in Warren's kitchen? Now Dracula was supposed to believe she was back here doing drinks the whole time. It took him a minute to see that it wasn't so preposterous. He sometimes forgot she was also Warren's mother. "Drink," she said—yelled—at him. Dracula sipped his drink like a seasick captain. He still didn't like that she was there.

So many people were there. As it turned out. Lucinda's mother. That mailman. He thought he saw the apartment manager. A thatch of towering blond that reminded him of the Russian. Were these friends of Warren's? He even saw the cop.

The cop was shrugging out with all the others through the back door, looking livid and clench-jawed, jostling away from the breaking static and stiff footfalls of his officially dispatched associates—now entering the other rooms, matriculating deeper and closer amid the manic disarray of foot traffic, to mutters of where's my purse and am I bleeding. Hissed pronouncements of hasty escape. *The cops are already here.* People slinking away through this kitchen door without their coats. Lucinda's mother holding the door open. "Come to dinner Sunday," she said. Dracula got out too.

Now he's here, taking the quick way home.

Dracula clutches the stale dog in his pulsing mitt, feeling huge as a vengeful deity, dented as a day-old doughnut.

This dinner is dreary. This life is weary. He can't decide if he's getting made fun of or being invited into some allegory of the night. *I must resolve my father's ash.*

"Excuse me?" Dracula swivels around.

It's unreal here, on the beach. He can't tell if there's an event or if everyone is sneaking home the same way. From the party. From all the parties. Some fanatic out here speaking conveniently to their moral dissolutions. Is that what this is? The voice is somewhat lost and recurring, like a sermon, or some hoax recording blasted on a grainy loop. It does not help him. Is he part of whatever this is or interloping as usual? The voice talks him into circles of evasive pursuit. *I am the mouth that molts. I am the dog that floats.* Dracula looks at his dog. Is it the dog doing the voice? Weirder things have happened. Tonight even. *I am the bone the bird flew home.* Well, it's a puzzle. Because Dracula's not. But he is going home.

The voice, whatever it is, seems to be having some kind of loopy fun at his expense.

Above him, the stars are the frozen dice of the sea, tossed up in that dastardly gamble. The problem here is that the other people besides him are all together in formations, here with each other in clumps and clusters that seem to make him the odd man out—couples clutching, bright vociferous youths in migratory flocks. He blunders by and they shrug him away like sea mist and shadow.

Is he even here?

"Found something!"

Dracula just did too. It's Lucinda's father, bending intently to his industry. The only other lone figure. He recognizes the pattern of hair swept across the head, the large lofted bottom, swaddled in sturdy fabrics.

The man glances up. "This is where we lost her," he grunts, possibly not recognizing him. Dracula squats down. He dips his hand into the hole. He pulls up three rusty nails, black as a mine mule.

"These are mine," he says, thinking of the three holes in his coffin. It took some wear and tear moving it in.

"You," says the man, looking sidelong, like he's just gotten some unwanted glimpse of his own sloppy reflection. "You're here?"

Dracula notes the big heap of seaweed nearby—a hole beside a knoll. He remembers this landmark from some other night.

"Get some light on the water!"

Dracula looks out over the water. *Don't you remember?*

"No," says Dracula. "I mean yes" is what he says to the man.

"The missing," says the man. "They're here."

"The what?" Is this a search party? Which missing?

"All of them. We're looking."

It does and doesn't look like a search party.

"It's a dinghy! No—something—"

Lucinda's father springs straight and goes striding. Dracula tosses a squeamish look over his shoulder as the voiceover commences. *I felt evicted in my bones as my bones reposed. The girl on a whim got inside. She looked at the stars, cold in their muffs of frost.* Dracula looks at the stars, cold in their muffs of frost. *She let out her breath and imagined herself dead.*

Now Dracula is walking. One foot in front of the other. He has a strange sense he knows something. He knows the voice. Is it the voice of his dreams? The coffin he lost? He's always losing coffins. Where does this idea come from? Dracula can't begin to remember.

He almost walks right up on two unsuspecting bodies. They are twined on a blanket and his foot touching it almost scares him witless. That's how close he is to them.

"Oh holy shit," says a voice.

Dracula is struck with a sense of unsettling déjà vu. The bodies, abstract and indistinct until now, jump apart.

"Oops," he says, with a swift intake of breath. He stumbles on ice-brittle limbs and swerves right into the seaweed and then face-plants into another long depression. He coughs sand out of his mouth and climbs out, sheepish. "Don't go that way," he says, stepping away. "There's a pit." They are already scrambling to pull on garments in the dark. The moon is hung between heavy clouds like a big bare hook. "It's going to rain," says Dracula.

"Hey would you get the fuck out of here?"

"Oh my God," says the girl, shining her flashlight into his dazed face.

"What—are those... ? This isn't Halloween, man."

"That's him. That's the guy," says the girl in a yanked-out voice.

"What guy?" His voice veers toward her in a protective way.

Dracula's never seen her before in his life.

"I know him," she says, shining the light defensively, like a torch to jab him back with. "He's the one I keep telling you about."

The man looks confused and unable to say it. Clearly he hasn't been listening. Clearly her voice is not being heard.

Clearly it's time for Dracula to run.

The Joke

*L*ucinda, looking out her window, feels like she is driving past a car accident. She has rubber neck. Except what's causing it is here in the car with her. She can see it in the reflection of her window. It's Rory, pretending to be Rory.

Who is this Rory person? Clearly sometimes he is acting as Rory when she thinks he's just being Rory. Everyone does that. She does it too. Not on purpose. It's hard to tell the difference.

The silence they have lapsed into is loud. Lucinda prefers it this way. There's not much time or space to talk in Rory's truck. The music is blasted, and the interior is bare and the kind of metal and cracked plastic that reminds her of outdated play equipment—shrieking merry-go-rounds and weather-beaten swings split like old gum, every squeal of protest loud. Lucinda sits on a flattened bench pad that barely buffers the frame and does nothing to absorb impact and sound, so they drive in a rattling echo chamber that funnels the wind through, and Lucinda has to hunch deep into her coat, and Rory is busy jerking the stick shift, making a motion just jarring enough to trench through any little conversation they may attempt and break up both their thoughts and words. It's always like this. Rory would rather pay attention to the physical feat of his own driving than have a conversation. Lucinda can sense the bodily attention it lets him pay to himself. She usually finds his absorption, right in front of her, fascinating—boorish in an almost good way. Tonight not so much.

She can hear the coffin rattling in the back—much louder than Dracula's—and it reminds her of something else. That she'd much rather be with him right now than Rory.

Once they got over the hump of his being Dracula, he was really the opposite of what she thought he'd be—an actual buffer to the pricks and pains of life, a thick and helpful hide. Lucinda is maybe realizing this right now. She seems almost to be learning some other way of being from him, now that she thinks about it, partaking bit by bit in a different kind of intuition. Is she finding a new and tentative faith for something? Whatever it is, it's not really Dracula that's the problem so much as his inkling of self, a smoky rendering that's not exactly ever complete. Slowly—in his own dark—he seems to be unfolding it, taking all the pain and haste out of it. She trusts him now because he doesn't even know he's doing it. This is why she loves him. She does.

Whether it's the effect of this or just the fact of going home after a long night, it's there before she can help it—this glub of elation that rises in her and then stays right there, sludging off her breath. She does and doesn't like the feeling. It's the kind of thing Lucinda almost wants to tell somebody about, but the only person she would tell would be Dracula himself. It's not that she needs to tell him or anybody. She also likes keeping it to herself.

Rory, who only enjoys talking smack about Dracula, would obviously not want to hear about it. She wouldn't want to tell him either. Especially not after tonight. He doesn't like to imagine her and Dracula as a couple. He tends on drives with her to recite little bits of research he's done—how Dracula killed this mother beside her baby's cradle, how he infested that village with rampant bloodlust, how he did away with this whole cloister of cheese-making monks. That's been a common theme lately. Rory is doing research.

Lucinda clears her throat. He has just fiddled the music down with an unsure opening of his mouth. She doesn't really feel like going into it or anything else he might be preparing to say.

"So." Her voice is a little bent and battered on the night's escapades. Why is it so worn? "Opening night," she says.

"Yeah." Rory blows a sigh. It sounds tired. "I really fucked up," he says. She's pretty sure he's talking about the play.

Now she's thinking about the play. She's thinking about how she made it, all the way through. Marty had hugged her right offstage, in the wings. He even pinched her cheek. He was never going to make a curtain speech.

"What do you think of Marty?" she says.

He throws the truck into third. "He's my uncle."

"What?" Excuse me? Why was this whole family continuing to grow like some creepy infestation, right in front of her?

"You didn't know?" he says with a smile. "Why do you ask?"

"I don't know." Now she can't say what she was thinking. "He looks like your mother."

"Yeah. Because they're twins."

Well. There's an explanation for everything. Lucinda doesn't mention how his mother was in the play. Neither does Rory.

"He says you're really talented," he says, chucking this out into the roaring silence. "Is this your first play?" The way his eyes scatter over her like dice makes her think he's embarrassed.

Lucinda is embarrassed too. She can't help it. She feels oddly bereft when she thinks of Marty saying this. Especially since he seemed to steal the play. Nodding in the dark, she realizes she needs to answer out loud. "Is it yours?" She knows it's not his.

"I did plays in high school."

"What plays?"

"Guys and Dolls. Streetcar Named Desire. Oliver. Grease. Our Town. My sister and I used to compete to see who could get more roles."

"Really?" Lucinda is pretty sure she's already heard this from Rory, or something like it. "That's a lot of plays."

Rory jams the stick into fourth and wipes his palm on his leg. "I always got dibs on the dumb sidekick or the goon. I was the fat guy in high school."

"Huh," says Lucinda, putting these two pieces together as though they were mysterious or unexpected. She can't tell if it bothered Rory to say that or not.

"Well not always," he says now. "I got some good parts." She suspects he wants her to ask.

She nods instead, a slow, contemplative up-and-down that seems to give him leeway to keep going.

As he goes, Lucinda thinks about this play, the one they've finally surrendered to the world. Rory is not exactly playing a goon, and his stature is closer to mythical than fat. He is a sad, sepulchral angel who has been browbeaten down from his princely perch and dropped into a dirty schoolyard full of scamps (one of which is played by Lauren). The children taunt him as they barrel up the slide and cross the monkey bars over his head, clearly affronted and terrified by such a lugubrious presence in their place of play, and they drop litter and pocket contents over him in their dismay at having an adult refuse to do anything about its wretchedness right in front of them. He is very pale. They might suspect he is an ethereal being but they have no idea that he used to be a pop celebrity. It wouldn't even matter if they did. The point is that every dead icon is a past occurrence, and even some-times an embarrassment to the new generation. They apply their perspective back and can't understand. Even if they try, and want to, they can't. Nothing human is truly immortal or everlasting. Rory plays his role with profound self-pity, as opposed to the bleak existential surrender Lucinda would have presumed appropriate, but Marty seems to like this. Lucinda finds it a bit sticky. It's very Rory.

She can't tell for sure, but right now she thinks that maybe as Rory speaks of his other plays his voice is smothering down a bright, boyish pride, something that perhaps he's learned he should cover over but doesn't really want to. He seems almost ready for her to make fun of him. Lucinda is once again wondering about Rory. What his life has been like. Who he is. Why he has these two distinct and dangling parts of his personality—this pained shard of optimism and that swift kick of brute belligerence. He is perfect for this character in the play. He does dumpy doldrums and proud perseverance as one and the same. Is perseverance just another stage of despair? Yes, says Rory. His brand of perseverance is embarrassing and full of the terrible sewage of self, the kind the world sometimes has to smear off its shoe with a shudder. He plays this tragedy with such secret optimism for his piteous plight that it gums up the message, Lucinda thinks. She feels like Rory's optimism is probably something he's been punished for all his life, and maybe that's why the belligerence is so quick to rear up. Of course she doesn't really know. She can't make assumptions.

They pull into the lot of the apartments and Lucinda shakes out her keys. She looks unseeingly at Rory. After tonight, she feels like she knows Rory much less than she did before, but also she knows more about him. It's odd. It's odd how knowing people works.

"What's this?" Lucinda says. It's a note, or something, stuck to his rearview mirror. *Beat that weakling!* and above it is a number: *315!!* Lucinda peers at it.

"Oh," says Rory, "I used to be friends with this guy. I keep that there for inspiration. One day I'm going to beat it and then beat his ass." He doesn't seem to realize she's confused. "Actually he's your neighbor." He says this like it's not a revelation.

"You mean—" her neighbor the Russian?

He darts a smile. "Dmitri? He dated my sister. The other one. The one you don't know."

Lucinda finds it amazing that he can say this with a big bland voice when he's also leaving so much out. That he took care of that sister's baby. That now it's Rory's job because he can't or won't. That they are both *Daddy*. That Daddy, whichever one or both, has been going in and out of her apartment with a key he stole to look for letters.

"Have you met him? I can't stand him," he says. He seems to be picking up her mood now like a rag in dirty dishwater. He makes a face.

Lucinda looks at him and through him. "Why not?"

"Eh." He cringes, as if he does and doesn't want to tell her. "Just stuff." She thinks he's thinking about his sister. "Weird things." Weird things. What kind of weird things? That's what Lucinda wants to know.

"I used to know this girl—she was roommates with my sister."

Lucinda thinks she detects an aluminum bend in his voice, some kind of warp of uncertainty. He rubs his hands on his pants. "She had this whole mirror thing with him where they'd tape each other singing in the bathroom. Like they actually tampered with the glass and had all this equipment—it was like karaoke hour—She was—" he swallows that as Lucinda skids an inward breath. He's talking about Vanessa. Isn't he?

"And then." Rory clears his throat. "He's also friends with Lauren's new boyfriend. They're always doing art together."

That is literally the last thing she expected him to say. "Art?"

"That guy—where you were tonight?"

Lucinda is still gunfiring heartbeats and trying to decide if she should say something.

"He was showing me this—pictures they do." He stubs a finger down between them. "Mirrors." He looks at her. "My sister actually gave them her placenta. Now they keep asking people for their placentas. That seems weird to me. Don't you think that seems weird?"

"Yes," she says. That is nothing if not weird. It also seems like something she's seen. Very much so. In those photographs in Warren's apartment. Where he was squeezing blood into buckets.

"It's part of some—I think they're into this lame Dracula thing." Rory looks at her, realizing his slip. "Oh," he says. "No offense." He almost seems to sneer.

Lucinda sighs. Okay. She gets it. Rory doesn't like Dracula. She's so sick of it—the way he always refers to him with mulish grunts and bursts of breath, calling him Bugs and Chopsticks. This is her boyfriend he's talking about.

Lucinda gets out of the truck. She grabs for the mirror. "Okay. Let's stick to the routine," she says, and without a look back she slams the door.

Lucinda remembers when she found the flyer for the community theater group. How Rory was the first one she saw when she walked in, slipping his hand through his hair like it was a fine silk. That's not exactly how he turned out to be. It was just one unreliable snapshot. Now she has many unreliable snapshots, of every one of the people who has recently arrived to meddle in her life. It seems like all of them are connected somehow.

But she doesn't have anything close to an answer for this. And she was the one who got herself into it. She remembers finding the flyer for the group in the book she got from her mother and took to the library. Somebody had been using it as a bookmark, or had folded it there for future reference.

Dracula, when he was trying to catch her, had fumbled it out of the back pages and dropped it. He stuck it in again.

Your father's in there, her mother had said. It was then that she had the thought. But she couldn't figure it out. It was just the sort of thing her mother might do for a joke.

"Is this yours? Do you want this?" Dracula asked, trying to give the whole thing back. She ignored him and tried not to take it until finally he forced it on her at the bus depot. They were playing Go Fish. She remembers the whole place smelled like a sulfur puff from a drain in there, like a gas leak.

It made her listless and grim, sitting in there with Dracula, thinking that her mother had done this, that she had locked her out, that Lucinda had nowhere to go. She could hear the squeak of rubber as people stood and idled and sat and waited to come and go. "Go fish," said Dracula. Lucinda rubbed her eyes. The light in there was like a heat lamp, roasting her eyeballs into old chicken nuggets. Lucinda went fish. Why did her mother even want her to think about her father? He was in the book somewhere. She never thought to look at the author.

Now Lucinda is glad the whole thing happened. If it hadn't, she wouldn't have written the play. She wouldn't have met Dracula. She doesn't know why she wants to be with him. She doesn't know why he wants to be with her.

It's just what happened. She would do it again. She will. She can already tell she has a second act.

Lucinda remembers the beginning—what she now thinks of as the first act—how she used to walk this path in the early days, when she would visit Dracula at the apartment before she lived here. She would cut across this parking lot with an engine revving in her throat, wondering where the feeling came from and trying to gulp great breaths to battle it back. As she opened the gate to get in, it actually hurt.

The routine she is doing now is the one she and Rory have gotten used to. She is on her way to go upstairs to check that Dracula is either gone or occupied indefinitely in the bathroom, and then she will come down and fetch Rory from the parking lot for the coffin. She hopes Dracula is not gone. She hopes tonight he's not occupied.

She remembers how when she used to see him Dracula never seemed to have the same feeling spluttering off of his face.

He would come to the door and give her a kiss, even if he was in the middle of brushing his teeth. Cavalier and presuming as the day he met her. It was like the moment they met they were already dating.

"Knock-knock," he used to say, as if they had a routine. He might say it whenever, just to remind her this was their thing. She remembers how disarming it used to be.

"Excuse me?" she would say. She even said it after she knew the routine.

"Who's there. Come on. I've got one."

"Who's there?"

"Needle."

"Needle who?"

"Need-le little loving?" Dracula was holding up his mending that night. She'd been there at least an hour. "I just made that up." He put the mending down.

"You just made that up, huh." She remembers her voice was aimed huffily into the fridge. That night she wasn't having it.

"It's like me. You know. Because." He pointed at his teeth. "You know."

"Ha ha," said Lucinda drably, because she already got it. "You know, you're going to make yourself sick." She said this with a stabbing gesture at the fridge. She'd been cleaning it for more than an hour and she was feeling more than a little irked. Dracula didn't ask her to clean his fridge. He didn't even want her to. He kept saying that over and over.

Now he looked at her. He was not going to get sick, his look said. It was just hard to embrace the monstrosity of someone who sat with his mending pinched between his knees. "You don't have to do that. I already said."

Lucinda shook her head. She did have to, because of herself. She had come over for the evening to get out of her house and accidently thrown herself into this grubby task impromptu and pissed herself off. Lucinda often did the same thing in her own home, though her mother never cared either way, and it always seemed the whole house would come right back undone around her while she worked. Even Lucinda herself would get into these diabolical funks and sabotage her own efforts—mats of hair and grime smearing a surface that she'd then bury in the shredded remains of one of her mother's magazines, torn vindictively and disconsolately, because now she'd have to clean that too—despising herself and hating those distant, dewy dreams of cleanliness. Why did she care? Why did she clean so much? Lucinda didn't know. She'd been doing it since she was young. But Dracula's pad—this was fresh, and in a certain manner attainable, because it was empty at least of her mother's insensible clutter, and since it was a new palette, a blank slate, something in her said it was possible.

The fridge she specifically attacked because when Dracula opened it she hadn't been able to stand seeing those dribbles of ground chuck he let fall right on the shelf, all raw and crusting, like nosebleed seepage. Worse, it came from those snack handfuls he would pull out all night long right in front of her, as if that wasn't a repulsive habit for a new girlfriend to behold. Well, she'd lived with things before. It had occurred to her all at once that Dracula was just and absolutely like her dad. All of them.

Now he was back to his mending.

Looking at him, she really didn't think it was going to work. He was cute but it was too much. Coffins in the closet. Pigeons in the tub. What else would there be? Hamburger breath every night and, for some reason, tremendous amounts of mending. Upon having that thought, Lucinda took closer note of his lap and wondered what atrocity he actually was mending tonight—some furry muff of fetid brown, rolled softly over his arm as he pricked the needle up through it.

"What *is* that?" she said.

"I'm making something. It's for Vlad."

Lucinda looked at him. "You're making a rotten fur tube for Vlad?" It almost seemed like another language coming out of her that she didn't understand, on many levels. Who would do that, even including her? She'd never made anything for anyone. Lucinda almost felt something filling her throat. It felt very much like that fur he was smoothing down over there.

"He's always so cold and you won't go anywhere without him so we never go anywhere."

They'd been dating, or whatever this was, for a month. He wanted to go somewhere? "Where do you want to go?" she asked around the feeling.

"I don't know, anywhere. Just for a walk. We could do that bike ride. Vlad could sit in a basket."

She felt a ferocious heat inside her then. She couldn't tell if it was good or bad. It was just the strangest feeling.

"Where did you get that fur?" She remembers coughing it out, sounding as if she were berating him just barely, and how she'd twirled her father's knife with a quiet hysteria on the counter, its tip digging up a little dust of Formica. The mark is still there.

"Remember that thing in the laundry room that we thought was a dead animal?" Dracula never followed up on that remark because he said, "Oh. I think I left my key down there."

"I'll get it." Lucinda needed the fresh air anyway. She needed to stop this immolating sensation from getting the better of her. She felt like it was somehow cremating her insides right away from her, leaving her a shell around a hiss of dry steam.

Dracula gave her a smile. An unassuming one.

On her way down the steps that night Lucinda couldn't help having a derisive conversation with herself. He is not that nice, she told herself. Or if he is that nice then he's a nitwit of some sort. This was definitely a possibility. Either way he is a blackbird pie—different on the inside from what he is on the outside. That is exactly what he was.

The Russian happened to be going up the stairs as she was going down. This was the first time she'd seen him. "They're broken," he said, in a huff.

"What?"

He didn't pause. "The machines." His tone told her that she was a further nuisance for not knowing what he meant. He kept going up floridly in those green swishy outfits she saw in hospitals, and his was big, voluminous as a parachute, so that what little space he gave her still made her slice her way down the wall at a slant. His elbow even thumped her in the arm. He didn't say sorry. She'd have to ask Dracula about him. How was it that all these belligerent cohabitants conspired to make Dracula look so much better? Lucinda felt like she had drawn the short straw that nobody wanted and realized it was a bit of good luck.

Now, being the bad girlfriend she is, it would normally be time for her to go flush her boyfriend out, like some vermin, from his own apartment. It's what she would be doing to complete the night's lie. But the lie had already been undone. Like a good dog Rory still waits in the truck. Now she can see from her spot on the path—a goulash of living room light is upstairs behind the curtains. Perhaps he is home. She could have left the TV on. Lucinda feels it, in her chest, like a tender brownout—her boyfriend's nearness. This feeling is so fickle for her. Sometimes she likes it and sometimes she doesn't.

Lucinda shifts her grip on the mirror. As she crosses to the stairs, it feels like some uncertain number of eons have passed.

Above her in the courtyard, the stars are out jabbing at the night sky with their feisty torchlight, as if stuck on the staffs of so many lost crusaders. She can see it in the mirror too. Emptily, as she goes, Lucinda gazes down into the pane. The face in the pane gazes blandly aloft, sinking up into the deep and constant fistfuls of heaven, and that's when something in her catches, the feeling of being lifted, to silent prevailing applause, as if she is finally here in the one place she will always, now that she knows her role, be going.

"Hi."

He says it before she even looks. He's holding something too. His hair is going up in the way it does. And he's coming from the strangest direction.

Acknowledgments

I have a few people to thank deeply for this novel. First I want to thank my editor at Unnamed Press, Olivia Taylor Smith, for seeing me through all the various stages of development and for bestowing upon me the great gift of time, which I couldn't have survived without. I want to thank Paul T., for answering my plea and reading this whole book when it was a ramshackle experiment, and then giving me advice that stuck the whole way through. Your generosity and insight helped me shore up my vision and kept me on track to the end. I also want to thank Ann A., who has been instrumentally in my corner, listening and advocating.

I want to thank my mother and father, for supporting me always and for understanding every time I dove back into my bunker for another indefinite bout of phone silence. I also want to thank my daughter and husband, for all the love and sacrifice you do every day to keep me writing and to keep our lives prospering. To my daughter, you give me mermaids and mermaids of love, and the truest companionship. To my husband, you give me everything over and over again, and you put the fangs on all my pigeons.

PHOTO BY TONY FRIEDHOFF

About the Author

Meghan Tifft is the author of *The Long Fire*, a semifinalist for the VCU Cabell First Novelist Award. She has an MFA in fiction from the University of Arizona and teaches at the University of Colorado. She lives in Colorado Springs.